OUTSTANDING PRAISE FOR CHARLES WILSON

DIRECT DESCENDANT

"Move over *Jurassic Park* . . . a terrific read, one done better with your door locked."
— *Clarion Ledger*, Jackson, Mississippi

"A story as technically correct as Tom Clancy, as terrifying as Stephen King . . . A surefire bestseller."
— Johnny Quarles, author of *Fool's Gold*

"Lean, tight and compelling."
— Greg Iles, *New York Times* bestselling author of *Spandau Phoenix*

"A story set so realistically in our city that there will be those in Memphis looking for a flash of blond in the dark."
— *The Commercial Appeal*, Memphis, TN

NIGHTWATCHER

"Splendid . . . A lean, tight, compelling story that was over much too fast. I wanted more."
— John Grisham

"Wilson throws one curve after another while keeping up the suspense like an old pro; the whole book rushes over you like a jolt of adrenaline."
— *Kirkus Reviews*

St. Martin's Paperbacks Titles
by Charles Wilson

DIRECT DESCENDANT
FERTILE GROUND

FERTILE GROUND

CHARLES WILSON

St. Martin's Paperbacks

FERTILE GROUND

Copyright © 1996 by Charles Wilson.

ISBN: 0-312-95859-5

Printed in the United States of America

St. Martin's Paperbacks edition/June 1996

10 9 8 7 6 5 4 3 2 1

To Linda

My thanks to those without whose technical help this would have never been a novel:

Dr. Craig Lobb, Dept. of Microbiology, University of Mississippi Medical Center, Jackson, Mississippi;

Captain Humburto Santiago of Sao Luis, Brazil;

Sheriff Ken Dickerson of Rankin County, Mississippi;

To Doug Faulkner of Enid, Oklahoma for helping me get the plane off the ground;

To Dr. Tereza Ventura-Holman of Lisbon, Portugal for helping me find my way around;

And to Alison Orr and Tommy Furby for their suggestions and readings.

Again, thank you all.

CHAPTER 1

The boxy gray helicopter, its long rotor blades thumping rhythmically, slowly descended toward the top of the rain forest. Delaney Jeffries stood in the big door at the craft's side and looked down at the mist shrouding the trees. The morning sun would soon finish burning the vapor away, but then the rains would come that afternoon and the condensation would be back again. It was a constant cycle, tropical downpours followed by a blazing sun, over and over again, creating a never-ending, sweltering dampness. He could feel it even now, the damp warmth mixed in the buffeting wash from the rotor blades whipping at his khakis.

Three weeks of it. Three weeks of his group and the groups from the other universities boating in and out of swamps and tidal flats and helicoptering into the interior of the forest. There had never before been so many Ph.D.s and top graduate assistants teamed in such a massive gathering of exotic plants. And there had never been so many people grown tired of it.

And after all the effort, had they found a specimen that might later yield a new medicine? Frankly he had reached the point of not really caring. Just let him get back home to a decent bed and air conditioner.

And then the helicopter stopped its descent and hovered.

"Ready when you are, Delaney," came the voice through his helmet's earphones.

He pulled the visor down across his face, buckled the chin strap under his firm jaw, slipped on his gloves, and moved to the very edge of the doorway. A hand reached out from behind him and checked the cable running from his upper body harness to an extension on the helicopter's roof. He felt a pat on his shoulder. He clasped the edges of the doorway, looked down at the trees for a moment, and then swung out into the bright sunlight.

In seconds he was lowered into leaves whipping wildly in the wash of the rotor blades. Twigs jabbed and pulled at his shirt and pants. Branches laden with dark growth slid across the visor. He glimpsed a wide tree limb coming up toward him, kicked out around it, and broke through the canopy into a dim twilight stretching to the ground a hundred feet below.

"I'm through," he said, and the cable increased its rate of descent.

In moments he had touched down. He quickly unsnapped the cable and raised his visor. "Take it away," he said, and the cable started back up.

"Here I come," said a feminine voice though his earphones. *"Catch me if I fall."*

He smiled and looked up toward the tree tops. A few feet off to the side of his ascending cable, a pair of boots kicked through the leaves and a pair of slim, khaki-clad legs followed. Then Jordan was through and, hanging forward in her harness suspended by a second cable, smiled down at him.

"It's beautiful," she shouted into her mike.

In seconds she was on the ground. She unsnapped the cable from her harness, slipped off her helmet and shook out her long brown hair, then walked toward a clump of tall, shimmering blue ferns growing at the base of a massive tree trunk at least twenty feet in circumference.

"Look, they're almost iridescent," she said back across her shoulder as she reached out to touch the narrow, featherlike fronds of one of the plants. Then she looked up at a shower of twigs and leaves coming from above.

Paul's muscular figure broke through the canopy. In addition to the revolvers they all wore, he carried a rifle slung across his wide shoulder and had a machete strapped to his waist.

Jordan walked toward him as he touched down and his cable went back into the air. The next time a cable came through the treetops, it had a bundle of small, shoe-box–sized specimen boxes and a radio directional beacon tethered at its end.

When the bundle was on the ground and the cable ascending again, Delaney looked up toward the helicopter. "See you in a few hours, Alex."

"Want to check the beacon, first?" the voice came back. *"It's a long walk out of here if we can't find you."*

Jordan set her helmet on top of the bundle, lifted the small walkie-talkie–shaped directional beacon, and flicked a switch on its side.

"Read it loud and clear," Alex said. Then he said something unintelligible to the helicopter pilot. The branches at the top of the trees swayed at a sudden increase in the craft's rotor wash as it turned and moved away. Jordan lifted one of the specimen boxes from the bundle and walked toward the ferns. Delaney looked past her through the massive, widely spaced brown trunks. Even with the distance between the trees, the cover of their intermingled, vine-matted tops virtually blanked out the sunlight. And the farther he looked the dimmer it was. Only a few hundred feet beyond the ferns it looked as if someone had turned off a light switch—only a deep darkness beyond that point. Paul caught a handful of the dirt at his feet and squeezed it into a mud ball in his big hand. "I doubt it ever dries out with the cover this thick," he said.

"Look," Jordan said. She pointed past the ferns to a

thick vine covered with orange flowers as it ran up the side of a tree trunk.

She was still in that position, her arm lifted in front of her, when a small dart thudded into the side of her neck.

She didn't fall. She didn't even jerk from the impact. Just a flinch, and her hand grabbing at her neck as if a bee had stung her. Her eyes widened at the feel of the feathery stub of the shaft, and she yanked it from her neck.

Delaney sprinted toward her. He and Paul reached her together. The color gone from her face, she stared at the three-inch dart lying at her feet. She tried to say something, but was in such shock her lips only moved without any sound coming forth. Paul raised his rifle toward the trees off to her side. Delaney grabbed Jordan's arm. The barely perceptible sound of a dart in flight whisked by his head. Paul's rifle fired loudly. Delaney pulled Jordan toward the cover of a wide tree trunk. *"Alex!"* he yelled into his mike.

Paul fired again.

"Alex!"

Delaney pushed Jordan behind the trunk. Her face completely pale now, she held the side of her neck. A trickle of blood ran between her fingers. He pulled her to him and held her tightly. *"Alex, Damnit!"*

Paul slammed into the trunk beside them. He stared at Jordan, then looked around the trunk. A dart whizzed by the tree. He raised his rifle and fired it rapidly three times.

"Alex!" Delaney said, still speaking loudly, still hoping to make himself heard, but with his stomach twisting with the knowledge the helicopter was probably too far away for the weak helmet radio.

"Read you, Delaney, faint. What do—"

"Get back here quick! Jordan's been hit with a dart!"

Alex didn't say anything in response. But Delaney knew he had been understood. Alex would have the pilot wheel the helicopter around in as short a turn as possible and come back to them with the craft's throttles open wide. But Alex would also know there was no use. Delaney caught Paul's glance. Paul knew, too. They all knew. Jordan knew.

It should have started already. The poison should have begun its spread within seconds of the dart hitting. He couldn't help but look down at Jordan's hands. That's how curare worked, paralyzing the extremities first, then spreading through the body, finally paralyzing the lungs, killing its victim by horrible suffocation. *God, please, no,* he thought, and he felt like he was going to vomit.

The sound of the helicopter reached them.

Jordan spoke in a voice so low he could barely hear it. "I should be feeling it," she began. "I . . ." He felt her shiver against him. "But I don't feel anything."

There was a sound of hope in her tone, beyond hope, pleading. She was trying to convince herself. Then the tops of the trees swayed a couple of hundred feet from them.

"Delaney," came Alex's voice.

"South!" Delaney shouted into his mike. "Come south!"

The swaying leaves moved toward them. The helicopter stopped while still at least seventy feet away. They didn't have time to direct it any closer. "Let the cables down." He caught Jordan's arm. Paul looked around the tree trunk.

Alex's thick shape broke through the matted cover above. He must have been coming down while the helicopter was still moving. He came down rapidly. He held the end of the second cable in his hand. Paul sprinted out into the open. Delaney urged Jordan after him.

Paul went on between the cables, past Alex. He fired his rifle repeatedly from his hip while still running, tripped on a vine, stumbled, sprawled forward to the ground, rolled, and came to his knees. He fired again, and then the rifle clicked empty. Delaney hooked the end of the cable to Jordan's harness. "Take us up!" he yelled, and grabbed for a spot on the cable above Jordan's head. It tightened. Paul dropped his rifle and sprinted toward them. Alex started up. Paul jumped and caught the cable behind Alex's neck. They started revolving. Delaney and Jordan went up straight. Paul tried to twist to look in the direction from where the darts had been fired. He had his revolver out and swept its barrel back and forth toward the ground. Delaney looked above them at the approaching canopy. Seventy-five feet to its cover. Fifty feet. Twenty-five feet. The pilot was pulling them up as fast as the winch would wind. Another few seconds without a dart finding them and . . .

Their heads and shoulders slammed into the first branches. Delaney tried to protect Jordan's face from the jabbing twigs with his gloved hand. Paul grunted. Alex grabbed him. But Paul hadn't been hit by a dart. A jagged branch had torn into his arm.

In a moment they were above the trees.

Even before they reached the helicopter it started moving slowly away. Delaney caught the edges of the wide doorway, pulled himself and Jordan inside, unsnapped her cable, and reached back for Paul and Alex. Catching Paul by the shoulder he pulled him toward the opening. Paul grabbed an edge of the doorway and swung his legs into the compartment. Alex came in and went to his knees. Delaney looked across his shoulder.

Jordan had scooted back against the far bulkhead. She was looking at her hand, raised in front of her. As he stared at her, her lip trembled, and he felt his heart twist.

Please, God, he prayed, *please.*

CHAPTER 2

The treetops flew past beneath the helicopter's open doorway. Delaney slipped a folded blanket under the back of Jordan's head. Her eyes came up to his.

"My hand," she said in a low voice. "It's . . ." Her lip trembled. She tried to flex her fingers, and grimaced. He felt his heart twist. He looked toward the pilot's compartment.

"Can't you get somebody on the damn radio?"

Alex was trying frantically.

Back on the ground in the dimness under the thick canopy, the bundle of specimen boxes, Jordan's helmet sitting atop it, was framed in a single ray of sunlight. Paul's rifle lay a few feet away.

A sound, faint in the distance, wafted softly through the tree trunks. A chant.

In the rhythmic tempo of a single stick sounding slowly against a drum, the words rose and fell.

A couple of hundred feet away from the specimen boxes and walking in a direction leading away from them, a short, muscular Indian, carrying a long blowgun and naked except for a thin loincloth, tightly girded, with long strips of cloth hanging down its front and back, moved slowly through the trees. His light brown arms and legs were streaked with narrow stripes of white paint.

A wider band of white crossed his forehead and curved down in front of his ears, continuing around the back of his neck and bordering his short, thick black hair. In front of him, a wall of wild thorns grew tall on the near bank of a stream.

A break in the wall created a passageway not much wider than a doorway and led through the thorns to the yellow-brown, slowly moving stream. He entered the water without slowing.

On his first step it came up to his knees. On his second, it rose to his waist. Fifty feet downstream, a twenty-foot-long crocodile lay in front of a similar tall growth of thorns on the opposite bank. The reptile's broad head rose sharply. The creature arched its upper body up on its stubby forepaws. Its long, sharply tapering mouth gaped. It moved with startling quickness down the bank into the water, and slid under the surface.

The Indian was up to his chest. He moved steadily but slowly, the water rippling gently around his broad shoulders and spreading out in wide circles toward the banks.

Two more steps, three, and the water shallowed. His body began to emerge once again. Ten feet from the bank he stopped.

The chant began again, muted now, much lower than before, almost reverent sounding. He took a step forward, the water dropping back to his knees, a second step, a third, and stepped up onto the sandy bank, stopping there, his heels only a few inches from the water. He waited.

A ripple behind him in the water.

"*Carbo veen craa.*"

The words came from behind a vine-matted growth of leafy cane fifty feet in front of him. He walked forward.

A tall Indian, the same white streaks painted across his long arms and legs and wearing a headdress of colorful bird feathers, stepped out from behind the cane. In his hands he held a narrow rock, nearly three feet in length and tapered to a fine point.

He waited until the squat Indian was nearly to him and then extended the rock rapidly out between them, holding it at the full length of his arms.

The squat Indian stopped.

As he did, two other Indians, similarly painted, sprang from their concealment to his sides. They had long blowguns in their hands and had them raised to their mouths, their cheeks puffed behind their hollow ends.

The squat Indian dropped to his knees, but his upper body remained erect, his gaze locking on the rock.

The tall Indian pulled it back to his own narrow chest and thrust it forward again. He began repeating the movement, over and over, in a pulsating motion, slowly at first, and then more rapidly. Then he suddenly stepped forward and raised the rock high over his head. The Indian on his knees threw back his head, arched his bare chest forward, exposing it, and threw his arms out to his sides.

The rock came down swiftly. Its chipped point, honed to a razor sharpness, stopped only an inch from the man's chest.

His face remained expressionless. He hadn't flinched. The only sign of fear were droplets of sweat that formed on his forehead. But they might have been from the oppressive humidity and heat.

The tall Indian stared hard at the kneeling one's face, continued to stare carefully at it for several seconds, then slowly pulled the rock back.

As he did, one of the Indians off to the side lowered his blowgun and, holding it out ahead of him like a long pole, moved toward the kneeling man.

The blowgun then came forward, jabbing the man in his chest. It was thrust forward again, digging into his neck. A third thrust went against his ribs, hard. The blowgun came forward still once more, twisting into the kneeling Indian's thick, dark hair, digging cruelly.

''*Forando bon*,'' the tall Indian said.

The torment stopped.

The kneeling Indian rose. The tall Indian stared at him for a long moment, then turned and walked silently toward the dark trees in the distance, the others following him.

The chant started again.

Delaney plugged the headset's cord into the socket in the bulkhead close to Jordan's head.

The Brazilian doctor was already speaking over the radio to Alex. *"How long since she was hit?"* he was asking.

Delaney answered. "Ten to fifteen minutes."

The doctor didn't respond immediately.

"Ten to fifteen minutes," Delaney repeated. "Her hands are tingling."

"Calm, yourself, senhor," the doctor said in a measured tone. *"The dart was not tipped with curare or she would not be conscious after this amount of time. But don't move her until I see her. She could have some cervical damage."*

Delaney looked down at Jordan. She had lifted her hand in front of her and was slowly clasping it and unclasping it. He caught it in his hand and laid it back at her side.

"The doctor says you're going to be all right. But he wants you to lie still until we get to the clinic."

An hour later, the coastline appeared through the open doorway. Delaney could see the small town in the distance. Its few, mostly wooden buildings sat along a ridge running above the ocean. The pilot flew toward the landing pad near the concrete docks.

"No," Delaney said. He pointed toward the square, one-story, tin-roofed medical clinic at the far end of the town.

The pilot looked at the narrow dirt road in front of the clinic. Directly across from the clinic, a building sat close to the other side of the road. A second-story balcony projected even farther out toward the road. He shook his head. "There is not enough room to land."

Alex stepped up behind the small dark-skinned man and, without saying a word, caught him by the shoulders and lifted him bodily out of the seat.

"No," the pilot protested, trying to reach back to the controls.

Paul caught his arm and pulled him back into the bay. Alex pushed the controls over hard.

In seconds, they were descending. The pilot's eyes stared wide at the upcoming street and the buildings close to each side. Alex went down between them without slowing the helicopter, and, its whirling rotor blades fitting with only inches to spare between the buildings, the craft bounced to a jolting stop.

Delaney caught Jordan's head, trying to keep it from moving. The dark-skinned young Brazilian doctor, his knee-length white coat whipping in the dying blast of the rotor blades, climbed hurriedly into the passenger compartment.

He looked at the thin line of dried blood on Jordan's neck as he knelt beside her. He smiled softly down at her, then reached out with his fingers and raised her eyelid, looking into her eye for a moment. "Are you experiencing any difficulty in moving your feet and hands?"

Jordan shook her head slightly. She raised a hand and flexed her fingers. The doctor laid his hand on her shoulder on the same side of her body as her wound.

He tightened his fingers slowly. "Does that hurt?" he asked.

She shook her head again. "More like tingles."

He smiled. "You're going to be fine." He reached to the back of her head. "Sit up slowly."

Inside the clinic, a squat Indian woman in a blue nurse's uniform waited at the entrance to a small examining room across the lobby. "She was hit by a dart," the

...aid as he walked Jordan past her. The woman's
...w wrinkled questioningly.

The doctor waited for Jordan to climb onto a narrow
examining table and then reached to a metal tray on a
small table and lifted a rubber hammer.

"Your elbow," he said.

Jordan held her arm out, and he lifted her forearm up
at an angle and cupped it in his hand. He gently tapped
the hammer against the apex of the bend. Her forearm
jumped.

He did it again, then reached for her other arm and
repeated the process. Nodding, he laid the hammer back
into the tray. "The tingling is shock to the nerve. But
the dart didn't go deep enough to cause any permanent
damage. You'll be as good as new in a few hours. Not
many people would hear that after being hit with an Indian's dart—hear anything again. Maybe it was dipped
improperly. Maybe the curare was old."

The nurse shook her head in disagreement. "The dart
was not dipped improperly," she said. "Not by one who
has hunted with it since a child. And time would make
no difference. The only way for the curare not to have
been present is for the dart to have killed before. Killed
more than once. To have killed often enough to have
expended the poison. But such a dart is kept in a separate
quiver until it can be dipped again." She looked back at
Jordan. "You are a very lucky woman. One whom God
surely protected this day."

The doctor looked toward the door. Paul and Alex
stood there. Despite the close proximity during the flight
to the clinic, it was the first time Delaney really took
note of Paul's wound. His sleeve was tattered. A jagged
cut ran six inches along his thick bicep. The shirt around
the wound and down to his wrist was dark with dried
blood mixed with dirt. Alex's wide cheeks had two long
scratches running down them.

"It appears you two came out the worse for the incident," the doctor said. "What happened?"

"Coming up through the trees too fast," Alex said.

The doctor smiled a little. "I would have been, too." He gestured with a sidewise motion of his head for them to come forward.

As they did, the nurse walked to meet them, glancing at Alex's cheeks and then reaching for Paul's arm. In a moment she was snipping the shirt's material from around his bicep with a pair of scissors she pulled from her pocket.

The doctor now moved an alcohol-soaked gauze to Jordan's neck. Delaney smiled softly when he caught her eyes, then turned and walked into the hallway.

At a window in the corridor, he took a deep breath, rested his hand against the wall and stared out at the research freighter moored at the dock down the side of the hill from the clinic.

Big doors at the vessel's side were open and carts carrying specimen crates were being pushed inside by dark-skinned workers. An occasional member of one of the research teams pointed out something or tagged a crate before it entered the ship. Then the opening of the clinic door drew Delaney's attention in its direction.

Police Captain Manuel Dominguiz, squat and wide-shouldered in a dark blue uniform, strode inside and walked toward him.

They shook hands, then Dominguiz looked toward the examination room. "The pilot told me of the incident," he said. "Your wife was a very lucky woman. An Indian wouldn't attempt to bring down a bird without his dart poisoned." His square face took on a questioning expression. "Strange also is the fact there has never been a report of a tribe living in the area where you were attacked. When I was a child, to come upon an undiscovered people was not out of the ordinary. But now, with slow-moving helicopters, prospectors swarming even the remotest area, and the satellite technology your government shares with ours, even the most isolated regions have been at least viewed."

Before Delaney could respond, Dominguiz added, "But then again, the forest *is* a vast place. Despite our technology, it no doubt still holds surprises of which we are unaware." He smiled at his next thought. "When I was that child I referred to, I remember standing on the beach, looking at the edge of the forest, waiting for a dinosaur to walk out of the trees to bathe in the ocean."

Paul stepped up beside them. He shook hands with the captain. Dominguiz looked questioningly at his bandaged bicep.

"I hung it coming up through the trees."

Dominguiz stared at the material of the shirt around the bandage. Though much of it had been cut away, what there was left was streaked with a mixture of dirt and dried blood. "I hope the doctor cleaned the wound well."

Paul smiled and held up a small bottle of penicillin capsules.

"Do not make light of infection in this climate," Dominguiz said. "The constant warmth and the rains don't only make the flowers grow. You are the one who shot at the Indians?"

"Indian," Paul said. "I only saw one. Just a glimpse of him. Actually just a flash of the white stripes he had painted across his body. I was mainly firing to keep him off balance."

"There wasn't only one," Dominguiz said. "Not with four of you, and you with weapons."

The rust streaking the side of the old freighter was apparent when you neared it. The company that had leased the ship for the expedition certainly hadn't had a luxury cruise in mind. But Delaney didn't care as long as the vessel could stay afloat until it got back to Miami. And had a clean bed, he thought. And air-conditioning. A blessed air conditioner. For the life of him he didn't know how people survived the summers here without it.

"Once I get in bed," Alex said, "I'm going to stay there until we arrive in Miami."

He looked like he meant it. Though noticeably over-weight, he normally stood straight and erect. Now he looked slumped. Worn out. They all were. Facing the incident with Jordan hadn't helped any. They all had been friends for years. Delaney and Alex had gone to college together—same major, same fraternity, same flying club. Paul had joined them in their research at the medical center over a dozen years before. Paul had actually been the first one to date Jordan. To Alex, Jordan was more like the sister he never had. Paul looked at his bandaged arm. Jordan did, too. "Is it bothering you?" she asked.

He smiled. "Itches."

CHAPTER 3

They sailed at dusk. Jordan looked from the bow at the rising moon bathing the town in a dim glow. Lights flickered in the windows of some of the homes nearest the beach.

"It is pretty," she said.

"Because you can't see the bugs," Alex said.

Jordan rubbed the top of her shoulder. "Bothering you?" Paul asked.

"About back to normal," she said.

Delaney looked above the trees behind the town. In the distance, a line of dark clouds moved rapidly toward them. "First night out is going to be stormy."

Paul scratched at his arm.

"First thing in the morning," Jordan said, "we need to change that bandage and check the stitches. Every morning. We don't need you coming down with an infection." She looked at Alex. "If it were you, I'd ask you to give me your antibiotics before you misplaced them." She smiled as she paused. "I didn't want to worry anybody, but every time you flew back to town I wondered if you'd remember where you left us."

"Funny," Alex said. "Just like my mother."

"Like anybody that knows you," Jordan said. She looked down at her khakis, soiled and wrinkled. "And me, I'm going to go take a shower. Become a woman

again before I forget how.'' She lifted one foot off the
deck and looked down at her boot. ''And if I ever wear
another pair of these again, I want one of you to get me
to a psychiatrist. Come on, Delaney.''

Reaching their cabin, Delaney held the door open and
Jordan walked inside. It was the same one in which they
had traveled from Miami, small with a bare steel floor
and steel walls, a smaller than normal double bed against
the rear bulkhead, and a tiny head off to the left. Not
much, and yet it looked like a Hilton compared to the
tents in which they had slept most of the last three weeks.

Jordan moved to the mirror over the small locker. She
raised her hand to her neck and pulled back the small
gauze bandage. ''Do you think it's going to leave a
scar?''

He smiled as he sat down on the bed. ''A few hours
ago you were worrying about dying.''

Her reflection frowned back at him from the mirror.
''I'm serious, Delaney. Do you think it will?''

''No. Come here.'' He held his arms out.

''I have to take a shower.''

''Then you'll come here?''

''Then it'll be time to go to dinner.''

Her smile told him she was teasing. He smiled and
laid back on the bed. ''You have to take a shower, too,''
she said.

He began unbuttoning his shirt. She walked toward the
head. ''Leave room for me in there,'' he said.

''It's a small shower,'' she said. But she left the door
open.

Back across the dark water behind the freighter, beyond
the small coastal town and deep into the forest to a spot
not far from where the helicopter had descended through
the trees, a wide mouth of a cave sat sunk into barren
rock halfway up the side of a hill.

Inside the cave, dozens of torches projected from the

rounded walls toward its center, creating an illumination
as bright as sunlight. The Indian who had crossed the
stream earlier that day walked a few feet ahead of the
tall Indian in the headdress of bird feathers. Behind them
came a young woman, her head lowered, crying, and a
small boy. They walked past a tall wooden cage built of
rounded posts tied together with twisted vines.

Inside the cage, a stocky, bearded white man held onto
a pair of the closely spaced posts and glared at them.
Dressed in tattered knee-length shorts and a yellowed
T-shirt, his hands gripped and regripped the posts, worn
smooth from his years of clasping them. His lips moved,
but no words came forth. The child looked at him, and
edged toward the cage. The man smiled.

Two long darts thudded into the posts on either side
of his face. He flinched, stared at the two white-streaked
Indians who had fired the darts and were quickly stuffing
another into the end of their blowguns. His fingers
clinched and unclinched. His cheek ticked. The child
walked back to stand behind his mother.

The tall Indian stopped at another similarly built cage
a few feet from the first and turned around. The Indian
following him reached out for the gate to the cage,
opened it, and stepped inside, pulling the gate shut behind him. He looked back toward the wide entrance to
the cave, spread his arms, and raised them wide above
his head.

"*Ponton ord rall,*" he shouted defiantly.

Several gray-haired women at the sides of the entrance
began to pull on long vines twisted into ropes. Two wide
doors of long timbers faced with thin slabs of stone began to swing shut.

Soon, the entrance looked from the outside to be nothing more than the continuation of the hill's barren rock,
sloping upward toward a crest thick with tall trees.

The knock on the door was soft. Delaney rolled away
from Jordan. "Yes," he said.

"It's me," Alex said.

Jordan slipped out of bed and scurried to the head.

Delaney pulled on his robe and opened the door.

"I didn't want to eat alone," Alex said. He looked into the cabin. "Where's Jordan?"

"She's taking a shower. Where's Paul?"

Alex smiled as the freighter rode high on a rolling swell. "A former marine. All the big stories. And now a little rough weather and he says he's not feeling well. He's going to skip dinner."

CHAPTER 4

The front stayed with them for eight days, the heavy rain seldom gone for more than a few hours before a new line of squalls moved through. But the night sky was clear now, at least directly over the freighter. A bright moon showed in the gap between the clouds that had just departed and the ones speeding toward them. Delaney leaned against the port rail and looked out at the rolling waves glistening in the moonlight. He wore a suit and tie. Jordan wore a green sundress with straps. She had replaced the gauze bandage with a Band-Aid. She turned to face Alex as he walked toward them.

"Paul not coming?" she asked.

Alex smiled and shook his head in amusement. "The marine's a casualty again. He wouldn't even get up and answer his door." He looked out at the waves and his smile broadened.

"It's not funny, Alex."

"It is to me."

Jordan frowned. "I'd be worried about an infection. He had a lot of dirt in that cut. But I've changed his bandage every day. The area around it is not even red now. He hasn't had any fever."

Alex still smiled. "It's not the red, it's the green at his gills. And you don't turn green from an infection."

Jordan looked toward the cabins. "It worries me most that it keeps hanging on—coming back."

Alex looked at his watch. "We going to stand here and talk about him or go eat with the captain? Paul's seasick. The coming back is when he gets out of bed and feels the deck moving."

Delaney smiled and moved toward the steps leading up to the captain's quarters.

Paul stared into the mirror in the head off his cabin. Sweat covered his forehead and shone from his face. Another wave of nausea swept over him. A sudden pain at the pit of his stomach nearly bent him double. He barely got his face over the toilet before he vomited again.

Jordan led them up the steel steps. The captain, a short, red-haired man in a full blue uniform with tunic, waited outside his door. He smiled politely as Jordan stopped in front of him.

"You're the team from Jackson, Mississippi," he said. "Dr. Jeffries."

Jordan returned his smile. "Yes."

He clasped her hand with his only hand. His other was missing, with his tunic sleeve folded across the stub and pinned. "See," he said and smiled. "I remembered without going back and looking at the roster. But it's not so difficult with someone as beautiful as you."

"Thank you very much."

He brought her hand to his mouth and kissed it, then released it and reached for Alex's. "And you are the male Dr. Jeffries or—"

"Alex Brister."

"Dr. Brister, then, glad to meet you." He shook Alex's hand. Then Delaney held his forward. The captain shook it. "And you are . . ."

"The male Dr. Jeffries," Delaney said.

"There were four of you, weren't there?"

"The marine," Alex said. "He's seasick."

Jordan frowned at Alex.

The captain looked toward the waves rolling past the ship. "I'm sorry that I couldn't do better with the timing of my invitation. But I would like to have all the teams to dinner and it looks like the weather is not going to give us a break." He stepped back and motioned with his hand toward the open doorway behind him.

The cabin was surprisingly pleasant, its steel walls painted beige, with the overhead, even the pipes crossing there, a soft white. The carpet was white, too, and thick. The spacious mahogany table, already set with food, filled much of the space at the center of the cabin. But there was still enough room for an easy chair with reading lamp in one corner and a straight-back chair and rolltop desk in another. A narrow passageway at the rear of the cabin led to what Delaney assumed were the captain's sleeping quarters.

Paul lay on his back on his bed, his eyes wide in horror at his thoughts. He tried again to force them from his mind. A pain doubled him over. He twisted, moaned, rolled over into a fetal position and pushed his face hard into his knees.

"So you find a plant in the Amazon and make medicine out of it?" the captain questioned.

Jordan was the one who responded. "Sort of. Plants are originally responsible for a large number of medicines—digitalis from the foxglove plant, penicillin from mold, and streptomycin and Aureomycin from mold, too. The idea of extracting medicines from plants came from legends of plants that a medicine man chewed and spit in a wound or mixed in a potion. There is no way to know how these people first discovered what worked and what didn't. But a lot of them did. Scientists have been trying new plants ever since."

"Spit in a wound?" the captain questioned.

Jordan grinned. ''Well, that's a little graphic, but it gives you the idea.''

Paul vomited violently into the toilet. His face twisted in pain. Glancing out of the head his eyes caught the light from the table lamp next to his bed—and it hurt.

His face twisted again. This time in anger. Jumping up from his knees he rushed into the cabin, grabbed the lamp and threw it smashing into the steel bulkhead.

Staring at what he had done, his lip trembled. He looked back at the bed and the sheets of notebook paper lying on the bedspread, pages where he had been trying to record what was happening to him. He stared at them. A tear ran from his eye down his cleaved, tanned face. He suddenly threw himself onto the bed, grabbed a sheet of the paper, crumpled it in his tight fist, drove his face into the bedspread, and started sobbing into it.

Delaney and Jordan left Alex at the bottom of the stairs leading from the captain's cabin. He walked toward his cabin. They moved to the rail. The moon was gone now and the waves were even tighter and higher now than before dinner. Close to the freighter, in the glow of its running lights, an occasional wave smashed itself into a white phosphorescence. Delaney slipped his arm around Jordan's shoulders.

The ship suddenly rode high on a large swell, then plummeted like a rapidly descending elevator.

''Oh, God,'' Jordan exclaimed and held her stomach. ''I shouldn't have eaten that dessert.''

Delaney smiled. Moisture peppered his face. He first thought it was spray from a wave crashing against the side of the freighter, but it was rain beginning to fall. A moment later it became a downpour. They rushed toward their cabin.

Down in the bowels of the ship, the rolling was not as pronounced as on the higher decks. But the heat and the constant clamor of huge diesel engines still made it the worst place to be, the stocky, bald-headed crewman thought to himself.

Then he heard the unusual sound.

A sharp crack of metal upon metal.

Loud enough to be heard above all the other sounds.

He turned his face, greased with a mixture of sweat and grime, toward the dimly lit steel walkway framed on each side by big crates stacked towering nearly to the upper bulkhead.

They were all lashed securely; it had been his job to make certain of that when they were loaded. Nevertheless, he decided he should check again. If part of the cargo broke loose there could be damage both to it and the ship. He started down the walkway, eyeing each crate individually, making certain the lashings were secure both top and bottom on all of them.

He heard the sound again.

This time, paying attention, he realized it came from near the stern, close to a darkened area where one of the overhead lights had burned out. Again, a sharp metallic sound—almost like somebody had slammed a pipe against the steel bulkhead. His eyes narrowing, he increased his pace.

In a moment he reached the dark area of the walkway and passed into it, disappearing.

For several seconds there was no sound other than that made by the engines and the working machinery.

Then came the piercing scream.

CHAPTER 5

The sun rose over a still-frenzied sea, its waves almost as high as the night before. But it had quit raining. Alex, his wide frame swaying slightly from the motion of the ship, walked toward the bow. Delaney, his elbows propped on top of the rail as he leaned back against it next to Jordan, smiled at Alex's appearance. His slacks and white shirt looked as if he had slept in them, and his short hair was unbrushed and matted, its ends sticking down from the sides of his head.

"What happened to you last night?" Jordan asked, also smiling.

Alex stepped between them, leaned across the rail, and stared forlornly in the direction of Miami. "No more jokes about the marine," he said. "I nearly died last night. Does it ever get calm out here?"

Jordan smiled again. "Now you know how Paul feels."

"Speak of the devil," Delaney said. Paul walked up the deck toward them. He looked a lot better than Alex. In fact he didn't look sick at all.

"So what have we got, a fake here?" Jordan asked. "Really on a diet just to make us all look bad, right?"

"*Me* a fake?" Paul said. His tone caused Delaney to look at him.

Jordan's smile faded.

Paul shook his head. "Hell, even the wind blowing makes me irritated with how I've been feeling. Sorry."

Jordan's smile came back.

Paul smiled now, too, as he looked at Alex. "What's wrong with you?" he asked.

"I'm sorry for teasing you, Paul," Alex said. "You don't know how sorry I am."

"Would you like to go eat some breakfast?" Paul asked, a grin on his face now. "I hear they have pancakes and syrup this morning. Maybe biscuits and gravy."

Alex's eyes closed at the thought.

Jordan shook her head. "Does one of you always have to be picking at the other?"

"Stop him, Jordan," Alex said.

She looked at Paul. "You do look a lot better."

"Yeah, except for the personality I think I'm back to normal. I hope."

Delaney noticed a crewman running up the steps to the bridge. The man hurried to the captain, standing on the observation platform jutting out from the bridge. Another crewman hurried up the steps. He had a pair of binoculars in his hands and another pair slung around his neck. He handed one to the other crewman and they moved to the platform's rail.

"Delaney," Jordan said. He looked at her.

"We're turning," she said.

They were, swinging back to the west, angling into the waves now rather than plowing directly through them. Delaney walked toward the bridge.

Jordan caught up with him as he reached the bottom of the stairs and started up them.

"What is it?" she asked.

"I don't know."

The captain turned toward them as they came up to him. They didn't have to ask. "There's a crewman missing," he said. "We've searched the ship. He must have been swept overboard during the night."

*   *   *

In the bowels of the pitching freighter, a large rat missing a right hindpaw awkwardly pulled itself up a leather binding strap which tightly secured three wide crates stacked one on top of the other. Near the top edge of the highest crate, the rodent stopped his progress and hung for a moment. His head lifted to look over the crate, his long snout sweeping slowly back and forth, his whiskers vibrating as he smelled.

Suddenly the snout stopped moving, the whiskers vibrated rapidly, black beady eyes stared at the form stuffed in the rear of the narrow space between the top of the crate and the upper bulkhead.

A clawed forepaw let go of the strap and reached over the top edge of the crate. Digging his nails into the soft wood the rodent pulled his thick body up onto the crate, and moved cautiously toward the form.

In a moment, made bold by the smell of death, the rat laid his whiskers back once more, opened his mouth, exposing curved, stained yellow teeth, bit into the soft flesh of a cheek, and began tugging at it.

Jordan looked at the crewmen staring through their binoculars in the hope of spotting the missing crewman. "We have some binoculars in the crates of supplies," she said. "We could help."

Delaney nodded.

Jordan turned from the rail. "I'll go get them."

"I'll go with you," Paul said.

At the entrance leading down to the storage decks, Paul held the steel door open. Jordan stepped over the raised lip onto the stairs. Paul closed the door behind them.

"Jordan."

She stopped and looked back at him.

"I am sorry for my tone a while ago."

"I wouldn't want to bet on my personality if I'd been seasick as long as you have." She started to turn back toward the steps.

"No, it wasn't that. It was you, really. You know how I've always felt about you—from the beginning."

She looked back at him as he continued.

"Just because it didn't work out . . . I mean at least you were around. When you were on the helicopter and I thought you might be . . . it nearly killed me not being able to say anything to you."

She stared a moment, then smiled softly. "Thank you, Paul." She was silent a moment. Finally she smiled again. "We better get the binoculars." She turned and started down the stairs.

CHAPTER 6

As Delaney came down the ramp into the Jackson, Mississippi, International Airport, he saw their two small children and Jordan's parents standing beyond the waiting area. Missey darted away from Mr. and Mrs. Daniels and, her little skirt flying out behind her, ran directly to him. He leaned to scoop her into his arms and swung her around.

"*Daddy*," she said, "I'm too big for that."

"You mean too fat or too old?"

Her blue eyes tightened and she pushed a lock of blonde hair back off her forehead. "Daddy," she said in a most serious tone, "I'm not fat."

"Seven's not old either. You never are going to be too big for me to swing around."

"Probably already hurt your back," she said, and pulled playfully at his tie.

Ryder, two years old and dressed in brown shorts and a white shirt, had finished hugging Jordan and now stared up at him. He reached down and caught the smiling boy in his arm and lifted him, too, then looked back at Missey in his other arm. "See, I can lift both of you."

He let them back to the floor when Jordan's parents stepped forward to hug her. Mr. Daniels held out his hand, and Delaney shook it, then hugged Mrs. Daniels.

"Did they give you any trouble?" Jordan asked.

Mrs. Daniels shook her head. "You know better than that; they were a joy. But we're glad you're back. We did so miss you two." She looked at the tiny indentation on the side of Jordan's neck and grimaced. "And that nearly frightened us to death when we heard."

Jordan touched her finger to the place. "Only ended up amounting to a Band-Aid and a tetanus shot. Didn't even need a stitch."

"You make it sound so casual," Mrs. Daniels said.

Delaney smiled a little. "I can promise you she didn't take it that easy at the time."

Minutes later, Delaney placed their last suitcase into the trunk of their car, slipped off his coat, and laid it on top of the bags, then walked around to the driver's door.

As he backed from the parking space, Jordan stared out through her window. "See Paul," she said.

His coat slung over his shoulder and his tie loosened, he stood beside the inner lanes of pavement passing in front of the terminal's lower level.

"You notice Beth wasn't here to meet him?" Jordan said. "I don't know what he's getting into by marrying her. She didn't say anything about it, but I could tell when we left on the expedition right in the middle of their planning their marriage, it upset her." And what was Beth getting into, too, with what Paul had confided on the ship?—*You know how I've always felt about you—from the beginning.*

There was no question as to how much that had taken her aback. Paul had not so much as even given her a friendly hug in all the time since they had broken it off. And then him saying that on the freighter, and his eyes looking into hers like they had—she realized she should have known all along. In fact, she should have known all along because he *hadn't* so much as given her a hug. She looked back across her shoulder.

Missey leaned over the seat between them. "I really did miss you," she said.

Jordan smiled. "We missed you, baby."

Missey's dark brown and black brindle boxer, Ozzie, was glad to see them, too. Between his eager prancing underfoot and a whirlwind tour of catching up on everything the children wanted to do—an impossible task—the weekend went quickly. Delaney especially rued not finding the time to take up his old Cessna. It had been something he had planned on the way others planned on relaxing with golf.

Finally, late Sunday night, they found a moment for themselves. Delaney held the door open as Jordan, carrying a tray with two glasses and crackers and cheese on it, stepped outside onto the courtyard that boxed in the front of their house. Although only twelve feet from the door to the tall stucco wall with its wrought-iron gate, and forty feet wide, it was an area of the house he enjoyed more than any other. He loved to sit out there at night, with the gaslight over the front door flickering on the cream-colored walls and casting shadows over the potted ferns. It reminded him of a courtyard they had enjoyed when they were in Acapulco on their honeymoon, and somehow it always made him feel like he was relaxing at some kind of exotic resort.

"It's a beautiful night," Jordan said as she settled into the cushioned iron chair next to his and looked up at the full moon and sparkling stars. She crossed her legs, her skirt moving up to the midthigh mark of her bare legs. He lifted his Bloody Mary from the tray and sipped from it.

"Did I fix it right?"

"Uh-huh." She always did. Of course she held her usual glass of orange juice in her hand. It had been like that since they had married, her orange juice and his Bloody Marys in the evenings, her orange juice and his coffee in the mornings. Even their taste in music remained different. His was varied and differed mostly according to the time of day. He liked tempered, slow music while he was eating breakfast, increasing the pace to faster tunes as he drove to his office and later in the day. Yet, the very first morning after they were married he had stepped into the kitchen to Three Dog Night's "Joy to The World" blaring from the radio as she fixed breakfast. It wasn't even seven o'clock.

And what else was different between them? He smiled. A lot of things. In fact their love of research was one of the few ways in which they were exactly alike. Ten long years of difference. Ten of the greatest years of his life. And he had almost lost her to a damn savage with a dart on their last day in Brazil. Her voice brought him back out of his thoughts. He had to think a moment to recall what she had said.

"Well, tomorrow the hard work starts. We have enough specimens being shipped in to keep everybody at the lab busy for months."

He nodded. "Assuming Carol has the culture mediums ready to go."

Jordan smiled. "When has Carol ever not had everything ready?"

He nodded. "Yeah. Maybe I should be worrying more about dead graduate assistants who didn't move fast enough to satisfy her." He glanced at his watch. Jordan sipped from her orange juice. Neither of them saw Missey's eye peering through the crack between the drapes inside the French doors leading from her room out to the courtyard.

Inside the room, Missey turned back toward the brindle boxer sitting beside her bed, waiting. "Path's blocked," she said.

Ozzie stared past her at the drapes. In a moment Missey hitched her nightgown above her knees and climbed back into her bed. "They'll go to sleep in a little while," she said. Ozzie crawled back into his accustomed place under her bed. Ryder lay asleep on his bed nearest the bathroom.

After a moment, Missey yawned and placed the back of her hand over her mouth.

"I'm sort of tired, Ozzie," she said. "Maybe we'll wait until tomorrow night, if you don't mind."

The brown and black mottled head poked out from under the cover hanging down off the side of her bed. But after awhile, with Missey not saying any more, Ozzie pulled his head back beneath the bed and went to sleep.

At the Port of Miami, the work of unloading the old freighter that had transported the expedition team members back from Brazil went on under bright lights. Forklifts and motorized carts carried crates of specimens and expedition equipment out the wide side doors on the vessel's dock side. A giant industrial crane towered high above the freighter and snaked large cables down into a cargo hold in the stern deck.

Inside the hold, grid-covered overhead bulbs gave renewed light on each deck, illuminating men hurrying about their work—except in an area on the lowest deck, where in a section nearest the stern, one of the lights, burned out, left part of a steel walkway in dark shadows. The sound of frantically scampering little paws came from the shadows. A moment later a large, bloodied rat dashed out into the light and jumped from the walkway into a cubicle formed where two large crates jutted out farther than the one in between. He scurried to the rear of the shallow space, sprang high, and grabbed a securing strap running up the front of the smaller case.

Behind him, a larger rat, slowed by the absence of a right hindpaw, leapt from the walkway into the space formed by the cubicle, and sprang up into the air onto the other rat's back.

The rat hanging by the strap squealed and twisted its head around as sharp, curved, yellow-stained teeth sank into the back of its neck. It hung on to the strap for a moment, then, burdened by the rat on its back, fell squealing back to the floor.

It was over in a moment, bits of dark fur mixed with blood splattered across the steel floor and onto the sides of the cases. But the crippled rat didn't stop then, continuing to rend and tear and rip at the smaller carcass until it was torn into bloody, stringy pieces.

Only a hundred feet away a fat, bald-headed crewman, his back to the scene of carnage, took a last drag off his roach, crushed it out in his hand and slipped the remnants of the marijuana into his jeans pocket. He waited until the cable being lowered to him had stopped, then caught it and hooked it securely to the clasps at the ends of the cables running underneath a pallet supporting another batch of crates to be lifted from the vessel.

Stepping back, he raised a small walkie-talkie to his mouth and said, "Take it away."

The cables tightened, caught around the bottom of the crates, and the load started up, tilting slightly and swaying. He stepped forward and looked up at the edges of the hole on the top deck, making sure the tilted load was going to clear the opening properly—and a body rolled off the top of the crates and, arms outstretched like a skydiver, plummeted toward him.

CHAPTER 7

Delaney pulled himself out of bed shortly after dawn, slipped on an old sweat suit and got in a few miles of jogging along the golf course behind his house. An hour later they delivered Missey to school at Northwest Rankin, and Ryder to Jordan's parents in Mill Creek. Then they drove the few miles into Jackson to the University of Mississippi Medical Center, a sprawling complex of teaching, research, and hospital facilities spread out across forty acres of gently rolling, tree-covered grounds northeast of the intersection of Woodrow Wilson and State Street.

Delaney parked in his reserved spot at the north of the complex and walked with Jordan back across the blacktop to the plant research center, a two-story structure not far from the seven-story university hospital.

A stack of the small crates of specimens they had collected in the rain forest had already arrived from Miami and sat in the hall outside the lab door. Carol, her broad brown frame encased in tight jeans and a sweatshirt emblazoned with the words ALCORN STATE, came down the hall pushing a small cart in front of her. It was stacked high with petri dishes, each covered with a glass lid.

"The last of the inoculated culture medium," she said as she stopped before them. She pushed a lock of her thick black hair off her forehead and nodded at the crates sitting against the wall. "We've barely enough cooling area for that bunch alone, and the invoices indicate they're only about a third of what will eventually come in off the freighter. I'm going to check with a couple of the other labs with cooling rooms and see if they can let us borrow some temporary storage space."

Delaney nodded. "Let me know how it goes. We might have to rent some refrigerated space somewhere else. Need to know by Wednesday, now. That's when the rest of the specimens are being flown in."

Carol nodded. "You'll know this afternoon."

Once inside the laboratory they moved to a long counter to the right of the door. It was the first in a line of identical counters running the breadth of the room. All of them were dotted with stainless steel sinks and various testing equipment ranging from simple Bunsen burners and light microscopes to high-tech equipment unknown only a few years before.

Several young graduate assistants standing around the counters moved into a group as Delaney started going over the procedures with them. First would be the cataloging and numbering of each of the specimens. Then each specimen would be divided into its parts—stem, leaves, and root for the plants, similar divisions for the molds and various other specimens. Each part was assigned a sub-number. Each of those parts would be further divided and assigned another sub-division number. They had collected enough of each specimen to do both the standard tests and some unique tests Jordan had designed. There would still be enough left over of each part of a plant or mold to use if something did show promise. It was nearly two hours before they left the work with Carol and the graduate students and moved into their office off to the side of the first counter.

A message from Mrs. Adkins, Paul's fiancée's mother, lay on Delaney's desk. It said to call her. *Important* was underlined.

Delaney dialed the number. Mrs. Adkins answered on

the first ring. "Oh, Delaney. I'm so glad you called. Have you seen Beth?"

"No."

He heard her plaintive sigh. "Delaney, I'm really starting to worry about her. She had to be here in New Orleans on business Friday when you all arrived. But she was coming on there as soon as she finished. Paul called Saturday and said she never arrived. Neither one of us have heard from her. I tried you all last night and this morning and your phone stayed busy. It must be out of order."

"No, it . . . you said she was supposed to meet him Friday?"

"Yes. She told me she expected to get back to Jackson around nine. Delaney, I'm so worried. Have you seen Paul this morning?"

"I assume he's lecturing one of his classes."

"He said he was canceling his lectures until she called. But he's not at home, either. I can't get any answer there now." There was a pause in Mrs. Adkins's voice. "He told me I should call missing persons here. He said he was going to contact them in Jackson. Delaney, I'm worried about a car wreck. I keep thinking about her lying out there in some bushes off the highway where nobody would see her. What am I supposed to . . ."

He heard the catch in her voice. She started crying softly. He closed his eyes. "I'm sure it's going to turn out to be something simple, Mrs. Adkins."

"I'm so afraid, Delaney."

He noticed Jordan staring at him with a look of deep concern. He shook his head. "Beth's missing," he mouthed, then spoke back into the phone. "Mrs. Adkins, let me get hold of Paul. See if he's heard anything yet. Then I'll get back to you."

He replaced the receiver and lifted it again, punching in Paul's number while he repeated the conversation with Mrs. Adkins to Jordan.

"Missey," Jordan said. "Bet she took our phone off

the hook so we wouldn't get a call to come in to work early.'' She shook her head. ''I'm not leaving home again, period. It's too rough on them.''

Paul's line was busy. Delaney tried it a second and third time, but it remained busy. He looked at Jordan. ''I think I'm going to run over there for a moment.''

Jordan wanted to go with him.

Twenty minutes later they drove down Paul's street in northeast Jackson. His car was not in the driveway of the small, redbrick home, and both garage doors were down. The front door was locked, too. Delaney left a note on the door telling him to call.

''What now?'' Jordan asked.

He wasn't sure. What did you do now? What would he do if it were his daughter missing instead of Mrs. Adkins's? *Go crazy, that's what.* He shuddered at the very thought.

That night they explained to Missey that they were waiting for a very important call, and told her why. The immediate deep concern in her eyes reminded Delaney how much she really was like her mother.

They had already called Mrs. Adkins back, and she hadn't heard anything yet. Paul's line remained busy. The operator had said there was nobody on the line.

Jordan shook her head. ''Actually I'm surprised Alex hasn't called us. You know he's heard about Beth being missing by now, as much as he's over at Paul's. He said he was seasick that last couple of days, but I don't know. I'm still not convinced Paul didn't catch something despite not having any fever. Maybe Alex's caught the same thing.''

As she paused, she shrugged. ''But, then again, knowing the way Alex is, if he was still feeling bad he would have probably called me by now, wanting me to come over and check on him.''

Delaney smiled to himself. She wasn't kidding. With

Alex's father and mother gone, and him an only child, he had adopted Jordan as the sibling he had always wanted, and that had gone on for years now. In fact, Delaney remembered Alex being the one who introduced him to Jordan.

"This new doctor that's here to work in research," Alex had said, *"well, I just met her, and you're not going to believe your eyes."*

And he hadn't. But Paul had already met her, even if only the day before when she had visited the center after accepting the position. And even if it had been only the day before, among friends anyway, that meant Paul had staked his claim first. Then, as things go, Jordan and Paul hadn't turned out to be right for each other. Delaney remembered knowing that Jordan was right for him though, and he had been right for her, too. They had both come to that realization even before she and Paul stopped dating. That was twelve years before, and it was the only secret either of them had ever kept from Paul. He was that good a friend—to both of them.

He glanced at his watch. "I think I'll run over to Paul's for a minute. See if he's there."

Jordan nodded.

Moments later he backed their Maxima out of the garage, drove up the street past a small walking park, and turned at its end onto the main street leading out of the subdivision.

A few minutes after that, a white Taurus turned in off the same street and drove to the side of the park, where it stopped at the curb.

Delaney found Paul's house completely darkened. The garage doors were still down and the front door still locked, though the message he had left pinned there was gone. He stopped at a pay phone and called home. Jordan answered on the first ring.

"You hear anything yet?" he asked.

"No," she said. "Paul wasn't home?"

"His car's still gone, but he's been there. He got my note." He glanced at his watch. "I think I'll call the hospitals. He could have found Beth there."

"Be careful."

He knew she was transferring her fear from what might have happened to Beth to her own family now—just as he was doing.

"You be careful, too. Make sure the door's locked."

A man in Castlewoods looking out his window at the white Taurus stepped to the switch panel next to the front door, turned on his yard light, and ran back to the window. The dark figure in the car looked his way. The car suddenly pulled out from the curb and went up the street toward the narrow fronts of the condominiumlike houses sitting close together in a row.

As the car neared the stucco front of Delaney and Jordan's home, it slowed. The man inside stared out the driver's window through the wrought-iron gate in the wall of the small courtyard fronting the house and saw Missey standing behind the glass doors of her bedroom, looking back out at him.

Suddenly an agonizing pain ripped through his stomach and he bent over, bumping the steering wheel and sounding the horn. He pressed on the accelerator and sped up the street.

Jordan heard the sharp sound of the horn. Her brow wrinkled quizzically. She rose and walked toward the front door.

Missey, in a long cotton gown and barefoot, met her in the hall. "It was a car," she said. "It almost stopped. But it didn't."

"Okay, thank you, baby. Now you get on back in bed."

Jordan opened the door.

"It went up the street," Missey said.

"Okay. Now you do as I said and get in bed."

Missey frowned.

Jordan placed her fists at the top of her hips and brought a theatrically stern look to her face. "Don't you frown at me, little lady."

Missey stared back at her, then, slowly, the corners of her mouth lifted, and she broke into a smile. She turned back into her room. Jordan stepped to the front door, looked out it for a moment, then closed it.

A few seconds later, the Taurus came back down the street, slowed, and turned onto the short concrete apron in front of their garage.

CHAPTER 8

On the lower deck of the old freighter berthed at the Port of Miami, a homicide detective looking for additional clues in the area of the murder, stared over the walkway rail at the fat crewman, on his hands and knees, scrubbing up the blood and dismembered body parts of a rat.

"What do you all keep on this ship, a cat or a mountain lion?"

The fat crewman stared down at the mangled remains. "We don't keep nothin'," he said, and took another swipe at the dried blood with his wet cloth. Then he grimaced and cussed. He had cut his damn finger on a piece of loose steel next to a rivet.

"Son of a bitch," he said and stood and purposely kicked his pail over.

The pink liquid splashed across the steel floor and ran slowly toward a side of the ship, settling into each crack and joint it passed.

The detective smiled, shook his head and started down the walkway.

Three levels above them, in the bright illumination of the industrial floodlights, two other men talked. One was the red-haired captain of the freighter. "We thought he had been washed overboard," he said.

The second man was middle-aged with graying dark

hair and dressed in a drab brown suit. He had been the first homicide detective on the scene the night before. He jotted the captain's answer into a notebook and glanced back toward the open hold leading down into the lower decks. "Whoever the crazy bastard responsible is, I hope he resists when we catch him. I'd like to be the one who catches him and have him give me an excuse." He shook his head in disgust at what he had seen. "Bit his face while he was strangling him; down on him like some damn wild dog—you know he's going to try to cop an insanity plea when we catch him. And we will catch him with all the prints he left."

As the detective paused, he glanced toward the hold again. "If that wasn't bad enough, there was the rats getting after the corpse. I seen one other like that, a prostitute whose body was dumped near a landfill. They go after the soft parts first—the eyes and the tongue. Makes you sick to see a bastard eaten up like that."

The captain's eyes narrowed. "His name was Bob Horne."

"Pardon me?"

"The bastard you referred to, his name was Bob Horne," the captain said, and turned toward the steel steps leading up to his quarters, leaving the detective staring after him.

Jordan heard the doorbell ring. Her forehead wrinkled— Delaney had a door key on his car ring. She came off the living room couch and walked up the hall to the front door. Looking out the peephole in the center of the door, she saw Paul standing outside the courtyard gate. She opened the door and hurried across the concrete to him. "Where have you been?" she asked as she swung the gate back.

"Looking for Beth," he said in a low, subdued voice. "At least when I haven't been on the phone calling all over hell."

Jordan felt a wave of sadness settle over her. "I don't guess you've heard anything?"

Paul was a moment in answering. "They found her car in South Jackson."

Jordan felt her throat tighten.

"They say it was broken down. I guess she was hitch-hiking on to my place. I guess."

"I . . ." What was there to say? Jordan thought. She shook her head a little. "I'm sorry, Paul."

He nodded without saying anything and walked on toward the front door. When he entered the house, Missey stuck her head out of her bedroom. "Hi, Mr. Paul," she said, looking up at him.

Paul looked at her. "What are you doing up this time of night?" Missey smiled, waiting for his next remark. He was always teasing her. But he said nothing else.

"Missey," Jordan said, "go on and get in bed now, and stay there. You have school tomorrow."

Missey frowned, but her head slipped back inside her room. Paul moved up the hall. "Where's Delaney?" he asked back across his shoulder.

"Actually he's out looking for you. We were worried when you didn't answer your phone. He'll be back soon. You want anything—a drink?"

He shook his head, walked across the living room carpet to the wide, plateglass windows overlooking the patio, and stared toward the golf course. Jordan saw his shoulders slump a little. She wondered what he was thinking, but felt awkward and didn't say anything. Finally, he faced back toward her. He looked even more haggard in the bright lights of the living room than he had in the dimly lit hall. His normally rugged face appeared to have sagged, he looked so tired.

"It's so bad," he said in a low voice, then his voice choked slightly, and the last couple of words he uttered were unintelligible. She saw his hand tremble. She felt absolutely terrible for him now. He started back across the carpet toward her.

At that moment the front door opened. Delaney came up the hall into the living room. "You heard anything about Beth?" he asked Paul.

"They found her car," Jordan said.

Delaney wrinkled his brow questioningly. "Was there—"

Paul shook his head. "Just her car." He glanced up the hall toward the front door. "I guess I'll be going."

Jordan shook her head. "You just got here."

"Yeah. I don't know, it's ... I was just driving around. I need to go on and get some sleep." He walked toward the hall.

Delaney walked with him, opened the front door, and led him out through the courtyard to the gate. "Paul, if there's anything at all that we can do ..."

"Appreciate it, Delaney, but what?" There was a momentary faraway look in his eyes. "What can anybody do?" Without saying any more, he stepped through the gate. After his car had backed off the concrete apron and turned up the street, Delaney stood a long time, staring at the red taillights until they were out of sight. He didn't notice that Jordan had stepped up behind him until she spoke. "Just driving around. I know how he must be feeling. I'm afraid it's going to be bad since they found her car."

He nodded without saying anything.

Jordan looked toward the French doors leading into Missey's room. "She was up when Paul came in. I don't know how she gets by on such little sleep. I'm dreading the time when she's a teenager. She can wait us out any night if she wants to."

He smiled. "She won't have to slip out. Not the way she can talk you into anything."

"Me?"

"Yes, you."

Jordan smiled a little, a wistful-looking smile. "Well, we tried for two years to have her, then went nearly another five years before Ryder. What am I supposed to do but spoil both of them?"

She glanced in the direction Paul had driven before she turned toward the front door.

In Miami the detective looked at the computer comparisons between the bloody fingerprints off the packing crate and the scientists' records. He looked up at the younger detective standing in front of his desk.

"Jackson, Mississippi," he said.

CHAPTER 9

Jordan stood next to her side of their bed. "I keep thinking about Paul coming over here," she said. "We should have made him stay for a while, talked to him."

Delaney had already slipped under the covers. He glanced at the telephone on her bedside table. "Why don't you call him? Maybe he'll talk to you when he wouldn't me."

"What do you mean?"

"The garage door was up. It was obvious my car wasn't here. I think he stopped to talk to you, then wouldn't when I came in. His pride, I guess, not wanting to sound whiny around me."

She frowned a little. "That's crazy, but, yes, that'd be typical of him. You too. Alex's the only one who will ever say anything when he is down." She reached for the telephone. "What do I tell him?"

"I don't know. You're the woman."

She frowned again and punched in the number.

Paul's telephone rang and rang. She was about to replace the receiver when the answering machine came on.

"Paul, this is Jordan. I know how you're feeling. We feel badly, too, not being able to help you. We're going to stop by there in the morning. Maybe we can think of . . . something, I guess. We love you and are thinking about you." She slowly replaced the receiver. "I couldn't think of anything else to say."

"That was fine—just let him know we care."

She nodded feebly and walked toward her dresser. In a moment she was unbuttoning her blouse and slipping it off. She stared back at him by her reflection in the mirror. "I wonder what he wanted to tell me?"

The figure was too shadowy to make out clearly as he stood in the bedroom of the darkened house. He pressed the message button on the answering machine:

"Paul, this is Jordan. I know how you're feeling. We feel badly, too, not being able to help you. We're going to stop by there in the morning. Maybe we can think of . . . something, I guess. We love you and are thinking about you."

The machine gave the date and time, then said, "*No further messages.*"

Off to the side of the bed on the floor, a blood-soaked sheet covered a slim figure. The only part of the body that could be seen was one pale hand sticking out from a corner of the sheet, and the long blond hair and part of the forehead that wasn't completely covered.

Directly across the hall in the adjacent bedroom, all that could be seen of a man lying off to the side were his shoes and trouser-clad legs, both soaked in blood.

Back in the room with the answering machine, the dark figure moved his hands to his head and began to shake it back and forth. A low murmur escaped his lips, then a louder sound, still unintelligible. He suddenly turned and strode back through the house and out the door he had entered only a moment before.

A few seconds later a car engine roared to life in the garage, and then the quick squeal of tires against concrete as the white Taurus reversed rapidly out of the garage into the street. As the car sped down the pavement, a next-door neighbor looked out his window, then let the curtains fall slowly closed.

*   *   *

Jordan faced the mirror as she unzipped her skirt and slid it down her bare legs. Delaney stared from their bed at her figure, hidden now only by the thin line of the back of her bra and her narrow panties. Despite their ten years of marriage she had changed hardly at all. Maybe a bit more filled out. She had been a little too skinny, anyway, especially her legs. Now they were fully formed, her thighs tight and rounded nicely as they tapered down from small hips to narrowing firm calves and slim ankles. Their shape made her legs appear long despite her barely five-foot-five-inch height.

She tilted her shoulder toward the dresser mirror, looking at the tiny indentation at the side of her neck. "I believe it is going to leave a scar. What do you think?"

"I think you're beautiful."

"Delaney, we're talking about my neck," she said.

"That, too. I always thought the only thing it lacked was a little dimple. Just didn't want to hurt your feelings by telling you so. Now it has one."

She smiled back at him from the mirror, reached behind her and undid her bra and laid it on the dresser. He stared at her reflection as she lifted a short gown from the dresser and slipped it down over her head. "Come here," he said.

She came around the bed to stand between his knees. At his slightly-over-six-foot height, his face nearly reached hers even sitting down. He slipped his hands around the small of her back, kissed her gently on the gown between her breasts, and pressed her toward him. She came easily into his lap, facing him, her knees out to each side of his hips.

She smiled a little now. "This is a lot better than having to worry about Paul or Alex popping into our tent, isn't it? When we were in Brazil I kept waiting for the flap to be thrown back." Still smiling, she reached to switch off the table lamp, then lowered her lips to his.

Delaney tugged her gown over her head and off her

arms, then turned her out of his lap to her side and laid her back against the mattress. When he leaned to kiss her, he slid his hand down her body. A slight moan escaped her lips pressed against his.

A moment later her hands elicited one from him.

Then she was pressing her body up against his and twisting at the same time, rolling him over onto his back—and she came up on top of him, staring down at him.

A minute later, the glow of soft moonlight filtering through the curtains at the side of their room silhouetted his tightly muscled body and her slim one, angled across the bed, straining together in dim relief.

Missey threw the covers back from her face, glanced at Ryder asleep in the next bed, and slipped to the floor. She carefully arranged her pillows and covered them with her blanket to make it look like she was still in the bed and, in her long gown and barefoot, walked toward the glass doors leading out onto the courtyard.

"Ozzie," she whispered.

The brindle boxer slipped out from under her bed and bounded toward her.

"Shhh," she said as she opened the doors.

Once outside, the light from the gas lamp flickering on her face, she quietly closed the doors behind her. Then she and Ozzie hurried to her left, past her Momma and Daddy's iron chairs, around the corner of the house and down the narrow walkway between the next house and hers.

Her small backyard was mostly a tile-covered patio, complete with a narrow lap pool. A few feet of grass ran from the patio to a black iron fence. She glanced back at the master bedroom and saw its lights were off. Ozzie already waited at the gate. She hurried to it. "Quiet now," she whispered, and swung the gate back. Ozzie darted down the steep slope behind the house and disappeared into the dark.

Missey smiled. Her mother had said it was too dangerous for Ozzie to play outside—there were too many cars going and coming in the subdivision. But how many cars would be out this time of night? And besides, wasn't it unfair for him to be cooped up all the time? Her mother said she was against that for zoo animals—and Ozzie was certainly more deserving than any zoo animal. Missey smiled again and raised her face out over the golf course at the bottom of the slope, looking at the dark outline of the ninth fairway. Bisecting it was a creek where she often found golf balls. Where the creek turned back to the right was a thick patch of woods and undergrowth paralleling the far side of the fairway. That's usually where Ozzie went to play, and sometimes a little farther. But he was always back in ten or fifteen minutes.

Then she heard the sudden agitated barking down on the course.

She looked that way. "Shhh," she said aloud though she was at least a couple of hundred yards from where he was.

Now a growl, barely loud enough for her to hear. It came from the course, too.

"Ozzie, will you stop it?" she whispered and looked back across her shoulder to her house.

But it didn't stop, instead grew louder and, suddenly, turned into the sound of dogs fighting.

Her eyes widened. Ozzie had jumped on another dog. "Oh, no," she murmured, and sprinted down the slope toward the creek.

The telephone rang.

Delaney moved away from Jordan's arms and reached for the receiver. "Hello."

"Delaney, this is Sheriff Langston. Have you seen Paul?"

"Yes, an hour or so ago. Is it Beth?"

"Where was he?" Langston's sharp tone took Delaney

aback. This was a man Delaney had known since child-hood.

"He was out here."

"Do you know where he went?"

"Home, I guess."

"He's not there now."

"Sheriff, what's going on?"

"Delaney, he's gone mad."

He sat up on the side of the bed. "What in the hell are you talking—"

"He killed his fiancée and another man."

Delaney felt the blood drain from his face.

"And he left a note on his desk about Jordan. I'm on my way out there now."

"Jordan? What do you mean a note?"

"I'll tell you when I get there. But if he shows up back out there before I do, shoot him before you let him inside. He bit his fiancée all to hell."

The line disconnected.

Jordan stared at him. "What?" she asked.

He was so stunned he just looked at her.

"Delaney, damnit, what is it?"

"Ozzie?" Missey questioned.

There had been no more fighting sounds since shortly before she ran up to the thick undergrowth at the far side of the fairway. But no Ozzie either.

Her brow wrinkled with the beginning of her worry.

"Ozzie," she called louder.

Still, he did not come to her.

The bottom of her gown was growing damp from the dew, and she lifted it up and walked across the narrow strip of concrete that golf carts used to travel along the course. Close up against the sidewalk's far side, the tall bushes and trees rose high and dark above her head.

"Ozzie, darn it, will you at least answer me?" She poked her face into the bushes.

The moon was bright, but the bushes were so thick

they cut off most of the light. But she had wormed her way through them when she and Ozzie hunted for golf balls. There were no thorns to tear her gown or stickers to hurt her feet. She pushed her shoulder past a restricting bush and stepped into the thick area.

"Ozzie," she called.

Her lip trembled. But she shook it off. He wasn't hurt. Maybe the dog who fought him was—but not Ozzie.

"Ozzie. Ozzie, will you please . . ."

A slight sound answered her this time. It had come at the same moment she was calling him and she hadn't been able to tell what it was.

"Is that you, Ozzie?"

The sound of a limb moving.

"Ozzie?"

The limb swung back to brush against another.

Her hands tightened at her gown.

"Ozzie, darn you!"

A sound suddenly closer now.

Missey turned and burst through the bushes behind her and out onto the golf course. She looked back across her shoulder, and then ran as hard as she could.

She heard something lunge out of the bushes behind her, but didn't even look back this time. *"Helllp meee!"*

It was right behind her.

"Helllp meee!" she screamed.

Then Ozzie was past her, bounding, looking back at her over his shoulder.

She stopped in her tracks. *"I hate you!!"*

Ozzie stopped and turned and faced her. His ears went up and he cocked his head to the side.

"Oh, I'm sorry," she suddenly said and ran to him. "Did you get hurt?"

She knelt and quickly felt over his shoulders. He pulled away toward the house. "No, Ozzie, wait a minute. I want to make sure you're not hurt."

He submitted to her feeling him over.

After a moment, she smiled.

Then she looked back over her shoulder toward the bushes. "I hope you didn't hurt anybody else's dog."

He licked her face.

She remembered her parents—and her screaming. She cupped her hand over her mouth and looked toward her house.

Fifty feet above the golf course, near the rear of her patio, a figure stared down at her.

Her heart stopped.

She was going to get it now. *Unless she acted hurt or something,* she thought.

But whoever it was, her daddy or mother, they had seen her running across the fairway. It would have to be something other than her foot.

What?

Somebody had tried to steal Ozzie and she had chased them away. No, that wouldn't work. Who was tough enough to steal Ozzie?

But she better make up her story quick. Whichever one of them it was at the rear of the house, they had started down the slope toward her.

Ozzie stared in the same direction, cocked his head, and raised his ears again. He let out a low growl.

"*No!* Ozzie. We're in trouble enough as it is."

The figure reached the bottom of the slope. She thought it was her daddy, but she wasn't certain. Then another cloud crossed over the moon, and the figure became only a shadow as it walked toward her.

"Missey!" her mother called.

"Missey!" her father called.

Missey's brow wrinkled as she saw them standing at the rear of the house near the lap pool.

Ozzie growled loudly.

Missey looked back at the figure, and her heart began to beat wildly.

"*Daddy! Momma!*" she called.

"*Missey!*"

They both came running down the slope.

The cloud passed from the face of the moon.

The fairway lightened, showing Missey on her knees, her parents sprinting toward her, and fifty feet from her, the figure walking toward her.

Mr. Paul.

Her racing pulse slowed. She came to her feet.

Ozzie stiffened, took a step forward, and growled louder.

"Shut up, stupid. That's Mr. Paul."

Ozzie growled again.

The sound that came from Paul was even deeper.

Missey's heart jumped into her throat.

Delaney, his pistol in his hand, sprinted as hard as he could toward the figure walking toward his child.

"*Get away from her!*" he yelled as loud as he could.

The figure immediately stopped and turned back to face him.

Paul!

Delaney's blood chilled. They were only twenty feet apart now. He stopped. "Paul, what . . ." The face contorted, the mouth gaped open. Paul uttered a deep guttural sound and ran at him as hard as he could.

"*No, Paul!*" Delaney raised his pistol. But he couldn't make himself fire. He dove to the side as Paul lunged for him.

"Paul!" Jordan screamed.

He groaned and lunged at her. She dodged him. His hand, crooked into a claw, swung back around at her. His face twisted back toward hers. Saliva flowed from his mouth. Her eyes widened. She drew her hands to her face. Delaney scrambled toward them. Paul groaned again, grabbed her arm and jerked her toward him, reached for her throat.

Delaney fired rapidly twice, then twice again.

Paul spun around, took a step toward him, seemed to hesitate a moment, swaying, looked at the pistol. Almost a realization of something seemed to sweep across his features, and he pitched forward onto his face.

"*Nooo!*" Jordan screamed.

"Daddy!" Missey screamed.

Paul convulsed and lay still.

CHAPTER 10

Delaney stared at Paul, sprawled on his stomach, his arms outstretched with his head out to the side and his eyes wide, staring blankly. "Daddy," Missey cried and ran sobbing to him. She flung her arms around his legs. He reached down and caught her and lifted her to his chest. She threw her arms around his neck. "Daddy, Daddy, Daddy." She kept shaking her head back and forth. He patted her back softly and looked at Jordan, her hands at the sides of her face and crying, too.

"Take her to the house," he said.

Jordan's hands slipped around to her mouth as she looked at him.

"Take her to the house," he repeated.

Jordan came slowly to him. As he pulled Missey away from his neck, Jordan looked at Paul's body and back to him. "You need to come, too," she said.

He nodded as he handed Missey to her, but made no move to follow them as Jordan turned toward their house. Then he looked back at Paul's body.

"Paul, what . . ." he started in a low voice. "My God, Paul, what happened to you?" He looked at the revolver lying where he had dropped it and shook his head slowly. "Beth, they said that you . . . how could . . ." Sirens came from the street past the ninth green. A sheriff's department cruiser sped by with its blue lights flashing.

He paid no attention to it and shook his head again. "Paul, please, what . . . my God, Paul, what caused . . ." Then he was silent in his shock.

The cruiser braked to a stop in front of his house. Seconds later flashlight beams swept back and forth in front of men running down the slope behind the house. He didn't know Sheriff Langston had stopped beside him until he heard the tall man's voice. "Delaney?"

Delaney looked at him. The gray-haired man staring back at him with compassion in his eyes had been his parents' best friend. "Delaney, let's go on to the house."

A deputy shined his light on Paul's face.

Delaney stared at the man. "You don't have to do that."

The deputy stared back at him. The sheriff looked at the deputy and shook his head. The light went out. Another cruiser sped along the street beyond the ninth hole.

"Delaney," the sheriff said in a soft voice. "His neighbors saw him going in and out of his house the last couple of days. His fiancée's been dead at least three. He had to be walking all over her. And there was a crewman found murdered on the freighter you all came back on."

Delaney stared at him.

The sheriff nodded. "The prints the killer left there matched with Paul's prints."

Delaney looked back at Paul's body.

"Delaney, God only knows why, but he went mad. Now you need to come on up to the house. You have a wife and child up there scared to death. And Jordan was his friend, too. She needs you more up there than down here."

In Miami, only the illumination of the moon was left to frame the large rat as he wobbled clumsily down the line leading from the vessel to the pier.

When he reached the bottom of the line and jumped off to the concrete, he left a faint smudge of red.

Moving in awkward short jumps due to his missing

right hindpaw, he traveled slowly down the darkened pier and toward the thoroughfare leading to downtown Miami.

Delaney stared up from the couch in his living room as Sheriff Langston handed him several sheets of paper folded in half. ''We found them in Paul's house. Like a diary he was keeping.''

Delaney unfolded the sheets. Jordan leaned closer beside him and looked down at them. Paul had started writing while still at sea.

First, there was the part where he began to suspect his sickness was caused by more than the waves. Delaney's eyes narrowed. Paul wrote that he kept getting sicker and sicker each night. He remained almost normal during the day, at least at first. Then even the days started to be bad. Not the nausea and pain that mixed in his stomach each night. Not the rage that always appeared then, he wrote. Rather a terrible depression and constant irritation—and his thoughts. He kept referring to them simply as thoughts. Then, suddenly, he was feeling perfectly well during the day. Delaney glanced up at the sheriff, and back at the sheet.

Twice on the page was the written promise by Paul that he was going to tell his friends what was happening to him, what the disease was doing to him.

Disease? Paul was referring to what was happening to his mind as if he were discussing a physical disease rather than a mental one. His doctorate was in biology, he had taught for years at the medical school; he would have known. But a physical disease, Delaney thought, affecting his mind—how?

Delaney looked back down at the bottom of the page. Paul wrote about killing the crewman. Delaney heard Jordan catch her breath over his shoulder.

He shook his head in confusion. ''How could he have done that and appeared so normal afterward? He . . . and acting normal again after Beth, too.''

"Normal?" Langston grunted. "If you'd seen her body and the man's . . . he evidently gave her a lift to Paul's. He was beaten to death; she was strangled—and bitten and scratched all to hell while he was killing her."

Delaney sat a moment, then slid the bottom sheet up over the one he had just finished. It was the worst part yet—how Paul, back in Jackson and knowing Beth was on her way, knowing what he would do when she arrived, had coldly waited for her. Those hours prior to her death were the last instance of his taking the time to write in detail.

But then there was the printing.

It said:

> I killed the crewman.
> I prayed to God to help me.
> That caused me to think about killing again.
> The devil has taken me over completely.
> Jordan keeps bothering me.

Delaney paused at seeing Jordan's name—and the final line on the page. *It's her fault.*

He slid the last sheet onto the top of the others. Only three words there, in big, bold letters printed in the middle of the page:

KILL THE BITCH

Delaney felt a chill run up his back. Jordan looked up at Langston, who shrugged.

"He played back your message on his answering machine." he said. "Did he write it after hearing that? Or had he already written it—before he came out the first time, prior to Delaney coming back to the house? And your fault—who will ever know what was going through his mind? All I know is it looks like you were lucky, Jordan." He held out his hand for the sheets.

Delaney handed them back to him. "I'll be going

now," Langston said. "You'll both need to come in sometime in the next couple of days and sign your statement."

Jordan nodded. Langston turned toward the hall. The deputy waiting there fell in behind him and followed him toward the front door. Jordan's father let them outside. He and Mrs. Daniels had arrived there only minutes after Jordan had called them. Mrs. Daniels stepped out of the bedroom next to the front door. She put her finger to her lips in a gesture for quiet, and she and her husband came up the hall.

"That Missey's one tough kid," she said as they stopped in front of the couch. "After she was sure you all and Ozzie were okay, she went right to sleep."

Jordan looked up at them and nodded. "Thank you."

"I guess we'll go now."

Jordan nodded again. As her parents walked down the hall toward the front door, Delaney leaned back into the couch and shook his head. "It doesn't make any sense, his coming after you, his going crazy in the first place. He was perfectly normal when we saw him. And what he had already done . . ." He shook his head in confusion. "Even back on the freighter," he added.

CHAPTER 11

Delaney sat in the living room the rest of the night. Shortly after eight in the morning, feeling no better, but starting to come out from under the shock of what happened, he glanced at his watch, lifted the receiver from the telephone on the coffee table, and punched in a number.

When a voice answered he said, "May I speak to Dr. Townsend?"

"I'm sorry, sir. He's performing an autopsy."

"This is Delaney Jeffries. He knows me. Will you ask him to call me at home as soon as he's able?"

Jordan's parents came for Missey and Ryder shortly after nine. It was another hour before Dr. Townsend returned Delaney's call.

"First, I want to tell you how badly I feel about this," Dr. Townsend said.

"Thank you, I appreciate that, doctor. Have you . . ." He took a deep breath. "Have you had time yet to do the autopsy?"

"He's the one I was working with when you called."

"Did you discover anything?"

"No sign of lesions or tumor in the brain, if that's what you're suggesting. In fact, nothing I could discern in any way that would have led to what he did. Maybe it was chemical. Maybe it just happened. There are examples all the time of a mental illness that pushes an individual to grossly distorted behavior, and yet there's nothing there to measure. Maybe the way I can best explain that to you is to have you think of someone who attacks their spouse in a rage of jealousy. That's certainly unbalanced behavior, yet there's no way to measure jealousy anymore than you can quantitatively measure love. I'm sorry, I know that's not much, but that's all I know to tell you.''

"Doctor, there's a chance he was coming after Jordan. I mean her in particular. That doesn't make any sense. She was the best friend he ever had.''

"Maybe that's part of it, Delaney. I'm not trying to sound like a psychiatrist, but I did have some psychiatric rotations in medical school. We all did. It's not uncommon at all for someone who has gone off the deep end to come after his closest friend. It's like it doesn't really matter what anybody else does to him. But then when a friend lets him down, or he imagines he did, then that's more than he can stand.''

"But Paul wasn't unbalanced. Not until now. We're not talking about someone who had a history of mental problems.''

"I'm sorry, Delaney. I've told you all I can.''

Still frustrated, Delaney slumped back into the couch. "Yes, sir, thank you. Thank you for returning my call.''

Mad, Delaney thought as he replaced the receiver, and only an hour earlier he had been sane at their house. It was Jordan's fault, Paul wrote; whatever was going through his mind he was coming after her. But not only her—mad before that too, killing Beth and the man with her. And yet Paul had been sane enough in one sense—enough to hide the man's pickup from view. It had been found locked in Paul's garage. Mad before that, too—the crewman. Mad, then sane—at least acting sane—and then back to mad, going back and forth and back and forth again. That was what stuck in Delaney's mind more than anything. It didn't make sense. Going suddenly mad at all didn't make sense.

Nothing made sense.

The doorbell rang.

It took him a moment to register the sound, and by then Jordan was already walking up the hall toward the door.

A few seconds later he heard Alex's voice.

He had known Alex would be there as soon as he received the news. And now, as emotional as Alex was, was he going to come in crying? That was Alex's way, but Delaney didn't know if he could take that right now.

He rose from the couch when Alex, his thick shoulders drooped and his wide face pale and drained, walked slowly into the living room. The tears weren't currently present but the eyes couldn't have been more red if he hadn't slept in a week. Alex came across the carpet to the couch and, without saying anything, hugged him. Delaney felt awkward. He patted Alex on the back. Then he was being released and Alex's face was directly in front of his.

"How, Delaney, how? What happened to him?"

Delaney shook his head. "That's been going through my mind all night."

Jordan squeezed Alex's arm gently. "Have you had anything to eat?"

"I couldn't, not now."

Alex did look terrible, Delaney thought, not only his bloodshot eyes and the shock across his face, but his whole appearance. His short hair was uncombed and sticking down at the sides. His clothes looked like he had slept in them, obviously clothes that he had previously worn that he had grabbed and slipped on before he hurried from his house. Delaney wondered how he himself looked. He was sure at least as badly.

An hour later, Delaney, now showered and shaved and dressed in jeans and a white shirt, walked across the grass to a beige and tan striped Cessna 310, a twin-engine plane he had owned nearly as long as he had been married. He drained the sump pump under each engine, checked the flaps and ailerons for easy movement, and looked down into each fuel tank to make certain they were topped off. A casual look over the props, then running his hand over them feeling for nicks that might lead to metal failure, completed his quick checkout. He came up onto the right wing, opened the cockpit door, and slid across the copilot's seat to the pilot's seat.

A minute more of checking inside the cockpit, and then, the Cessna's throttle open and its engines roaring, he released the brakes and the plane jumped forward down the start of the long runway. With two thousand plus feet of runway behind him, he pulled back on the yoke and the old craft lifted off and up into the sky.

In a few seconds the town of Madison had become a place of toy buildings, and he banked right through a thin, wispy cloud and headed in a wide turn across the Ross Barnett Reservoir, the twenty-mile-long, thirty-three-thousand-acre lake northeast of Jackson.

And then he let go. Not sobbing even then, but tears running from the corners of his eyes and down his cheeks like water dripping fast from a spigot. The only words he said were, "I'm sorry, Paul," first in his mind, and then aloud.

"I'm sorry, Paul."

That night was unusually cool for a late August evening in central Mississippi. It had been cool that way ever since they arrived back from Brazil. The Channel 16 weather report had said the area was on its way to setting a new record. There had only been fifteen days above ninety the entire summer, with only seven more days left in August. Cooler weather normally set in by the middle of September. The old record had been set in 1974, with only forty-two days above ninety that year.

"It's been like fall all summer," Jordan said as she

handed him the Bloody Mary she brought out to the rear patio. She had her glass of orange juice.

She settled back into a chair across the round wrought-iron table from him. "And we spent a month of it in the rain forest," she added. "Just our luck."

He looked out across the ninth fairway illuminated by the bright moonlight and immediately felt uncomfortable again. That's how he had been feeling ever since he had come out to the patio. In fact, even before that. Every time he stood at the windows and looked at the spot where Paul died.

How long would that last? With the view there, right at the back of the house, there was no escaping it—as he had escaped the spot where his parents had been killed. Though the drunk had run the stoplight on the same street Delaney had been driving to school each day, he hadn't had to look at it for over a year. That was how long he took a detour. Never emotional about it, he simply wasn't going to drive by the spot. Then one day he finally did.

A year? A year of looking at the spot in the middle of the fairway. Or would seeing it every day make it take even longer for the horror to recede from his mind? Maybe never, he thought, and started to look away, but then saw movement near the bushes on the far side of the fairway. His stomach tightened involuntarily.

"What?" Jordan asked, and looked across her shoulder in the direction he was staring.

He realized then it was a couple walking slowly along the golf cart path. Jordan looked back at him. But she didn't dwell on the reaction he had shown, instead said, "You know, I think I would like to go out and eat tomorrow night. Get away from the house, relax a little. I might even get drunk. That would blow your mind, wouldn't it?"

"Jordan, I keep wondering if Paul was coming here to get us to help him? Whatever was wrong with him he obviously had his sane moments. He was at least thinking

about coming to us about what was happening to him—
he wrote he was wanting to. Maybe he was going to say
something to you before I came up, and then couldn't go
through with it. He came back, maybe to try again, and
this time he went—''

"Delaney, quit torturing yourself. I told you, whatever
the reason he came, he ended up meaning to kill us.
We'll never know why, but that was what he would have
done."

He sat a moment in silence, then raised his Bloody
Mary and sipped from it. Jordan looked at him. "Now
how about going out to eat?"

He nodded.

"You want to invite Alex?" she asked. "He could use
a break, too."

He nodded again. It would be after the funeral. That
was tomorrow, too. He was certain he would need a drink
after that. He looked back across the table at Jordan.

"How do you go to the funeral of someone you shot?"
he asked. "Paul's mother is going to be there. I keep
thinking about that. How am I going to face her?"

He found out the next day he didn't have to. When
Paul's mother had been told what happened, she had collapsed screaming. Afterwards, she refused to accept either her son's death or that he could have done what he
did. She was currently in an extreme depressive state in
St. Dominic Hospital under round-the-clock watch. So
was Beth's mother, suffering a possible mild heart attack
after identifying her daughter's body at Paul's. All these
things passed through Delaney's mind for the hundredth
time as the pallbearers carried Paul's casket past him.
Alex was one of them, and Delaney saw his eyes come
around to him.

He found himself feeling the need to break eye contact
and had to make an effort not to drop his gaze toward
the ground. He had felt that way when others had earlier
glanced in his direction, even though he knew the looks
weren't cast in anger or even doubt. He hadn't been in-

vited to be a pallbearer, but that wasn't a slight either. It just wouldn't have been right. He wouldn't have accepted anyway after being the one who fired the shots. Everybody knew what had happened, that there had been no choice, and nobody was casting blame. Then, trying to force the endless thoughts from his mind, he looked back at the small crowd assembled for the graveside service. Too small, not over twenty mourners there at the most. Paul had been outgoing. He had lots of friends. But where were they?

At home, not wanting to be seen at a funeral for a crazed, vicious murderer like Paul, he knew. And they would have been seen, too. The cameras were there from every station in Jackson, and a couple from out-of-town stations he didn't know. Friends, he thought again.

He was bitter for a moment, then it passed. People will be people. That was true everywhere and under every circumstance. Let a problem arise and see how many friends you really have. Maybe it was a tribute there were twenty there. Twenty was a large number. Of really close friends.

Then Reverend Williams began to pray, and Delaney bowed his head.

CHAPTER 12

As the graveside service ended and Reverend Williams stepped around the end of the flower-covered casket to shake hands with Paul's uncle, Delaney saw Alex coming toward him and Jordan.

"Hey," Alex said in a subdued voice, and nothing more. Delaney wondered if Alex could have said anymore without crying—up close he looked even worse than he had carrying the casket, his eyes still bloodshot, his whole face drained and tired looking. Somehow seeing Alex's continued suffering made Delaney feel even worse than he already did.

Jordan smiled softly at Alex and patted him on the shoulder. Then the three of them turned and started toward the line of cars parked along the road.

Alex glanced back over his shoulder at the grave. "I guess every time I drive into the medical center I'm going to think about the professor that's not teaching there any longer. He really was a good one."

They continued toward the cars. Delaney glanced back at the grave. Paul's uncle stared in his direction. He was the only kin Paul had left, other than Paul's mother. The lone childless uncle. The bloodline was coming to an end. Damn, he needed that drink and a helluva lot more. He looked past Jordan to Alex. "We're going to go out to eat tonight. We'd like for you to come along."

Alex didn't answer immediately. Jordan said, "Please. We'd really like to have you."

"I really don't feel up to it, Jordan. I'm going to have to get some sleep."

"It'd do us all some good," Jordan said. "You need to try and get your mind off it for a little while anyway. To just go back to your house and sit . . ."

Alex pondered a moment. "Can we make it early then? I am going to have to get some sleep."

Jordan nodded. "How about seven? You'll be home in bed by nine."

"Make it six-thirty."

"Fine. Is Nick's okay with you?"

Alex nodded and closed her door.

As he walked off Jordan looked after him. "He's keeping it all inside him. You can see in his eyes it's about to kill him. Go home and sleep, he said. That's a joke. He doesn't look like he's slept since it happened."

Delaney heard her talking, but he wasn't really paying attention to what she was saying. He was looking back at the gravesite and Paul's uncle still staring his way.

God, how could the man keep from hating him?

"Are you going back to the lab?" Jordan asked.

"I need to keep my mind on something."

"I probably do, too. But somehow I want to be with the kids right now."

When Delaney entered the lab, there were several students there working, watched over by Carol's stern face. They didn't look up. But that wasn't because of Carol, he knew. They didn't know what to say. What was there to say? He tried to force his mind to quit dwelling on such thoughts. That's why he was at the lab in the first place.

Moments later, having left the coat and tie he had worn to the funeral hanging in the office and now wearing a thigh-length white lab jacket, he was into his work with a vengeance—jumping from milking the extract from one section of plant to crushing and grinding another—and it began to work, his mind going long stretches without visualizing the look on Paul's face.

In an hour he had moved to one of the simpler first steps in trying to discern a new medicine. Infectious bacteria, already growing in a transverse section across the upper part of a culture medium contained in a petri dish, was removed from the incubator where Carol had placed it. Wearing a mask, he ran a swab along the bacteria, then made several sweeps of the swab up and down the lower clear half of the medium, these longitudinal sweeps implanting some of the bacteria in a new position.

Now a milky extract from one of the plant's leaves was brushed over half of the transverse section and completely over the longitudinal swaths.

If the extract showed an inhibitory action against the bacteria, it might show up in the coated half of the transverse section, either stopping or slowing the bacteria's growth. Maybe the extract wouldn't have the quality of attacking the already established bacteria, but it might have a prophylactic effect, preventing the new swaths of bacteria from taking root in the culture medium.

And then, as hard as he was trying not to think of anything but the lab work, the look on Paul's face just before he collapsed jumped back into his mind. After the shots were fired the look had seemed to change from one of rage to wonder. Questioning maybe. Realizing. A sad look sweeping over it. And then he had fallen and convulsed.

At seven thirty, Delaney sat in a booth beside a short wall running up to the second level in Nick's, a noted restaurant off Lakeland in Jackson. He had ordered the crabmeat-stuffed eggplant, while Jordan and Alex had ordered the fish of the day.

Even though he hadn't been any more certain than Alex that he was ready for eating out, he found himself not only enjoying the food but actually relaxing to a degree. He lifted his Bloody Mary and sipped from it. Coming towards him was a doctor he knew vaguely. The man nodded and smiled as he went past.

Delaney caught himself trying to remember the man's specialty. Now he did. A *gynecologist.* If the man had been a psychiatrist he might be of better use at the moment, he thought, and smiled a little to himself. Actually smiled, he realized. Well, that was a beginning, and he had to begin again. He heard laughter coming from the partitioned lounge area to the far side of the restaurant and wished he could do that too. Then he felt a sudden surge of guilt at wanting something so simple as to feel better. His mind swirled again, and he took a deep breath and lifted his glass back to his mouth. Jordan smiled at him, then went back to her conversation with Alex across from her.

Delaney noticed another man sitting at a far table close to the hostess's podium. He remembered him almost immediately, the owner of a car dealership in Jackson. The one where a few years before a salesman had tried to sell him and Jordan an "especially good deal on a used car."

It had been a two-year-old Lincoln. It had been beautiful—black cherry with a muted red leather interior.

It also had obviously been wrecked at one time. One side of the driver's door fit slightly looser than the other side. There was a faint difference in color on one of the panels, and an almost indiscernible tilting of a piece of chrome. Obvious. Not only wrecked, but whatever hit it had come hard.

He looked at another couple as they came down the tables. He remembered the man from a photo he had seen in the *Clarion Ledger.* An oil man named McGowan. Delaney thought he looked younger than his photograph. Then a waitress leaned to place warm rolls on the tablecloth.

Delaney glanced at Alex, picking at his food. His fish

had hardly been touched. And now there was a strange look on his face. Not sad so much—more like he was sick.

Alex noticed the stare. A small, halfhearted smile came to the wide face. "Paul, I guess," he said. He looked down at his plate for a moment, then stuck a fork into the fish. In a moment he was eating rapidly.

"I guess I just have to force myself," he said.

Then a blond was passing the table, and Beth jumped into Delaney's mind. Her mother had taken her body back to their original home in South Carolina for burial. Then he visualized Paul again, and couldn't shake the image.

How in the damn hell did you just go mad?

In Miami, it was only barely dark, but the old wino had nothing to stay awake for. He drained the last bit from his bottle and laid it beside him, then turned on his side in the large shipping crate and pulled a stained blanket up over his shoulder.

The big rat squealed its fury as it sprang through the air toward his face.

The wino reacted in a drunken stupor, first thinking somebody had pitched something into the crate with him. Then the curved, yellow-stained teeth sank deep into his cheek and he screamed and beat at the thick body with his arm.

The rat hung on even harder. The old man grabbed it and tried to pull it loose. The rat snapped at his hands, and he threw it from him and scrambled out of the crate.

The rat came back hard again, charging on three legs. The wino kicked as hard as he could, catching the creature under its chest and propelling it backward into the brick wall at the side of the alley.

The rat slammed to the concrete, rolled over, came to his paws, and the man was stomping it, the rat biting at his soles as he did. Even as the creature's back broke and it fell to his side, it kept snapping at the man's soles, snapping until there was no breath left in its body.

The old man stumbled back and reached a hand to his cheek. Blood poured from under his palm to his chin.

CHAPTER 13

Crushing, grinding, filtering, stirring, heating, mixing—Delaney still trying to keep his mind busy. Then Alex strode from the hallway into the lab. Several of his students followed along behind him.

"Hope you don't mind," he said. "I wanted my class to get a firsthand look."

Jordan smiled and came off her stool to face the students. Alex introduced her and Delaney, then walked to the specimen boxes sitting on the counter and turned back to face the students.

"This particular batch of specimens might not yield anything," he said. "The odds are that it won't. New finds don't come easily. In fact, if there were some way to bring back a specimen of every single plant from the rain forest, from all of the rain forests all over the world, there still might not be any results."

The students listened intently now. Even Carol. Alex was considered one of the top instructors at the center, and also one of the most demanding. Only the serious students enrolled in his lectures, and the looks on the faces of the ones present told Delaney they were another top group.

"But that doesn't mean anything," Alex went on. "Even if there's not currently a plant in any of the forests that will yield a new medicine, there will be some day.

That is the beauty of the rain forests. The plants there are constantly mutating, producing new plants with different makeups and extracts. A cure not there today might be tomorrow. Will be some day. So long as the forests are left alone to keep producing. Doing what for centuries they have . . .'' He paused a moment. "Doing what they have for centuries," he added quickly.

At the pause, Delaney had looked directly at him. Alex glanced at him but quickly was back in his lecture to his students. "So when someone tries to tell you there's no proof we're having trouble with the ozone layer, that nobody has proved the worth of the rain forests in regard to that problem, tell them that's not the problem worth arguing about. Tell them that what is really important is the one fact that stands without doubt. The forests *are* where we will eventually find many new medicines. It's been true in the past and it will be true in the future. Provided, again, that the forests are preserved for that benefit.

"And, finally, bear this in mind. Many diseases are fast becoming immune to current antibiotics. All diseases eventually will. That's the nature of what happens when an antibiotic is used. The most susceptible organisms causing the disease are killed. But there are a few that are resistant enough to survive, especially when the prescribed antibiotic is not taken full term or in strong enough dosage.

"These resistant organisms, without the competition of their weaker cousins, multiply rapidly, eventually causing a new, more resistant strain of the disease. Even stronger antibiotics are then called for, and the process repeats itself—the most resistant organisms remain, multiplying into an even stronger causative agent. Eventually, there is not an antibiotic strong enough to deal with the disease. That eventually happens to every antibiotic, always has. And, if there is no new antibiotic to treat the disease, the patient will die. Synthetic antibiotics are being developed in the laboratory. Yet, alone, they will never be sufficient in and of themselves. The bottom line is very simple—no rain forests, no new medicines from flora, and man could well go the way of the dinosaurs. Which, by the way, might have well disappeared due to the simplest of killers, little germs less than a hundred millionth of their size. I—''

The unexpected pause again, this time accompanied by a sudden motion of his hand toward his stomach. But it never quite reached there. Delaney saw Alex's eyes come to his again.

Alex smiled a little. "Every time I eat a damn burrito for breakfast."

Several of the students smiled. Alex looked back at them. "Well, that's enough boring talk for today." He glanced at his watch. "Oh, and I'm going to be late for an appointment." He gave a polite smile toward Jordan, and walked toward the door.

The students looked after him for a moment, then slowly began to break into small groups. A couple of them stepped to the counter to take a closer look at some of the specimens. Delaney heard one of the female students say, "That would make a hell of a patio plant."

After a minute, the remainder of the students started for the hallway. Carol and the graduate assistants were back hard at work.

Delaney continued to stare at the empty doorway.

Alex's face, he thought. It had reminded him of when Paul had looked so bad back on the freighter, the same look that Alex had carried the last couple days back into Miami—and now again. He looked toward two young black students on their way toward the door. He walked rapidly after them.

"Just a moment, please."

The two looked back at him.

"Has he been acting sick? I mean before now?"

"Excuse me?" the taller of the two students said.

"Alex. Dr. Brister. Has he been acting sick since he's returned? During his lectures?"

The student looked puzzled. "There haven't been any lectures. Today is the first time Dr. Brister has been back in class."

Sick the last couple days of the cruise.

Last night at Nick's, still pale, picking at his food like he didn't want it—then eating it rapidly after being noticed. Almost forcing it down.

Now, suddenly bringing his students by the lab—he had never done that before. Not in over a dozen years of his lecturing only a building away. But now he had. Almost as if he were trying to prove something.

Like he was okay.

But he wasn't okay. The abrupt stops in his lecturing, once reaching toward his stomach.

Paul's seasickness, his apparent seasickness had led to . . .

Delaney felt the most frightening feeling he had ever experienced wash over him.

He finished explaining his thoughts to Jordan. She shook her head almost before he was through. "Worry can make you sick, Delaney. He's terribly upset over Paul, too. Go look in the mirror, you don't look so good yourself."

"But I'm not sick. And I haven't been sick since we came back. He was sick the last two days of the cruise, then something else kept him from class the next day, now sick again—sick enough to reach for his stomach as if it were bothering him too. Maybe sick like Paul was."

Jordan frowned. "Delaney, don't say something like that. Don't even suggest it. Two people going mad within days of each other—from a sickness? Crazy."

"I know."

The Rankin County Sheriff's Department and jail was located in Brandon, a bedroom community a few miles east of Jackson. The jail was housed in the top two stories of a three-story brick building. It sat at the end of a narrow blacktop bounded by the old Rankin County Courthouse on one side and a few small businesses and an attorney's office on the other side. Delaney had been there some time now, in Sheriff E. B. Langston's office on the building's first floor, half sunken in the earth.

"I don't know," Langston said, shaking his head slightly.

"I know it's a one-in-a-million shot, Sheriff. God, I hope it's not even one in a million. But after Paul's writing about how he stayed sick, I can't ignore what I'm thinking."

Langston didn't immediately respond. He had been like that ever since he had started listening, seldom saying anything at all, a skeptical expression across his face much of the time. But once or twice he had raised an eyebrow and seemed to be listening more intently. Now he clasped his hands in front of him on his desk.

"Okay, Delaney," he finally said. "I'm going to bite. Sure's hell I'm going to regret it, but I'm going to bite anyway. So what do we do now?"

Before Delaney could respond, Langston said, "But first—" He lifted a small sheet of blue paper from his desk. "It might go a ways to telling why Paul came after your wife. Or you. It's something he'd been thinking on for a long time, anyway." He held the sheet out. "A deputy found it in a drawer at Paul's."

It was from the type of memo pad used at the medical center. It had been folded, was faded with age, and worn from being handled. It had his name printed with an ink pen at the top. It said:

Delaney:
I've gone over to Paul's to break it off. That's the only way to be fair. But I don't want him to

*ever know it had anything to do with us. I don't
want to hurt him like that.*

Love,
Jordan

CHAPTER 14

Alex's house was located off a street intersecting with Highway 80 in Pearl, a fifteen-minute drive from Castlewoods. It was a small, one-story yellow brick, with only a few shrubs around it. It was dark—only the glow of a night-light barely perceptible through closed drapes behind a big picture window at its front—but Alex's brown Buick sat in the carport. Sheriff Langston drove by twice without stopping. Delaney didn't speak. He was still thinking about the note of a dozen years before.

As they passed the house a third time, Langston shook his head. "I just don't know. I mean, even if you've hit it right on the head, how can you expect to just walk in at anytime and catch him in the act—I mean acting the way you say?"

Delaney forced his mind back to the present. "In Paul's letters he kept referring to the disease affecting him worse at night. When I thought back on it, we never saw him at night all the way back to Miami. We invited Alex out to eat last night. He insisted on setting a time where we could eat and be gone before dark." He paused a moment as he thought. "Hell, I don't know. I'm putting all this together, and I just don't know."

Langston glanced at him, then faced forward toward the windshield again. He ran his fingers through his grey hair and shook his head. "Hell, Delaney, when I first read that stuff Paul wrote, I thought it was the ravings of a nut. So you come by and tell me maybe it's not.'' He tapped his fingers nervously atop the steering wheel. ''Hell, I don't know, Delaney. I can understand the need for preventing panic, but if there is something wrong with him, why not simply take him out to Whitfield and let them isolate him in one of the criminally insane wards there until something can be figured out?''

Delaney shook his head. ''And have everybody in the county—hell, the whole country—knowing about the disease in a couple of days? If I'm right, you can keep him in jail without anyone knowing why until Washington can take over—somebody can take over. We don't do that, and the word gets out that it is a disease, that everybody who was on the freighter might be capable of spreading it, and some nut'll end up shooting one of them.''

''So we expose ourselves to it?'' Langston asked.

''Neither Jordan nor I have been sick. If it is a disease it's either not communicable—they caught it from something they did or ate or . . . God, I don't know, but as I told you, at the very least it's not easily communicable or Jordan and I would have the same thing. And somebody is going to have to be the one to take him into custody—if I am right.''

Langston was quiet for a moment. ''We keep adding, *if you're right*. Assuming you are, why do you think he's just going to walk peacefully out the door with us?''

''You don't know how much I'm hoping, Sheriff. Hoping I'm crazy as hell. Hoping that if I'm not, he can be reasoned with when he sees he has no other choice.''

''Like you reasoned with Paul.''

Delaney stared across the seat.

Langston stared back at him. ''Don't be playing sad games with me, Delaney. I'm telling you how it might end up if you're right. And maybe that's the best thing that can happen—if you are right.''

''Sheriff, Paul was my friend, and Alex is, too. I've

known him since college. It's for him is why I'm here—
I don't want him to end up like Paul did. I want him to
be in custody not only before he can hurt anyone else,
but before he gets hurt himself. We have to find out.''

Langston was quiet for a few seconds, driving another
block while he thought. Then he stopped the car, backed
into a driveway, and pulled back out on the pavement in
the direction of Alex's again. ''Okay. I'm going to pull
off onto that street a couple houses down from his. We'll
come back on foot. That way if it turns out you're right,
we'll take him out his back door and no one will see us
with him.''

When they parked, Langston opened his coat and undid the safety strap on his holster. Delaney opened his
door. Now that they were about to find out, he felt his
pulse increase. His prayer was that he was completely,
ridiculously, crazily wrong.

A moment later they hurried off the sidewalk and toward the front of Alex's house. Delaney pushed the doorbell.

Langston looked at him. ''What are we going to say
if you're wrong?''

''Tell him you're following up on Paul. Ask him a
couple of questions about what he observed on the
freighter. Tell him you'd been questioning me and I came
along.'' Delaney rang the doorbell again.

Langston glanced over his shoulder at the dimly lit
street behind them. He shook his head slightly. ''Pearl
police come by and see us standing here with my car
hidden down the block, what am I going to tell them,
that's what I'm really wondering—that I'm helping out
the son of an old friend of mine who's come up with a
nutty idea? Elections coming up, the word will be out
I've flipped my lid.''

Delaney still wondered if it was he who had gone
crazy. But even if he was proven wrong, would that be
the end of it, or would he want to check Alex out one
more time? And then once more, and once more? How

many times would he have to see for himself before he became convinced his thoughts were really ridiculous? He shook his head in irritation with himself, and pushed the doorbell again.

Alex, sweat covering his body and soaking his underwear, peered through the blinds of his bedroom, twenty feet from where Sheriff Langston and Delaney stood at the front door.

He watched Delaney push the doorbell button once again, listened to the chimes, then turned and walked slowly out of the room toward the rear of the house.

Delaney tried the doorknob. It turned. He looked at Langston. "Breaking and entering," Langston said.

"You're the sheriff."

"Where's my warrant? And what judge would be nutty enough to give me one?"

Delaney looked at the rear of Alex's Buick protruding from the carport. "If he's not here, where is he?"

"You don't ever go anyplace with friends?"

"I don't think he has." He pushed the door open.

The living room was dark.

He snaked his hand around the doorframe and found the switch panel. The light came on.

Before them lay a living room hit by a tornado. A broken lamp lay on the floor beside the couch. The coffee table was on its side. At the rear of the room the wall had holes knocked in the plaster. Delaney's stomach tightened. Langston touched his coat over his holstered automatic.

Alex stepped out the back door and walked toward a line of hedges. Just before reaching them, he stopped.

He stood for a long moment, then turned and faced back toward the house.

*   *   *

Near the hallway's entrance, Langston veered out toward its far side and leaned his head forward, peering cautiously down it. "Bedrooms are down here, I guess."

Delaney nodded. "Two bedrooms and a bath."

"There's four doors."

"A hall closet."

Langston moved his coat back out of the way of his holster and stepped into the hall.

The first two doors, across from each other, were half open. Langston stepped to the one on the left, looked back at the one on the right, and reached his hand out and pushed on the one nearest him.

Even with the living room light behind them it was too dark to see any more than the shape of a bed against the far wall in the room. Langston glanced back over his shoulder toward the end of the hallway, then reached around the doorframe to the light switch.

The light came on.

To the right of the bed was a partially open closet door. To the bed's left was a closed door.

"A bathroom," Delaney said.

They stepped inside the room.

Alex came through the front door. He walked to the edge of the hall, peered down it, then went on into the kitchen.

Langston stepped out of the last bedroom and turned up the hallway. At the edge of the living room he nodded across the carpet to a wide doorway bisecting the far wall.

"What's that to?" he asked.

"A family room."

Langston looked to his left into the kitchen. "Is there a dining room?"

"Between the family room and the kitchen."

"You know if he's here, he knows we're here," Langston said. He looked at the overturned coffee table.

Delaney caught the strong odor of vomit. Despite

having stood in the same spot when he first was in the
living room, he hadn't smelled it then.

Langston's nose moved. "Do you smell that?"

Delaney nodded.

Langston looked toward the family room. "If you'd
ever been around a drunk tank you'd know there's a
difference in old vomit and fresh vomit. Fresh just
washes over you with a bitter, strong wave." He pulled
his automatic from his holster.

"Alex," Delaney said.

Langston looked at him.

"Alex, this is Delaney. I'm here to help you."

Langston looked through the kitchen to the back door.
"I'm going to go through the family room. But I can't
be two places at once. If we both go in there, he can go
around through the kitchen and get out the back door."

Delaney looked into the kitchen and nodded. He
stepped toward its door.

"If you want," Langston said, "I can stand here and
watch both places until you go down to my car. There's
a shotgun in the trunk."

Delaney shook his head.

"Are you sure?" Langston asked.

Delaney nodded.

"I'd at least get something in my hand."

Delaney looked at the straight-back chair setting
against the wall a few feet from them. He walked to it,
picked it up, glanced toward the entrance to the family
room, and came back to Langston. Then he walked into
the kitchen, partially lit by the light from the living room.

The doorway into the dining room was open, but the
dining room was dark and the light didn't penetrate that
far. Delaney saw the light switch back at the door to the
living room. He stepped to it and turned it on.

Its light shone into the dining room. A short wooden
table with six chairs sat in clear view. He could not see
around the corners to each side of the door. He moved
toward the room.

A couple of feet from the door, he stopped, lifted the chair in front of him, and cautiously leaned forward.

The light came on in the family room. Langston appeared in the doorway on the dining room's far side.

"So where is he?" he asked. He walked to the door to the backyard.

It was unlocked. He opened it. "Saw us coming and went out here?" He stepped into the doorway and looked toward the hedges.

Delaney didn't see Alex coming up behind them.

"God, help me Delaney!"

Delaney whirled.

Langston stumbled backward to the outside step, and grabbed for his gun.

Alex held his hands high over his head. *"Help me, please, God!"* he screamed. He fell to his knees. His big body quivering, he stared up at Delaney. "Please," he said. "Please. You have to do something."

CHAPTER 15

It was nearly dawn. It was also chilly, and Delaney rubbed his arms with his hands as he glanced behind him at the jail, then looked back up the narrow blacktop leading to the Confederate monument at the very center of Brandon's compact downtown. The lone, slouched soldier at the top of the tall structure stared forlornly in the direction of Jackson. It was almost as if he were waiting for Jordan, too. And then Delaney's thoughts were back on the disease.

For that's what it had to be with two people exhibiting identical symptoms within a matter of days. And within a matter of days from returning from Brazil. They had to have caught it there, and not while they were on the freighter, because Paul had become sick almost the moment they cruised out of the small port town.

Something in Brazil. Something somewhere in the rain forest, in the swamps, or in the trees or the coastal town. Yet something that struck Paul and Alex at different times?

But why at different times? They had been everywhere together. And that thought brought back one that made him nervous the first time it had passed through his mind—where had Paul or Alex been that Jordan and he hadn't? Nowhere.

But he forced that out of his thoughts and tried to

focus on a reason for the difference in time between Alex and Paul showing the first signs of the disease. They could have contracted it at the same time, and Alex's immune system was enough stronger than Paul's to have held the disease off longer. Then his mind was going back to Jordan and himself again—and now there was the added thought of them having been around Missey and Ryder.

"Damnit," he muttered aloud, trying to drown out his nervousness. He felt his breast pocket for a cigarette. It was the first time he remembered doing that since he had stopped smoking—ten years before. But he wanted one now—it was surprising how much. Then headlights swept across him as one of the department's cruisers turned onto the narrow street and drove up the blacktop toward the jail. When the cruiser parked in front of the building, he walked to meet the uniformed deputy stepping from it. He was an older man Delaney had never seen before.

"You don't smoke, do you?"

The deputy stared at him a moment, then reached into his shirt pocket. "Marlboro Lights," he said, and held out the pack.

Delaney took it, pulled a cigarette out and handed the pack back.

"You have a light?"

The deputy reached into his trousers this time, producing a chrome-plated lighter. He flicked it and held the flame out. "Want me to thump you in the chest to get you started?"

Delaney forced a smile, leaned forward and puffed. The first drag flooded his lungs. It didn't make him choke as he had imagined it might after going without one for so long, nor did it taste bad. In fact it tasted even better than he remembered.

"Thank you."

The deputy nodded and walked toward the jail. Before

he went down the concrete steps into the building, he glanced back across his shoulder.

Probably wondering who that fool is, Delaney thought. *I wonder what he would be thinking if he realized the danger he might have been in by coming close to me?*

In fact, that's one of the reasons he waited outside the jail for Jordan. Too many people inside had stopped to talk to him. And though he had told Langston he didn't believe the disease was easily contagious, if contagious at all since he and Jordan hadn't come down with it, there was always the possibility.

Because of that possibility, Alex now sat as the lone inmate in an otherwise empty cellblock. In the end they had decided that Langston would tell his deputies that there was a possibility the prisoner was infected with some kind of contagious disease. Without any further explanation, it would be assumed that the disease was of the normal variety and had nothing to do with why Alex was under arrest in the first place. But it was adequate to create a reason for keeping Alex isolated, away from other prisoners as well as the deputies until someone capable of handling the situation could arrive to take charge of him. Langston said he would be the one to feed him until then. Why not? he had said nervously. He had already been exposed to him—if there were any danger in it.

Was it contagious?

Whatever *it* was.

He took a deep drag off the cigarette, blew the smoke out slowly, and tried to think in a logical pattern. Assume Paul had it first. Alex caught it from him later. That would explain why Alex took longer to develop the disease. And that would also lead to it being obviously contagious. But then why hadn't Jordan and he caught it?

So not contagious between humans? Then how did Alex come down with it? Again, had Paul and Alex both picked up something at the same time and Alex's body resisted longer? Could a body resist something like that?

Contagious, he thought again. At least the sheriff didn't have children to worry about. He was a widowed father whose only son worked as a disc jockey in Nashville. Despite how down Delaney felt, he couldn't help but smile at the sheriff's words about his son earlier that night. "He hasn't been back to Mississippi since he started making big bucks. My luck, little big shot will get fired today and be down here tomorrow."

The noise of a car turning onto the street pulled him out of his thoughts. Jordan drove toward him. A figure sat across the seat from her. Delaney took a last quick drag off the cigarette and flipped it out to the side, then walked toward the car as it stopped.

Dr. Darrell Rogers, his long face highlighted by a pair of gold-rimmed glasses, stared out the passenger window. As Jordan stepped from the other side of the car he opened his door. He had obviously dressed quickly, his graying brown hair uncombed and mussed, and the white shirt and dark slacks he wore wrinkled, as if they were what he had worn the previous day.

"Delaney," he said, and nodded his greeting rather than offering to shake hands. Then he looked toward the jail.

"I don't know," he said as he brought his face back around. "A physical disease affecting the brain sufficiently to drive a person mad is one thing. That's not rare. Not even to the extent of Paul's attacks mimicking those of an animal's. Criminally insane patients with the same propensity have been legion over the decades. On a lower level, lycanthropy is a recognized mental disease that causes those suffering from it to mimic the actions of wolves—crawling on all fours, howling at the moon, salivating. To the extreme, the Metheny case in northeast Arkansas in the early fifties comes to mind as the one most comparable to Paul's. There, a man growling and salivating attacked and killed a child and mutilated a young woman before being shot to death by officers he attacked when they cornered him later.

"Yet for a person to be driven mad enough to exhibit that kind of behavior—whether symptomatic of a physical disease affecting the brain or a purely mental condition—and then experience periods of control as Jordan described when he visited your house . . ." He shook his head.

"So you're saying it's impossible?"

"Delaney, after thirty years as an infectious disease specialist, I don't categorically state anything anymore. You want impossible? Last year an older couple coming back into New York from a safari in Africa suffered a virus-related disease in which they hemorrhaged from the ears and nose while their blood was clotting in other parts of their body. No way in hell to treat that kind of disease—you give blood thinners for the clotting and the person suffering from it hemorrhages to death, you give something to clot the blood to stop the hemorrhaging and they collapse with a stroke or a heart attack. That's impossible, but it damn sure happened. And immigration doctors are seeing new diseases every day now—diseases that were thought impossible a few years ago. No, I'm not going to state categorically that it's impossible for there to now be a disease that drives its victims mad as a rabid dog, and yet allows them control at times. But I am saying it's highly improbable."

Before Delaney could respond, Darrell continued. "And yet I'll admit I can't see two friends only coincidentally going mad within days of each other, either. I called Atlanta and spoke with Dr. Feltenstein at the CDC. He was at first as incredulous as I had expected. But when I explained about Paul and Alex exhibiting the same physical symptoms—he said for us to go ahead with testing Alex's blood like you've suggested."

As he paused, he looked toward the jail, then back around. "One more time, Delaney, to make sure I'm absolutely certain—neither you nor Jordan have felt sick in any way?"

"No."

"I mean felt anything unusual at all?"

"No."

"And you were with both of them the entire expedition?"

"Every minute, traveled over every inch of ground they did. Touched the same things. Ate the same things. Face-to-face with them almost every minute on the way there and back."

"Then with your not showing any symptoms, even if you're correct about it being a disease, it's likely not airborne."

"You know better than I do that isn't completely definitive at this point."

Darrell smiled a little. "That's all I need to be reminded of when I'm trying to get up my courage. On the way over here I was asking myself how in hell did I get so lucky as to be the one who was going to expose myself to it. Well, let's get on with it." He started toward the steps leading down to the jail's first floor.

On the way up in the elevator to the cellblocks, Jordan lifted the cloth-wrapped package of syringes and tubing out of her purse. Delaney, standing next to her, saw her eyes come around to his.

"Is he any better than when you called me?" she asked.

"He's still damn near catatonic. It started right after we arrested him. Paul didn't act . . ." He shook his head in irritation with himself. "Listen to me starting to say how Paul acted. We don't know how he acted except when he wanted us to see him, do we? But Alex's nearly like what you would expect to see of a catatonic in a mental institution."

Darrell entered the conversation. "That's behavior a little more in line with a person's later exhibiting aggressiveness. A disease could work on the brain to the point of causing a near catatonic depression, then finally express itself in excitatory rage. But, again, the reverting back to calm behavior after the patient has once become wild . . .'' Darrell shook his head.

Delaney noticed Jordan staring at him strangely, but in a way different than if she were reacting to Darrell's statement about Alex. ''You haven't been smoking, have you?'' she asked.

He narrowed his eyes as if puzzled at her statement, and then shook his head. ''I don't smell it. Maybe one of the deputies was smoking in here earlier.''

She continued to stare at him until the elevator door opened on the second floor. The booking area was small, with plaster walls and a counter behind which the jailer stood. A door past the far end of the counter led into the cellblock. Delaney looked at Jordan. ''Maybe you should wait outside while Darrell and I draw the blood.''

''That's silly, Delaney. I've been exposed to him as much as you have. What difference is one more time going to make?''

He didn't know. How could they know anything for certain yet? But she was a scientist, too. She knew what the risks were. And, the main reason he didn't argue with her was that she had already told him over the telephone she wasn't going to be held back. Not back from anywhere you're going to be, she had said, and there wasn't any way to dissuade her when her mind was made up. He had learned that a long time ago. He stopped at the door leading into the cellblock.

''It's not locked,'' the jailer said without making any move to come out from behind the counter. He was obviously heeding the sheriff's warning to the letter. Delaney pulled the door back and they walked slowly down the dimly lit hall.

Alex's cell was at the very end of the block on the right. It was cast mostly in shadow, only a bare glow of the rising sun coming through the barred, screen-covered opening high in the center of the rear wall. Alex wore a loose red jumpsuit as he sat at the rear of the cell on a narrow lower bunk, a couple of feet from a small lavatory and a toilet without a lid. He had been sitting the same way ever since he had been brought to the jail— in the middle of the bunk, his legs pulled up to his chest with his arms around them and his face pressed down against his knees. His head didn't come up as they stopped in front of the bars.

Delaney waited several seconds. Just before he started to speak, Alex's head moved. Barely. More movement. His eyes came up over his knees and he stared at them.

"Alex," Jordan said in a soft voice. "Do you mind if we speak with you for a minute?"

He didn't answer, didn't move at first. Then, still staring at them, he released his knees and his legs slowly straightened, his feet slipping off the bunk to the cement floor. He sat that way for several seconds. Then, visibly taking a deep breath, he stood and walked slowly toward them.

Delaney noted the perspiration beaded on Alex's wide forehead, the paleness. Yet there was something suddenly much better about his looks than a few hours before. Even better than a few minutes before when Delaney had left Alex and walked outside to await Jordan.

Alex stopped at the bars and looked directly at Jordan. "You have to help me," he said in a low voice. It was the first time he had spoken since he had been handcuffed at his house.

Jordan spoke softly. "We're going to, Alex. That's why we're here."

Alex's hands raised nervously from his sides to clasp the bars. If anything the sweat across his face was thicker now. Yet, there was still so much difference—life in his stare, his body somehow appearing more erect. Like Paul, Delaney remembered, when they were still on the freighter. The nights had been ones of rage according to his letters, but during the day, when they were seeing him, there was only the gray appearance of deep seasickness.

Jordan held the cloth-wrapped syringes in front of her.

"We want to take a blood sample to see if there's a causative organism."

Alex stared a moment before speaking. "That's what it is, isn't it? A disease. I mean not really a mental disease." He nodded then. "I know it's physical, I can tell."

Darrell's eyes narrowed.

"We're guessing, Alex," Jordan replied. "You know that as well as we do. But we think there's a good possibility."

Delaney kept thinking how Paul had deceived them on the freighter during the day. He looked at the morning light growing brighter outside the barred window.

"Alex, how long have you felt this way—been sick?"

"I don't know. It's . . . I just don't know. My mind can't think."

Can't think? Paul had catalogued every detail from the first moment he suspected what was happening to him. But why would Alex lie about something so simple? He stared at the sweat on Alex's wide forehead. It wasn't faked. The almost involuntary clasping and unclasping of the bars wasn't either. But it might not be so much from fear of what had happened to him as from the rage, requiring that much effort to control now, much as Paul's had. Maybe Alex didn't answer truthfully because he didn't want to be asked any more questions—didn't want to be forced to keep expending energy on speaking, needed it all to hold back what he had become. Jordan had unwrapped the syringes and was stepping closer to the bars. Delaney visualized Paul on the golf course— grabbing for her.

"Jordan!"

At his sharp tone, she stared at him. He held out his hand for the syringes.

"I'll do it," he said.

"Delaney, I—"

He kept his hand out.

She handed him the first syringe and a bottle of two

percent iodine. He turned back to the bars.

Alex slowly rolled up his sleeve and stretched his arm through the bars.

"Delaney," Jordan said. She held out a pair of surgical gloves.

He held out each hand in turn as she slipped them over his fingers and up his wrists. Stepping to the bars he kept a cautious stare on Alex as he wrapped the rubber tubing around the thick arm, cleaned the spot where he would insert the needle, then brought the syringe forward.

In a moment he had filled the syringe's vacuum tube and reached back to Jordan for another one.

"I hope it turns out it's just chicken pox gone bad," Alex said in a low voice.

Delaney stared directly at him. Alex had a weak smile on his face. Even under the circumstances, he really had tried to make a joke. Which was the man who contained the murderous rage, and which was the one who had just attempted to be lighthearted?

And was there still a difference in the two?

CHAPTER 16

In Miami, the old wino stopped in front of a one-story redbrick building and adjusted his clothes, a faded white dress shirt with a hole burned in the pocket by cigarette ashes, and a pair of dark cotton trousers rolled up to the correct length. A pair of dirty white tennis shoes completed his ensemble. As far as the jagged bite in his cheek, there was nothing he could do about that. He touched the wound tenderly and looked up at the sign above the doorway. BLOOD BANK, it said in simple block letters.

He opened the glass-paneled door and stepped inside.

It was a rather bare-looking place, three plastic-covered couches against the back wall and a desk and chair off to his right. A stocky Hispanic dressed in khaki shorts and a muscle shirt lay on one of the couches. A short, middle-aged nurse with blonde hair handed the Hispanic a glass of orange juice, then walked toward Henry.

"Yes, sir?" she said as she stopped before him.

"Where do you want me to git?" he asked.

She stared at his cheek for a moment. "Have you given blood here before?"

"Plenty of times."

"I see. I don't remember you."

"Gave here, gave there, whichever place was closest

when I took a mind to. Besides you don't remember everybody walks in here anyhow."

"No, sir. I'm certain I don't."

"You don't want to be discriminatin'. Laws against that, you know. Just 'cause I don't look up to your fancy."

"Looks don't have anything to do with it, sir. I needed to know whether you've given blood before so I can get your records."

"Well, git 'em then."

The nurse frowned. "What's your name?"

He brushed a lock of his thin hair off his forehead and stood a little straighter. "Henry B. McKinley the third."

She asked him his Social Security number. She inquired if he had any identification and wasn't surprised when he said no. "I'll only be a minute," she said.

It was more like fifteen minutes, as she not only used a computer to check the information he had given her, but then attended to the greeting of two other arrivals. He began to grow jumpy, irritable in fact, staring at her and wiping the back of his bony hand against his dry mouth as he waited. Then she was motioning for him to come over to one of the plastic-covered couches.

He winced when the needle went into his arm. The nurse shook her head. "You have almost no veins left."

"You found one, didn't ya?"

"I—"

"After stickin' 'round on me enough. 'Bout time."

The nurse stared at his cheek again. "How did that happen?"

"What difference does it make?"

"It could."

He stared back at her a for a moment. "I fell on a piece of glass."

"Have you had a tetanus shot?"

"Yeah."

"Where did you get it?"

"Hell, I don't know. A clinic."

"Uh-huh. And the doctor just left the wound like that? It's going to leave a terrible scar."

"Ain't nobody puttin' stitches in my old face. Not no kinda way."

"And no bandage either, huh?"

"I took it off. It itched." The wound really had, but of course there had been no doctor, and no shot. One thing he didn't like was needles. Especially if you couldn't at least get a few dollars out of it.

The nurse continued to stare at him. "Well, maybe you did get it cleaned. But I'm going to clean it again— and give you another tetanus shot."

"No you're not."

"Yes I am."

"You wait and see."

"If you want to donate any blood I am."

"What do ya think I'm doin' right now?"

"I'll throw it away."

His thin eyebrows knitted. "You can't do that."

She straightened and folded her arms across her chest. "You want to bet?" She knew what was going on. The local crime boss was a philanthropist of sorts, and enjoyed having a reputation of giving back to the community. Five dollars went to everyone who donated a pint of blood—twice a month like clockwork. She knew it was wrong to be accepting blood given under those circumstances. She had informed her superior. But he didn't want to get sued. "You can't just up and be accusing people these days," were his exact words.

She knew what he really meant. He was afraid of losing his job. And that was possible. The money the crime boss gave to the derelicts left them in his debt. Come election time he would send one of them into each voting station and have them bring a blank ballot back out. The ballot would be marked in whatever manner the boss wanted, and then carried back inside by the next man in line, who would deposit it in the box and bring his own blank ballot back out. Everybody voted a hundred percent right that way. Except, of course, the first man, who got a check by his name on the voting rolls, but never did actually vote.

The check beside the name was important too. It was a system designed by the voting officials to make certain there was no fraud. And that was the purpose it served for the boss, too. A name on the voting rolls without a check beside it following an election meant there was now a man who would no longer be paid for his blood.

And with the power the block vote brought the boss, there were certainly politicians here and there who could cost her superior his job.

It was a business, all around.

Delaney held the laboratory door open as Darrell and Jordan stepped inside. Jordan turned on the overhead lights. Darrell stared around the wide, deep room for a moment.

"Normally we would establish laboratory procedures until we make certain about the blood one way or the other," he said. "But quite frankly, since we have already been exposed to any causative agent there might be—if it is airborne—the only thing I can think to do now is be certain we don't contract it in any other manner. We'll wear gloves, make certain we don't sustain any cuts or needle pricks, and wear masks in case our working with the blood should cause a dispersement which hasn't already occurred."

He looked toward the closed door behind him and then to the windows on the far side of the lab. "As an extra precaution we'll keep the windows closed permanently and the door closed as much as we can. We need to put something around the sides and bottom of the door. I guess we need to seal off the air-conditioning vent, too. You have any tape?"

"Boxes of surgical tape," Jordan said, and walked toward a closet near the rear of the lab.

*   *   *

It took them a half hour to complete sealing off the lab—
at least as best they could given the circumstances in an
old laboratory not meant to be used for what they were
preparing it for. Jordan moved to a drawer at the end of
the first counter and pulled out two packets of masks and
gloves. Darrell walked to her as she began unwrapping
them. Delaney knew that the masks, though better than
nothing, were no more a guarantee of safety than the
flimsy tape around the windows and door. If the agent
was airborne, and was a small bacterium, or an even
smaller virus, it would slip between the weave in the
masks like a bird flying through big open windows. He
looked back at Darrell, now moving toward a light microscope sitting in the middle of the first counter. In a
minute Jordan came across the floor, held out a mask and
gloves, and Delaney took them from her.

CHAPTER 17

After the old wino stepped out of the blood bank, the nurse looked back at the pint of blood he gave. She wished there were some way to stop this, but what could she do?

That would be discrimination, she thought and smiled. That's what he had said. Under his gross exterior there remained at least a spark of intelligence. She wondered what Mr. Henry B. McKinley, III, had done in his better life.

Henry touched the fresh bandage adorning his cheek as he made his way across the street toward a set of wooden exterior steps leading up to the second level of an old, two-story masonry building. He was early, and there was no line waiting on the steps. That pleased him. He couldn't take waiting much longer.

After climbing up to the landing, he pushed a battered door open and stepped inside a room that was unfurnished except for a wide, worn desk against the far wall—and a narrow-faced man with a long nose sitting in a chair behind it.

Henry handed the man the slip of paper the nurse had given him. It indicated he had donated blood. The man slipped the paper into the top center drawer of the desk and pulled out a stack of one-dollar bills.

He counted out four.

Henry took them into his hand before he spoke. "Supposed to be five."

The man's eyes narrowed. Henry's expression didn't change. Slowly, the man slipped another bill off the stack.

Henry said, "Thanks," when he took it into his hand.

The man stared at Henry all the way to the door. Finally he dropped his gaze and shrugged. He hated letting the dollar go, but to have gone ahead and forced the wino to let him keep it might have caused a scene. At the very least the bastard might have complained about it on the street. And, besides, in any business you're not expected to make a profit on every deal. The majority of winos, homeless, and assorted other derelicts, took the four dollars in their hand and left without comment. And, without their comment, how was he to know he had accidentally shortchanged them? Even Uncle Carlos, who had gotten him the job for that section of the city, knew he was notoriously bad in math—and didn't pay much attention to details, either. So if the word did get back to the boss, the shortchanging would only turn out to be an ignorant mistake on his part. He looked up as the next derelict opened the apartment door and walked across the floor toward him.

He was a tall black man dressed in worn bib overalls over a yellowed T-shirt. There were always quite a few blacks coming through the door, most of them Haitians. Some days as many as a third of the total. The next largest group was Hispanics of one sort or another, most of them from Central and South America, hardly ever a Cuban. Then there was the occasional Asian, throw in one or two nationalities he couldn't quite figure out, and a sprinkling of whites, like that dumb wino who had just left. He wondered if blood mixed, or if the blood bank had to keep each kind separate. Damn, that would be a big job. He was glad he didn't have to think about something as complicated as that. He held out his hand.

"Give it here," he said.

The black man handed him the small piece of paper.

Outside the apartment, Henry fingered the bandage the nurse had taped over his cheek after cleansing the wound. She hadn't been such a bad old girl. Reminded him a lot of his daughter—except fatter. And still alive—his daughter had been killed in a car wreck nearly ten years ago now. His used-to-be-daughter, he thought, like his used-to-be-wife, both gone now—the wife, he supposed, still married to the used-car salesman she had run off with. That was eight years ago. He barely remembered, and didn't give a damn. And, since he didn't give a damn, he managed to keep smiling as he walked across the street toward a little, red-faced man sitting on the steps of an old, dingy tenement building on the far side of the pavement.

The man raised his head and shook his blond locks back off his shoulders at Henry's approach.

Four dollars were held out toward him. The little man took them and reached into a cardboard box sitting off to the side. He lifted out an offbrand wine and extended the bottle up toward Henry.

Henry made no move to take it. "I gave you four dollars," he said.

The man stared for a moment, then reached back into the box for a second bottle. When he handed it up along with the first bottle, Henry took them into his hands, slipped one bottle inside his hip pocket, and opened the other and took a long swig.

Then, destined to be happy for the next couple of hours, and with a dollar's profit in his pocket to boot, he started down the trash-littered sidewalk. For a moment, he thought once again of his used-to-be-wife and his used-to-be-daughter. He decided the daughter was the one better off—she didn't have any more troubles in store for her. He paid no attention at all to the growing pain in his stomach; the cheap wines he consumed had made stomach pain his nearly constant companion for years.

Delaney, a light sheen of perspiration across his forehead from the increasing heat in the air-conditionless laboratory, leaned back against the closed hallway door and looked at the stocky, middle-aged FBI agent who had arrived shortly after they had. His assignment, he had explained in a no-nonsense tone, was to make certain that none of them left the building again until Darrell had finished examining Alex's blood. So the CDC's Dr. Feltenstein, despite his initial doubts, was taking no chances; if the madness did turn out to be caused by a disease and was communicable, he intended it to be spread no further—at least by any of them walking out among the public.

But what about the agent himself? Delaney wondered. What had he been told? He obviously had been told something from the manner in which he had purposely remained a few feet away from them since he had arrived. He currently stood at the far side of the lab, leaning back against the wall, his thick arms folded across his chest and staring blankly at the far wall.

Jordan sat on a lab stool, one of her legs crossed over the other and her elbow on the counter. She stared at the agent for a moment, then slipped to the floor and walked across the hardwood floor toward the doorway. Delaney looked across his shoulder at her as she stopped beside him.

She spoke in a low voice. "If I were Darrell, I don't know if I would've become involved with this or not. But at least he knew what he might be getting into." She nodded toward the agent. "Look at him. All he's done as a precaution is not get close enough to touch us. He doesn't have a clue of the other possibilities."

Delaney looked at the man. "It doesn't really matter, does it?"

She knew what he meant and nodded her agreement.

Who, with any scientific understanding at all, wouldn't know? he said to himself. If it were a disease and could be transmitted through the air, then all the families of all those who had been on the freighter, all those scientists' colleagues, and all their students, had now been exposed. Each one of them who went to the grocery store would have exposed hundreds more people. And what about those passengers on the flights on which the various team members had flown home, and then those passengers spreading out at locations all over the country to expose still others? If it were airborne, then there was no statistically scientific reason to worry about the agent contracting it. He would only be one more case out of literally thousands catching it, and then the hundreds of thousands after that.

But then that was the worst-possible-case scenario, and the one thing making it highly unlikely was the fact that still neither Jordan nor he had shown any symptoms.

His thoughts were interrupted by Darrell looking toward them from the stool where he had been studying Alex's blood under the magnification of a light microscope. He removed his glasses and ran his fingers through his hair.

"Well, if there is something, it's not obvious," he said. "No characteristic bodies, nothing. Of course any signs could be localized in the brain, only latent systemically." He thought for a moment, then slipped off the stool and, carrying a sample of Alex's blood, walked toward a centrifuge which was set up on a short counter next to the far wall of the lab.

Soon he was straining the sample prior to using high speed centrifugation. Delaney didn't need explained to him why Darrell did that. Next would come the placing of a small volume of the pelleted sludge of the blood into a bedding material. A slice of that would be inserted into the electron microscope farther down the wall. Were the causative agent of the disease a bacterium of any normal size at all, and indeed present systemically, Darrell would have likely already discovered it using the light microscope. That left a good possibility that the agent, if it was indeed active in the blood, was a virus. In addition to rendering their masks virtually useless if it was, they would also then face another problem, maybe a hopeless one. For while hundreds of compounds could be used to attack bacteria successfully, there were very few that could be used against a virus. Even those few compounds were mostly only effective as a vaccine, stopping the virus in its incubative or latent stage. Very seldom was any treatment even partially successful in combating a virus after it had already manifested itself in a disease.

Then he caught Jordan glancing at him, and he forced a smile as if what was on his mind wasn't, even though he knew she was as aware as he what the possibilities now were.

CHAPTER 18

Darrell looked back at them from where he had been working at the electron microscope. His expression told them what they feared before his words did.

"It's a virus."

Even though he'd known what was going to be said, Delaney still felt his stomach tighten. Jordan glanced at him. Darrell didn't waste any time, walking to a small, stainless steel container on the first counter and opening it. When he faced back toward them he held a syringe in his hand.

Delaney moved toward him, rolling up his sleeve as he walked. Jordan lifted a short section of thin rubber tubing off of the counter and tied it around his bicep. Seconds later he watched the needle slide into his vein and the vacuum tube fill with blood. Then it was Jordan's turn. No one said a thing. Darrell turned toward the electron microscope.

When Darrell had properly prepared the samples, he inserted one of them into the electron microscope. Delaney saw Jordan glance at him again, the silence continuing. He walked toward one of the windows at the side of the lab and looked out through the panes. His prayer this time was every bit as strong as it had been on their way back over the rain forest to the hospital after Jordan had been hit by the dart.

*   *   *

Though the wait wasn't as long as before, since Darrell was more efficient now that he knew what he was looking for, it still seemed forever before he faced them again. This time they knew before he spoke—a smile was across his face.

"No sign of your having contracted it," he said to Jordan, "neither of you."

Delaney hadn't realized how tense his muscles had been until he now felt them suddenly relax. He saw Jordan close her eyes, her lips move in a short prayer. But when her face came up, instead of happiness there was the saddest look he had ever seen across it.

"There's nothing that can be done for Alex, is there?" she said. "Not if it's a virus."

"We can't be certain of that," Darrell said as he mopped at his damp forehead with a handkerchief. "An attenuated antibody might prove effective. There are other possibilities." He looked toward the doorway to their office.

"Is there a telephone in there?"

Jordan nodded, and he moved toward the office.

Delaney stared after him, thinking. An attenuated virus was a live virus whose pathogenicity has been removed, making it unable to cause a disease, but still retaining its antigenicity, so the immune system would recognize it as a foreign invader. It was then injected back into a subject's body. The idea was to cause the immune system to work even harder, producing extra antibodies against the newest invaders. But that process was, again, usually only successful when undertaken after a human was infected with a virus but before it had already multiplied and spread into an active state, obviously not the case where Alex was concerned. What else to do? Darrell had said "other possibilities." But what?

Delaney didn't have the slightest idea, and he doubted that Darrell did either.

*   *   *

Nearly a half hour passed before Darrell came back out of the laboratory office. "I've talked to Atlanta and Washington. They're going to be climbing all over this as soon as we can get some samples of Alex's blood to them. In the meantime, they want us to be working on it concurrently."

Us, Delaney thought. Any insistence from Washington or Atlanta along the line of testing had only to do with Darrell and his worldwide reputation. Who had ever heard of the Drs. Jeffries, plant biologists? "What do they think we're supposed to do?" he asked.

"Be of some help with your brains and hands, for starters," Darrell said.

When Delaney kept staring, Darrell added, "Believe me, I'm not all that thrilled about my being involved in this either. But, quite frankly, it's either this or they're going to quarantine you; me too if I hadn't agreed to work on it. They're setting up quarantine procedures on everybody who was on the freighter—to give the incubation period a few more days, to be absolutely certain it hasn't already spread. And I really am going to need some help," he added.

"What do you want us to do first?" Jordan asked and walked toward him.

"They want ninety to one hundred ccs of Alex's blood sent to them on the first plane out of here."

"We have some sterile shipping containers."

Darrell nodded. "Good. One thing more. There's still the need to keep this quiet—Washington stressed that. We're not going to be able to do that if we call all over the center asking labs to send us the equipment we're going to need, especially if we have to ask them to leave it outside the door. And we're going to have to remain cautious until we determine with certainty that there is not any chance of it being airborne contagion." He shook his head as he paused. "In a way that isn't really gaining us anything, is it, not with all the people that have already been exposed to it? Still, I wouldn't feel right wandering the halls now that I've been in here and possibly exposed. We're going to need someone to go back and forth for us. Somebody we can trust explicitly to keep their mouth shut about what we're doing."

"Carol," Jordan said. She bit her lip as she thought. "Damn, we're going to end up infecting everybody that we can trust if we keep this up and . . ." She shook her head and walked toward the office and the telephone there.

Delaney might have been imagining it, but when Carol appeared outside the lab door a few seconds after the FBI agent left for the airport with the samples of Alex's blood, her complexion seemed a little lighter than usual. She was definitely nervous, clasping her hands together in front of her as Jordan explained the first piece of equipment Darrell had requested.

When Carol went back down the hall, Delaney, looking through the glass panels in the doorway, saw her look back twice over her shoulder.

"She's scared," Jordan said. "But so am I. She'll do fine." She glanced at her watch. "What are we going to do about the graduate assistants? They'll start pouring in here in an hour."

Darrell smiled. "Pull the shade on the door and put a sign outside the glass saying the lab is closed until next week. If they're like any assistants I've ever had, they damn sure won't be asking any questions about why they're getting a week off."

They waited until Jordan had locked and shuttered the door leading into the hallway, then moved to the room at the rear of the laboratory.

Animal cages took up the entire back wall and most of both side walls. The cages ranged from those large enough to house dogs down to ones small enough to contain a single white rat.

Darrell pointed out rhesus monkeys, guinea pigs, and rats, three sets of each, quite a large number of sets on which to run the initial tests, but this was different from most experiments. There wasn't time to wait and see if some difference in one of the animals, genetic or otherwise, might prevent it from contracting the disease.

Delaney moved to the first cage. Jordan helped him move it back into the lab. Meanwhile, Darrell strained a sample of Alex's blood to remove contaminants and bacteria and leave a now light-pink solution loaded mostly with the virus.

Delaney, his mask still across his mouth and nose and now wearing heavy gloves that came up to his elbows, gathered one of the rats into his hands. Darrell injected it with the filtered blood, the most likely way to guarantee a quick infection.

The second rat they swabbed heavily with the blood. The animal would lick some of it off. It wouldn't definitively be a case of the virus taken in through the skin. But if the animal did come down with the disease, they could separate the actual manner of the transmission later.

The third rat was put in a special cage, one with a small tank on it affording it an independent air-recycling capacity. The rat was placed on one side of the cage divided from the other side by a simple wire mesh barrier. A portion of Alex's blood, heavily diluted with a neutral, sterile liquid, was placed into a petri dish on the unoccupied side. A tiny fan hovered above it, spinning slowly. The cage was then placed in an oven set at a temperature slightly above that of a hot day. A simple device really, much like a humidifier. Now all the rat had to do was sit on the other side of the wire mesh from the blood and breathe the vapors coming up from the dish and being recycled, passing through his lungs time and time again.

The guinea pigs were all treated the same way. Then the monkeys.

CHAPTER 19

It had been twenty-four hours since they had first entered
the lab, and fourteen hours since they had exposed the
last animal to Alex's blood. Delaney sat at the first long
counter in the laboratory and forked the last of the scrambled eggs into his mouth. Darrell and Jordan had already
finished with the breakfast Carol had delivered to them,
and Darrell was now in the office talking on the telephone to Atlanta again. Jordan, fresh looking after bathing from a lavatory in the bathroom at a rear corner of
the lab, was now preparing different culture mediums in
petri dishes. But she prepared only mediums containing
living cells, like those in the animal blood they were
using. For unlike bacteria that grow on almost anything,
viruses can replicate only on living cells. Delaney sat a
moment longer, took a last sip of his coffee, then stood
and walked toward the towels and fresh clothes lying on
a chair near the laboratory door.

"I'm going to clean up," he said.

She nodded. "It's already starting to get hot," she
said. "I believe it's going to be worse than yesterday."

The temperature did grow hotter, their bodies growing
damp with their perspiration and their hands constantly
staying slippery under their latex gloves as they mostly
spent the time inoculating culture mediums with Alex's

blood. But the work paid off. By late that night they had learned something definite. Time and again the virus had immediately expired when exposed to any culture medium except the blood itself—in fact, quite specifically, the virus grew only on T lymphocytes. But not any other medium at all, no matter whether it contained living cells or not. Even the open air killed the virus immediately. In fact, the blood smeared on the coats of the animals now contained nothing but dead viruses. When the blood coagulated, the virus died.

Darrell looked back at the cage of the injected monkey. "I want to get a swab of his saliva." When he started toward the cage the monkey started screaming.

"Hey, fellow," Darrell said as he leaned toward the cage, "we're not going to use a needle again."

The monkey screamed even louder, and raked at the front of his cage with his thin fingers. Suddenly he grasped the wire tightly and bared his teeth.

Jordan stepped up beside Darrell. Delaney thought of Paul's letters. He looked at one of the laboratory windows and the darkness outside. The night. He turned back toward Darrell now reaching for the growling monkey's cage.

"I think he's reacting just like Paul and Alex." He nodded toward the windows. "It's night."

Darrell stared at the monkey. "It hasn't been much over thirty hours. I want to get another blood sample."

Jordan stepped to the injected rat's cage. The small animal looked up at her, spread its mouth wide and made a deep hissing sound, then bit hard at the wire covering the front of its cage. "You're going to be right, Delaney."

Darrell slipped on a set of the heavy gloves and reached for the door to the monkey's cage.

"Be careful," Jordan said.

Darrell smiled at her, then cracked open the cage and grabbed inside for the monkey, catching it around its neck and back. It squirmed and tried to pull his hands loose as he lifted it outside. Delaney lifted a syringe off a metal tray lined with them.

When he moved toward the monkey it seemed to know what was coming and started struggling even harder in Darrell's arms. The animal's teeth started snapping; it squirmed harder and harder, causing Darrell to have to grip it extra tightly to keep it from breaking loose. Its tail came up and lashed at Darrell's face. Jordan grabbed the tail and a foot, extending the leg as Delaney leaned forward with the syringe. The monkey started screaming.

It was several hours before Darrell had finished his search with the electron microscope. He pulled off his glasses and nodded. The virus was now present in the blood of every one of the injected animals—the monkey, the rat, and the guinea pig.

Jordan shook her head in confusion. "They're already saturated with it. There wasn't any latent period at all."

"Look on the positive side," Darrell said. "We know that the virus can be transmitted to lower animals, and so we can test now for a cure."

"A cure?" Jordan questioned. "Just like that? We can't even cure the common cold."

Darrell stared at her. "You want to go to Alex and say, it's a virus, we're just going to have to let it run its course? Besides, this isn't only about you and Delaney and Alex. If it was, with all due respect, I wouldn't be down here taking a chance of going mad. We know you're not infected and I thank God for that. Not only for your sake but because that makes it highly likely the virus isn't airborne. But it's for damn sure transferred some way, or Alex and Paul wouldn't have become infected. Now we need to know how it is transferred before somebody else ends up contracting it. Do you know what it could mean if that happens—if it starts spreading?"

In Miami the freighter captain frowned and rubbed the stub of his left hand against his chin as he stared at the yachts moving too close across his vessel's bow as it passed into the open sea.

But as irritated as he was, his thinking was nothing compared to the thoughts of the fat crewman lying in his bunk in the crew's quarters below deck. He stared once more at his throbbing finger, and cursed again.

Damn highfalutin professors that we brought back from Brazil, he thought. It had to have been one of them who had snuck a critter on board. What else could it have been that tore all the rats into so many pieces? And he had been the one his son of a bitch of a captain had ordered to clean the messes up. Probably something like a Tasmanian devil, he thought. That's what probably did all the killing. He had seen one of those ferocious little things before. Mean as hell, ate twice its weight in meat a day, and attacked anything up to the size of a small dog. It had escaped, and the scientist responsible for it had been afraid to mention anything—the penalties for bringing animals out of the Amazon were damn tough.

Then he wondered if the Amazon even had Tasmanian devils? No matter, he thought. It was something like that for sure. And that wasn't the point, anyway. The point was his slicing his finger, and that was somebody's fault. The damn scientists' fault. The damn captain's fault for having him do it. And what about all the other bastards on board? Had one of them offered to help him with the nasty work? No, of course not. All of them thought they were too damn good.

And his anger grew and grew and grew.

It was forty-six hours since they had first entered the lab, thirty-eight hours since they had first placed the animals in contact with Alex's blood. After Darrell had called Atlanta once again, they had run smears on all the animals, this time taking sputum as well as blood samples. Still, the only ones to harbor the virus were the injected animals, and it was present only in their blood. Darrell raised his face from checking the last plate in the EM.

"It's a little premature to say categorically it can only be transmitted blood to blood," he said. "But I'm becoming more certain of that every minute that passes."

Delaney stared at the injected monkey, huddled at the rear of its cage and staring out at them with its fangs showing. That the virus brought on the disease so quickly had given them their most important knowledge to date, other than the original finding of the virus itself. "Darrell, if it causes that kind of reaction that fast, then it's logical that Paul was reacting to something that happened shortly before we boarded the freighter."

Jordan bit her lip in thought. "Blood to blood, but it had to come from something first, some way to get into Paul's . . ." She narrowed her eyes. "The monkey was already reacting to the virus before we tested him. The symptoms were almost immediate. Paul became sick the first night on the freighter—just a few hours after . . ." She nodded at her thoughts racing ahead of her words. "Did it enter his system when he cut his arm coming back up through the trees? The virus is in the trees? On the leaves? That would make the timing right. His open wound would have allowed a portal for the virus to enter." Her brow wrinkled. Her hand went to the side of her neck. "The same time I was hit with the dart."

Darrell stared at her. Delaney did, too, but he was shaking his head. "You tested negative."

"You don't have to prop me up, Delaney. Maybe I didn't contract it then, but there's a good chance Paul did." She paused a moment. "But if Alex was infected then, too, then why did he take so long to come down with the symptoms? And he wasn't cut. Yes, he was— his face was scratched coming back up through the limbs. But still, he went nine days before he started getting sick. Paul, the injected animals, they all took about the same length of time for the virus to manifest itself. Why didn't Alex? Was he infected later, by Paul, in some way? Or is it the difference in their immune systems?"

Her eyes narrowed. "It's been over two weeks for me.

But if there are differences based on immune systems—
and that's a definite possibility—then I could still get
it.''

Delaney felt his stomach turn nervously. He looked at
the monkey. The animal's eyes slitted as it stared from
the rear of its cage. There were certainly differences in
immune systems. Some people infected with HIV developed full-blown AIDS within a matter of a few years,
while some had gone ten, fifteen years before developing
it—some had gone that long and still hadn't developed
the disease. He looked at Jordan.

She was quiet now. Her eyes were narrowed again.
But this time it wasn't at some deep thought she was
having—she was staring intently at the monkey. Suddenly she jumped to the side, reached her hands up above
her head and slapped them together.

Darrell stared at her. She faced him and held out her
hand. In her palm was a minute spot of blood—and the
flimsy remains of a crushed mosquito.

"Damn," Darrell said, and looked at the monkey.
"We keep the door closed in case it's airborne, and mosquitos don't even occur to me. No insects occurred to
me. A blithering high school biology student would have
thought about them and I didn't.'' He looked toward the
windows on the near wall. In addition to the tape plas-
tered around their sides, they were all tightly closed and
all had screens. He looked toward the door into the hallway, also closed. But it had been opened more than once.

"The odds are remote of a mosquito transmitting the
virus. But I should have taken better precautions. We
should have been fumigating this place on the hour.''

He bit his lip in thought. "The cellblock, too." He
shook his head in irritation with himself. "I should have
thought," he repeated, and walked toward the telephone
in the office.

Delaney walked toward the windows. *Remote*, Darrell
had said, and it was. The HIV virus wasn't transmitted
by mosquitos. Delaney wasn't up enough on the world

of medical practice to know if any viruses were. But *some* diseases were—malaria, for one. It wasn't impossible. And if it was possible . . .

He shook his head at the thought—and the thought of Paul lying on the golf course only feet from the creek that ran through it, and the tall grass in the damp areas close to the slope that ran up to the houses. Tall grass and water that could breed mosquitoes. His house. Where his children were. Trying to shake that unnerving thought from his mind, he looked out a windowpane into the dark night.

Then he suddenly visualized Paul falling when he ran from the trees shooting in the Indians' direction, visualized the dirt on his sleeve when he came to his feet. *On the same sleeve the jagged branch had pierced.*

Alex had hung on to Paul as the cable had pulled them back up through the tree tops. Alex came into contact with the dirt on Paul. The twigs had scratched his face.

He tried to think what they had learned to this point. Their tests had shown the virus nearly immediately died when exposed to air, but maybe mixed in the dirt smeared on Paul's arm it had lasted at least for a few minutes.

That's all it would have taken, to have stayed virulent long enough for Alex grasping Paul to have gotten some of the dirt into the scratches on his face.

"The soil," he said. "The virus could be in the soil."

"Paul's shirt," Jordan said.

Darrell looked at them from the office doorway.

"Paul fell," Jordan explained. "When we were at the clinic his shirt was streaked with dirt. I never touched him. But Alex rode up the same cable with him."

Darrell's head disappeared back into the office.

Jordan's mother, in her bathrobe, yawned as she filled a glass with water at the sink. Her gaze went past the counter dividing the kitchen from the dining room into the darkened living room. Her eyes narrowed with her thought. She took a quick drink from the glass, placed it on the ceramic tile next to the sink, and came around the counter on her way through the dining room and the living room to the hallway.

Seconds later she quietly cracked open Missey's door. The French doors were open, the faint glow of the dawn shining into the room. She hurried past the end of the bed to the doors and out onto the courtyard.

Back to her left, Missey sat in the farthest heavily cushioned, wrought-iron chair. Ozzie sat beside her in the chair.

"Missey?"

The blue eyes looked her way, but Missey didn't say anything.

"Missey, what are you doing up, child? And in your gown. You'll catch your death of cold."

"I'm afraid I'm not ever going to see Mommy again."

"Oh, child, of course you are."

"I'm afraid I'm not ever going to see anybody again," Missey said in a low voice.

Mrs. Daniels, preoccupied with the first statement Missey had made, didn't register the added remark. She knelt by the chair. Ozzie leaned across Missey to try and lick Mrs. Daniels, and she pushed his head to the side with her hand.

"Baby, of course she's coming back. She has something very, very important to do right now. But it won't be long. Can you understand that?"

Missey didn't say anything.

"You need to come on into the house now," Mrs. Daniels said. "Your Momma and Daddy will be back before you know it. Then they won't ever leave again."

Missey stared back at her grandmother.

Darrell stepped from the hall into the laboratory and quickly closed the door behind him. He carried a quart jar. Several mosquitoes hummed behind its glass. He smiled a little.

"Security guard in the parking lot thought I was crazy, running around trying to catch these things."

His amused expression went away. "So now, we place some blood in with them—and then pray."

CHAPTER 20

There were no live viruses found in the mosquitoes despite their having ingested the contaminated blood, so the disease couldn't be transmitted by the insects. But hardly had Delaney breathed a sigh of relief over that when Darrell found viruses in the injected animals' sputum, and in highly concentrated quantity.

Darrell touched his upper lip with his tongue as he thought. "The virus can't live inside a mosquito. But it can in an animal. And now, if it's spread from the blood into the saliva in the injected animals, why can't it be introduced directly into the saliva—by licking or eating?"

Jordan walked toward the rear of the lab. In a minute she returned carrying the cage containing the monkey whose coat had been smeared with Alex's blood.

She set the cage on the first counter as Darrell pulled the heavy gloves up over his forearms. "The only thing," she said. "If the virus dies when exposed to air, how could it live long enough on the outside to be picked up—at least by licking?"

"Maybe it can't be," Darrell said. "At least under most circumstances. But stop and think about a blood clot. Think of it as a big round ball. No, think of it as bigger than that. Think of it as a domed stadium. A virus at the center of the blood clot would be like a baseball suspended at the center of a domed stadium. Maybe all the virus around it would be dead, but it might be protected long enough by its own surroundings to survive for a while—an hour or two, maybe days, if the clot stays moist.''

In a minute they had both a blood and saliva sample. He began preparing them for use in the electron microscope.

While he did, Delaney and Jordan used a syringe to introduce contaminated blood directly into the uninjected animals' stomachs, to replicate them eating the flesh—and thereby the blood—of an animal already contaminated with the virus.

It wasn't long until they knew. "It's there," Darrell said. "Concentrated in the saliva and only lightly in the blood, but it's present. So it can be introduced both ways, into saliva and spreading into the bloodstream, and into the bloodstream and spreading into the saliva. And it lived long enough on the coated animals to infect. With it only lightly in the blood of the uninjected animals, and already in a concentrated form in the saliva of the injected ones, it looks like it takes longer going from saliva to blood. We'll need a sample of Alex's saliva to be certain it's the same in a human, if his saliva is infected now, too, but I can't see the results being any different.''

Delaney stared at the monkey whose coat had been smeared with the blood. His blood was infected now, but not yet in as concentrated a form as in the injected monkey. And not showing any rage yet. He looked at Jordan, and experienced a thought that created a sinking sensation in his stomach. The dart had only made a tiny wound. The deep scratch on Paul's arm could have allowed a multitude of viruses entry—like the multitude of viruses they injected into the animals. Yet Alex's face, only scratched, might have allowed only the slightest of viruses to enter, taken days longer for the multiplication into disease that finally overpowered the body's defenses.

And maybe Jordan, her tiny wound, maybe it allowed even less of the virus to enter.

Then he felt even worse as he saw her rolling up her blouse sleeve. Darrell didn't need any prompting. He was already reaching for a sterile needle.

In a few seconds a syringe was again filling with her blood.

And the wait started again. And again it didn't take Darrell long. But again it seemed like forever. And he was turning back from the electron microscope.

"Negative," he said.

Jordan's relief showed only imperceptibly in the slightest relaxing of her face. Delaney took a deep breath. It must be like being a prisoner on death row who keeps getting last-minute reprieves, he thought.

"Delaney," Darrell said.

Delaney looked at him. Darrell was rolling up his sleeve. Jordan now held the syringe in her hand. Darrell shrugged. "We need to check ours once again, too," he said.

Delaney moved toward the counter. It was a logical cautionary step. Yet, somehow, he didn't in the least worry about what the results would be, not his and Darrell's. They would be negative. They would continue to be negative. It was Jordan who kept worrying him. Why? Because of the dart wound, or because of some sixth sense he had? Or was it because he hoped so much she didn't come down with it that he couldn't stop worrying about it?

"The changing back and forth from rage to seemingly normal during the day," Darrell said, "that's still the most confusing aspect to me. Granted, the brain is the least understood part of the human body, but there are basic underlying premises. You destroy a part of the brain that contains an inhibitory area, and an excitatory area takes over. A person reacts in a dramatically different way than before, and in the cases of severe damage, sometimes goes mad. But when something like that does happen, the person doesn't jump back and forth from his new behavior to his old. But Alex, as well as Paul from what you've told me, not only demonstrates a changing back and forth from daylight to dark, but can even control his rage to some extent during the night— Paul not charging madly out of his cabin on the freighter at night to give himself away, his managing to stay in control at your house, in fact his being able to be focused enough to drive all the way from Jackson to Castlewoods."

Jordan had an idea. "Instead of the disease destroying an inhibitory area, couldn't it affect some excitatory area to the point of creating a nearly overwhelming urge, but only nearly? The injected animals showed the rage almost immediately. But humans—we're a higher order of intelligence. We're not only governed by instinct and urges, but are conditioned by environment, too. Couldn't this give us the ability to hold off on acting out the rage—at least for short periods when we'd appear normal?"

"Anything's possible," Darrell said.

"Maybe a little more than possible," Jordan said. "To some extent the disease almost mimics temperature, with the rage tending to rise at night and fall during the day. Maybe at night is when the disease peaks to the point it can't be contained anymore. But then Paul controlled his, didn't he?"

Darrell's forehead wrinkled with whatever passed through his mind. He looked at a thick book lying at the end of the first counter.

It was a copy of a *Journal of Extreme Psychiatric Aberrations* he'd had Carol bring him from the medical school library. He had spent every spare moment since then reading through it, but it hadn't mentioned any mental illness similar to what they faced. Delaney had thumbed through the volume. It was mostly couched in highly technical psychiatric jargon, with a large number of charts and graphs. One of the chapters discussed lycanthropy. He had read it carefully. But other than a short paragraph discussing the Metheny case there was nothing in it that seemed even to approximate what Paul and now Alex suffered—and no other chapter heading listed a mental disease even remotely similar.

Darrell walked to the volume. He thumbed backward through its pages, found what he was looking for, and studied a passage for a moment.

"In 1943," he said across his shoulder, "a South American industrialist with pro-Nazi leanings was killed in the crash of a private airplane leaving an airport outside Rio de Janeiro. The pilot survived long enough to say that the industrialist had suddenly gone mad, demanding that the plane be turned around and landed at the very moment it was taking off. He actually tried to yank the stick around, there was a fight, and that was when the plane crashed. A young boy was subsequently found dead inside a closet in a hotel room where the industrialist had spent the previous night. The boy had been sexually assaulted and bitten repeatedly before being strangled. The case is lumped into a chapter which mostly discusses the perversions attributed to many members of the SS during the war. Biting is not an uncommon event during a sexual attack. It happens in both heterosexual and homosexual rapes. What I kept wondering about every time I read this case was the fact that the industrialist committed a heinous crime the night before—in his hotel room where he knew he would be found out. It's like he didn't care. That reminds me of how Paul acted in leaving the bodies lying in his house. And then this sentence intrigues me. Listen to it:

" 'Though it is thought that the industrialist was in Rio de Janeiro meeting with Nazi agents, he used as a cover story that he was in the country to check over his vast timber holdings in the Amazon.' "

Darrell raised his face from the book and looked back at them. "I wonder if any of these holdings were in the area where you were, and if he might in fact actually have checked on them—personally went there?''

Jordan looked puzzled. ''You're saying this might have happened before?''

CHAPTER 21

The coast guard cutter came fast, slicing a phosphorescent white spray out to each side of its bow. On the bridge, the cutter's commander raised a mike to his mouth.

"Freighter bearing southwesterly, this is the U.S. Coast Guard. We request that you heave to and await further instructions."

"Heave to for what?" came the freighter captain's response back over the radio.

"Our orders are to interdict you and detain you at your present position until further notice."

"What in the hell are you talking about? We can't stop. We have penalty clauses on this cargo."

"I sympathize with your situation, Captain. But I have my orders. I'm certain something will eventually be worked out."

"Worked out! The government? Bureaucratic wrangling with a bunch that don't know a ship full of cargo from a barrel full of shit. Penalty is going to amount to twice what we've made on the last two runs."

The coast guard commander looked at the officer standing next to him, then spoke back into his mike. "Again, I'm sorry."

The freighter captain, his jaw tightening, raised the microphone to his lips again. "Hell, what are you, the

American Coast Guard or the Cuban? Hell, on second thought, Castro's bunch wouldn't even do this to us. I tell you what, I'm not stopping until you deliver me written authorization for your orders. How do you like that?''

"I'm sorry, Captain, but I don't have written orders. Still, you have to heave to.''

"You watch.''

There were several seconds of silence. The coast guard commander's voice again:

"Captain, my orders are to interdict and stop you— by any means necessary.''

The freighter captain banged his stub against a chart table. "Why, you toy soldier son of a bitch, you threatening me, a United States citizen?''

No comment came back from the coast guard cutter.

The captain fumed, stared toward the cutter a long moment, then looked at his first mate. "Damn, I ought to do it,'' he said. "Make a run for Mexican waters and see if the bastards want to chase me and risk an international incident.'' He angrily slammed the mike back against the radio.

When the roaring of the props suddenly stopped, the fat crewman lying in his cabin in the crew's quarters tightened his eyes questioningly. Then he was immediately back to thinking about the pain in his throbbing finger and the sickness he had been experiencing. He saw the brown face peer around a corner of the doorway into the cabin. The Vietnamese smiled, sniffed the marijuana odor, shook his head in amusement, and moved down the passageway.

The fat crewman jumped from his bed and rushed out into the passageway.

"What does that mean?"

The Vietnamese stopped and turned around. "Do what mean?''

The crewman walked towards him, strutting, his thick shoulders rocking from side to side.

"You damn Vietnamese come to the damn country," he muttered. "Fifteen of you live in a shack. Make a little money. Buy a stinkin' fishing boat. Suddenly you think you're better than us."

The Vietnamese spread his hands out to his side. "Man, I not buy no boat. I work like you."

The fat crewman was now nearly on him. The Vietnamese stepped back. The fat crewman kept coming. "Prick, little geek," he suddenly said, and swung.

The Vietnamese ducked easily. "That's gook, not geek, you ignorant fat prick," he yelled, and kicked the crewman hard between the legs.

The crewman grunted and bent forward, but managed to grab the smaller man. His heavy weight forced them both backward, and they slammed to the floor of the walkway.

The Vietnamese drove his hard fist into a fat ear. The crewman bit into a brown shoulder. The Vietnamese howled and jammed his thumbs into the man's small eyes. The crewman yelped and rolled off the Vietnamese onto his back. The little man scrambled to his feet and kicked him in the side of the head and stomped his face. The crewman grabbed his leg. The Vietnamese yanked it back, the crewman's fingernails tearing thin strips of brown skin down his ankles.

Another crewman stepped out of his cabin. He was young, blond, and well muscled. He hurried to them, stepped across the body of the fat crewman, and held his palms up toward the Vietnamese. "That's enough, old buddy," he said.

The fat crewman bit his ankle. The blond yelled and kicked his leg loose and stomped the crewman.

Another older crewman ran up the passageway between the cabins. "What in hell is going on?" he yelled and pushed the blond away from stomping the crewman on the deck. The blond swung and hit him hard in the face. The older man went backward, then yelled and lunged forward, tackling the blond, their bodies slamming hard to the deck.

"Stop this!" the first mate screamed as he rushed up the passageway.

Soon he was in the middle of the fight, fists hitting, teeth biting, feet stomping—and blood flying everywhere.

In Miami, the old wino felt the first sharp pain. He stopped abruptly on the sidewalk and raised his hand to his chest. A second pain shot through him, causing perspiration to break out on his forehead, and he felt dizzy. A mailbox was only a few feet away and he moved unsteadily to it and rested his forearm against it.

A young black police officer, coming down the sidewalk from the other direction, hurried to the wino.

"You okay, old timer?"

Henry looked at the young man strangely.

"I said, are you okay?"

The dizziness receded as rapidly as it had come. There wasn't another pain—and *he was* Henry B. McKinley, III. Leaving his hand against the mailbox for support, he straightened and nodded.

"I'm perfectly okay."

The officer still showed a concerned expression.

"I'm perfectly okay," Henry repeated.

"I can run you down to the emergency room."

Henry forced his body more erect. "No, don't need to."

The officer stared at the red coloring marking Henry's face. Too red. "It doesn't cost anything. They can check you out and I'll bring you back here when they're through."

Henry stared back into the young man's face. Its square jaw and broad cheek bones reminded him a lot of his son's face. His used-to-be-son, he thought, before the boy left a note saying he was sick of all the drinking and left town. Never heard from him again. There should have been more loyalty than that between blood, he thought, at least a second chance. Especially for someone who had already lost his daughter and had his wife leave him. But his used-to-be-son never came back, never even called where it could be explained that the drinking was going to stop—if he would just come back. Now he couldn't come back, his used-to-be-son. He was dead— killed by some crackhead in an argument over money, is what he heard.

The young officer, patiently observing the old man, now seeing the red coloring starting to recede, asked again, "You sure you're all right?"

Henry simply nodded this time. The beginning of a heart attack? he wondered. Maybe an actual heart attack that had already taken place—and what damage might it have done? And what difference did it really make? he thought. Maybe it would be better anyway, just to kick out and go. And who gave a big rat's ass?

He smiled at that thought, a one-sided sort of sarcastic smile. He had handled that fat rodent handily, hadn't he? Then the smile went away as quickly as it had come. He really didn't give a damn. What was there to give a damn about? He wiggled his legs a little, to make sure they would be stable under him, and pushed away from the mailbox and walked slowly past the staring officer and down the sidewalk. Who really gave a damn? he thought again, more wistfully than he would ever admit. Not his used-to-be-son or used-to-be-daughter, they couldn't. And not his used-to-be-wife. Damn sure not her.

A block farther he reached inside his worn coat for the bottle there. But it was empty and he pitched it into an alley to his left.

He had gone almost a full block farther when he felt the next pain so bad he had to stop.

But it, too, passed, and he still didn't give a damn, even welcomed anew what the pain might mean, and he walked on down the street.

And he suddenly felt terribly angry.

CHAPTER 22

Delaney had been in the bathroom, bathing as best he could from the lavatory, cooling his face and body as much as anything—from the sweltering heat in the laboratory outside the door.

He looked at the water in the lavatory. Strangely he pictured a volcano erupting and those living around it running everywhere looking for a source of water with which to extinguish it. That was as good a comparison as any to how they were acting in trying to find a cure for a virus. *Who are we trying to fool?* he thought.

And then he realized he kept hearing voices outside in the lab. Strange voices. When he stepped out of the bathroom he was surprised at the presence of two men in suits talking to Darrell and Jordan. One of them carried a large black suitcase. He walked across the floor to them.

The taller of the two, a wide-shouldered, middle-aged man with graying brown hair, turned to face him.

"This is Dr. Feltenstein, from the Centers for Disease Control in Atlanta," Darrell said.

"I'm here to take charge of this operation," Feltenstein said. "My colleagues and I have spent the last eighteen hours straight discussing the findings to date, and concur that the virus is almost certainly transferred only by body fluids. You and your wife not being infected is one of the most certain signs of that.''

He glanced across his shoulder at the man who had been standing next to him, an older man in a loose brown suit who was now walking toward the office on the far side of the lab.

"So now it appears we're down to two remaining problems. First, how varied is the incubation period in individuals? Obviously, based on the difference in the first subject showing symptoms almost immediately, and the second, this Dr. Alex, uh . . .''

"Brister," Jordan said.

"Yes, Dr. Alex Brister. The difference he exhibited in not showing symptoms until days after the first subject shows there is still something we are not certain of. Now as you three have concluded, it might hinge to a great extent on not only the strength of the individual's immune response, but how massive the original infestation is. But that's only what might affect the onset of the symptoms. It still doesn't answer the question of how long a time this difference might span.''

As he paused, he openly looked at the spot on Jordan's neck, and Delaney felt irritation sweep over him.

"So," Feltenstein continued, "how long do we wait before certifying an individual past the danger point no matter how minute the possible original infection?

"And the final question, how do we eliminate the virus at its source in Brazil—whether it's in the Amazon or elsewhere? It's most certainly there somewhere. And since not everyone over there is running around mad, I have to tentatively conclude it's in the isolated area where you came down when you were collecting plant samples.''

"Did Darrell tell you about the soil?" Jordan asked.

"Teams were already on the way to test the area. We relayed the word to them. And that brings me to something else. Indians fired those darts at you. An Indian, anyway. First thing I was concerned about was, did we have some lost tribe running around out there maddened as a March hare? That hardly seemed likely. Why, if infected, wouldn't they have killed each other out? Then I wondered if maybe they had developed an immunity to the virus? And, if they did, then that led to the thought that we conceivably could make use of their immunity to create some kind of vaccine, maybe even a cure.

"But there are no Indians. None. We've had helicopter patrols searching for signs. Satellite imagery shows no evidence of heat radiation—campfires—in a hundred miles of there. There is a river a half mile from where you came down. I can only conclude a hunting party from a known tribe came down that river, were frightened at your rappelling down through the trees, and fired at you. All the hell I'm hoping for now is one of them didn't contract the virus. We have medical teams at this moment checking every village up and down the river within five hundred miles of there."

As Feltenstein paused, he shook his head. "That would be hell, wouldn't it? The spread would have begun. What would we do, try to take an entire tribe into custody—or eliminate them?"

In Brazil, four American army helicopters flew in close formation. "We're over the location, Colonel," a pilot reported.

Inside the passenger compartment of the lead helicopter, the ranger colonel came back with a, "Roger. Radio each of the other pilots to remind their teams to be on guard against the possibility of Indians. Just because none have been sighted to date doesn't mean they aren't there. And we're going to be on the ground, face-to-face with them if they are." He reached for his helmet, looking much like a deep-sea diver's helmet, except that it was made of lighter material with a bib coming down around its neck. He already wore a white protective suit. He stood and pulled the helmet down over his head. It sat at a strange angle, its clear visor facing out to the right, and he snapped it forward into place, a click indicating it was securely locked. The metal tank on his back quickly hissed compressed air into the suit, inflating it.

In moments, all four helicopters were hovering only a few feet above the tops of the trees, the turbulent wash from their rotor blades causing the sea of green leaves below them to whip wildly. Double cables snaked out of the open doors of the helicopters and soon, eight men, all in similar white protective garb, were sliding down them.

Another eight men followed, and then eight more. Some of them had chainsaws in addition to the air tanks strapped to their backs. Some had automatic weapons slung over their shoulders. A couple of them carried nothing. They were the officers.

Soon the sound of a chainsaw revved into gear. Others quickly followed. Within a couple of hours, a rough clearing had been made by dropping a number of the great trees outward in a fan-shaped fashion. Then, one at a time, the helicopters carrying the various testing equipment and more soldiers, scientists, and heavily armed army rangers, had touched down in the clearing. Now, each in a bulky white protective suit, the men started about their assigned tasks, the rangers fanning out in a protective circle around the expanding perimeter, the army engineers starting to take soil and plant samples. And this was happening for miles in every direction, helicopter flights bringing in more rangers to clear landing sites, then the rest of the equipment landing. In all, the total number of men was to reach nearly a thousand before night fell.

Not an Indian was seen the entire time.

At the Port of Miami, Father Eli Dunnigan gestured repeatedly with his hand, cleaving the air with the signs of the cross he made toward a departing cruise ship, though the group of his parishioners, off on a holiday, had already cruised out of sight.

Finishing his blessing, he tarried a moment more, watching the white ship grow smaller as it passed out onto open water, then he turned and stepped into the street on his way across it toward his car.

He never saw the car coming, only heard the screeching of its brakes.

And then there was the thud.

CHAPTER 23

The ambulance, its lights flashing, sped through the streets of downtown Miami. But there was no accelerator-to-the-floor emergency in the driver's mind. He looked back over his shoulder through the little glass window to Father Dunnigan.

The old priest lay prone on the stretcher. But his eyes were open, his thin hands propped casually between the pillow and his head as he spoke to the attendant leaning over him.

"The Lord was certainly watching over me," he said with a smile and a twinkle in his eye. "It is hard to realize how fast things can happen."

The attendant nodded. "Not only you, Father. After sliding sideways into you, the driver went across the sidewalk through the plateglass window of a diner. When he opened his door, a half dozen little girls from a Brownie troop were sitting so close they had to move their chairs before he could step out of the car. Not a scratch on him. Not a scratch on anybody." He smiled. "Except maybe a few on you. But that's all. Praise the Lord."

"Bless you, my son."

The ambulance sped on up the street, the loud siren continuing to wail, its shrill, grating sound reverberating down a nearby alley—more than the old wino sitting inside the packing crate could stand. Sweat popping out on his forehead, he slapped his palms to his ears, and moaned.

A brown face lowered to look into the packing crate. "Big hangover, huh, old man?" the Hispanic said and laughed.

The wino slowly lowered his hands from the sides of his head and stared at the youth. The youth's dark eyes looked around the wino, staring at each part of the inside of the crate. "You ain't maybe got a little money stashed in there, huh?"

The wino glared back at the youth.

A second face appeared outside the crate. This one was a wide-faced blond with a thick forehead. "You ain't speaking to us, old man?"

The wino, his face reddening, his hands starting to clasp and unclasp, slowly extended his thin legs out of the box. The blond stepped on his ankle, then held out his hand. "Money, money, money," he said. "Or maybe we'll see if those are false teeth or real." Then the boy shook his head and grinned. "No, not falsies, they're too yellow for that."

The wino suddenly lunged for the boy's leg. The blond barely jumped back in time to keep from getting bitten. "Why you old bastard!" he yelled. The wino came out of the box and stood.

The blond stared at him. "Try to bite me, will you? Hell, I'll leave you with no teeth at all."

The wino growled and reached out his hand. Both boys stepped backward. "Now, listen, you old bastard . . ." the blond started, and could say nothing more as the wino lunged at him.

The boy dodged. The wino came on. The boy took several steps back and drew a knife. "You son of a bitch!"

The wino looked at an old, rusting metal chair sitting next to his crate. He reached and lifted it in front of him.

The Hispanic started to say something, but stopped as

the old man twisted the chair in his hands, bending the metal backrest down over the seat, and pulled hard, ripping the screws loose from the chair and tearing its back off.

The boys' eyes widened.

The wino threw the rest of the chair to the side, raised the twisted backrest over his head, and charged. They turned and sprinted for the end of the alley, him chasing close behind them.

Ahead, a wire cyclone fence stretched across the alley, blocking their way. Both of them jumped high, caught their fingers in the wire and scrambled up it. The wino slammed the back of the chair into the wire under their feet, and jumped to grab the blond's ankle, but missed. They went on up the fence and over its top.

And he climbed after them.

"Crazy son of a bitch!" the Hispanic shouted. The wino moaned loudly as he reached the top of the fence, and the youths ran hard for the other end of the alley.

The wino, salivating and breathing hard, his face now fairly glowing with a red color, jumped to the ground and ran after them.

They looked back over their shoulders. Suddenly the wino put on a burst of speed and, to their shock, started closing the distance between them. The youths burst out into the street at the end of the alley and ran wildly between passing cars across the pavement.

The wino started shuddering now as he ran, his eyes slitting and saliva running freely from the side of his mouth—and he suddenly stopped. He threw his hand to his chest and his eyes widened with a different pain. He staggered out of the alley past a startled couple, took another step and shuddered again, then dropped to his knees in front of an old woman. She stumbled back out of his way.

He stared ahead of him across the street, then groaned and pitched forward onto the sidewalk, his hand reaching out and clasping the woman's ankle. She screamed.

He shuddered, then convulsed, groaned into the concrete, convulsed again, and lay still, his hand falling away from the woman's ankle, his eyes open, staring blankly.

His red coloring immediately went away.

The black suitcase carried by the man who had arrived with Dr. Feltenstein had contained a fax machine. It was now hooked into an office phone line and manned by the man, sitting in a chair in front of the desk. Jordan lay a few feet away on the couch. She was supposed to be taking her turn at sleeping but her mind wouldn't let her. A virus, she thought again. That human beings still existed at all was due only to the fact that over ninety percent of all viruses, spores, and bacteria were harmless to man, a couple more percent comparatively minor in what they caused, and only a bare one or two percent really a problem. Of course that wasn't how it had always been. Many of the organisms were harmless now only because of the initial price that had been paid. Virulent ones had caused terrible plagues in past centuries, wiping out literally millions of people, sometimes in one episode. Then a few with genetic immunity survived the diseases and they passed the immunity to their children, and the once terrible killers had been tamed.

That could happen to this virus too, whatever it was. Maybe it had already happened in the past, creating some terrible plague, then humankind developing an immunity. Or maybe even the body developing a killer cell to wipe it from the face of the earth—except for an isolated area of the vast Amazon.

Had it lain there, somehow reproducing itself? Or, like the spores and bacteria found in Egyptian tombs, had it formed a protective envelope around its viral body and waited without oxygen or subsistence for centuries, but always ready to strike again if disturbed?

Perhaps, over the long years, humankind, no longer

needing the special protection of the immunity against that particular organism, had lost or had bred out the ability to fight back.

Now the virus was exposed again. How many millions might end up paying the price if it did get out? Or, if it was a virus new to man, would any price be high enough? Would it sweep the earth clean of humankind before going back into its dormant stage?

These scenarios—and knowing any of them might be possible—caused her to shudder. Then, despite how active her thoughts were, they momentarily lost out to her drowsiness. She closed her eyes to rest them for just a moment and, without meaning to, fell fast asleep.

"Uuu," Father Dunnigan said.

The doctor smiled apologetically. "Little tender there, huh?"

"Yes, my son, a little."

"Your kidney is bruised. That's where you were hemorrhaging. It's stopped now. Yet to be extra cautious, we're going to administer you a pint of blood."

In Washington, D.C., President Richardson thought about the old freighter. If the damn thing had sunk during a hurricane or some other blessed event when returning from Brazil, the world would be a hell of a lot better off. But it was too late to pray for that. The damn thing hadn't sunk, and now he had no-telling-what on his hands.

He looked at his watch, shook his head, and leaned back in his big, overstuffed chair. Reaching out his long arm, he punched the button to a private line.

In a moment he had his chief of staff on the other end. "Am I ever going to get brought up to date on this damn virus mess?" he roared.

"Yes, sir. I was about to call you. As I told you earlier—and it's even more certain now—it appears that the virus can only be passed through direct blood-to-blood or saliva transfers—body fluids. So, we've got contain-

ment in the form of the only one infected now safely in
jail. As an added precaution, all the scientists who were
on the freighter are in custody and being held incom-
municado at the moment—except for the ones in Jackson
whom Dr. Feltenstein recommended being allowed to
keep working on this along with Dr. Rogers. Dr. Feltenstein is of course having their blood tested daily since
there is still some chance that they could come down
with the disease, Jordan Jeffries in particular. She's the
one who sustained the open wound in Brazil. Coast
guard's halted the freighter. Their instructions are to
quarantine it at sea until further notice. We have people
on the ground in the Amazon trying to determine how
widespread the area of infection is, if that's where it was
contracted instead of on the freighter. And the latest word
from Dr. Feltenstein is that the source is likely in the soil
in the Amazon. Assuming that, then hopefully the area's
not all that big. We'll have to find a way to sterilize the
ground. That's going to take some thinking. I have people on it now. I guess last is to keep trying to find a cure,
though Atlanta's of the opinion we can forget that.''

"What about the Indians? Anybody seen one of the
bastards?''

"No, sir. Not yet.''

"How could there be any? With the way I understand
this works, it looks like they would have killed each
other off.''

"Dr. Feltenstein theorizes one possibility is the infection wasn't as devastating at first—maybe thousands of
years ago. Maybe the virus was in a less virulent form.
Maybe it's mutated to its present state. Under that circumstance, Indians in the area might have been able to
develop an immunity to the first virus, one that works
now with the mutated strain. But he readily admits he's
just guessing. And there haven't been any Indians found
to date.''

"What are we doing about the tribes up and down the
river?''

"Monitoring them continually. That'll be ongoing for some time, but it looks as if we came out lucky; we're pretty close to being able to say with certainty we have the disease contained to the man in the Mississippi jail. And that's the key. The whole ball game in a nutshell. Containment."

On the freighter it took four men to force the raging, fat crewman into a makeshift brig they had fashioned by hastily emptying a cold-storage locker.

After the door slammed shut behind him and was locked, they could hear him beating with his fists on its other side. One of the crewmen wiped blood off his busted lip. "Lunatic bastard!" he exclaimed.

A man the fat crewman had attacked in his bunk stood at the doorway to the area. He held his hand against a bite mark on his neck, slowly seeping blood.

CHAPTER 24

In the hospital in Miami, the young doctor shook his head at the sight of aging Father Dunnigan slipping on his clothes. The priest looked back across his shoulder at him.

"I'm fine, my son," he said. "There's barely a sore spot left in my old body. But it is old. I don't know how much time I have left. And there's so much to do. The Lord's work, my son, the Lord's work."

Minutes later, Father Dunnigan stepped onto the sidewalk at the bottom of the hospital steps. He took a deep breath of the fresh air tinged with the odor of salt. He really hadn't felt any pain as he had dressed, none after stepping off the elevator and walking to the front door of the hospital, and none going down the steps. The Lord was merciful in His blessings.

Across the street to his left, an older couple waved at him.

"Good afternoon," he called back. "Isn't it a wonderful morning!"

Then he felt the sensation in his stomach, only faint, almost unnoticeable. But he was alert to such feelings because of his problem. When he arrived home he would take a dose of Maalox and the sensation would be gone. He smiled at his next thought. Seventy-six years old and his only health problem of any kind was a minor stomach problem; technically a pyloric constriction and a duodenal ulcer. He still didn't even have to wear glasses— except when reading. How many others his age were so lucky?

The Lord *really was* merciful in His blessings.

Jordan looked at Sheriff Langston. She had a syringe ready.

"Alex," Langston said.

Alex looked in his direction.

The sheriff pulled a set of handcuffs from beneath the tail of his coat. "I want you to place your arms through the bars as far as you can reach and press your wrists together."

Alex walked to the front of his cell. His thick arms stretched forward and his wrists went together. Langston stepped a measured distance forward and snapped the cuffs into place.

Alex smiled.

As Jordan stepped forward Delaney moved with her.

"Alex," she said, "this might be a waste of time, but it can't hurt anything."

"I know," he said.

Delaney, cautiously keeping his eyes on Alex's wide face pressed close against the bars, reached out and tied the rubber tubing around his thick bicep. Jordan quickly found a pumped vein and slipped the needle into it. The attenuated virus contained in the sterile solution ran into Alex's body. Would his immune system now produce additional antibodies to respond to this new band of invading contaminants, and in doing so help to fight the virus affecting him? Or was his system now at full blast—hopelessly overextended already?

"Wasn't chicken pox, was it?" Alex said.

Jordan smiled softly. "No, Alex, it wasn't. We're going to give you a few minutes after this, then we want to take another blood sample."

He smiled back at her, the gesture camouflaging his real thoughts. *Her standing there only a quick grab away. It would be no trouble to yank her against the bars, lift her chin up, find her throat with my mouth, my fingers digging into her eyes. Show her how it feels. Show Delaney why he should be trying harder to find a cure. But it's not time yet.*

He shifted his eyes to Delaney—the one who was really at fault from the very beginning; he was the one who organized their group in the first place. He was staring back. On guard. Alert. But nobody was alert every moment.

He forced his smile to stay in place. It was his shield. But he couldn't hold it much longer, the saliva building up within his mouth would soon start trickling out into view.

Then Jordan was finished with the injection and stepped back from the bars. Delaney looked away for a moment, and with Jordan not looking either, Alex swallowed.

The sheriff stepped cautiously closer now. Alex smiled as Langston undid the cuffs and they fell away. He noticed Delaney was staring again.

Trying to see through his shield, he knew. More than anyone else, he was trying to see. The bastard, he thought, and smiled once again, then turned back toward his bunk, the back of his head shielding the sudden tight squinting of his eyes and his lip curling above his teeth.

"Here's the mop, Alex," the sheriff said.

Alex knew he couldn't turn back at that exact moment, couldn't force his features to relax again so quickly. He tried as hard as he could, focusing.

"The mop, Alex."

Finally, he felt his muscles begin to release their tension. His lip slowly slid back down his teeth. He turned, smiled, walked to the front of the cell, and reached for the long handle as the sheriff extended it through the bars.

He immediately moved to his lavatory, wet the stringy head, and began swishing the mop over the concrete floor, but out of the corners of his eyes he stared at Jordan preparing the fresh syringes. Then his attention was attracted to the opening of the door at the end of the cellblock. A deputy stood in the doorway.

"Your daughter is on the phone," he called down the block. "I told her you were busy right now, but she says it's important."

Delaney saw Jordan's eyes come around to his. "You go ahead," she said. "It could be something about Mother or Dad."

"One of them would have called."

"Go on, Delaney, you don't know."

He hesitated a moment, looked at Alex, then back to her. "I don't want you drawing the blood until I'm back."

She frowned a little, but nodded.

He turned and strode up the cellblock toward the door.

Alex looked back at Jordan.

Delaney stopped in the booking area outside the cellblock. The jailer was talking on the only telephone behind the counter. Delaney looked toward the deputy waiting for the elevator, and then hurried in its direction. In a minute he reached the bottom floor and went straight to Langston's office. He saw a pack of Winstons and lighter on the desk next to the telephone, grabbed the pack, and fumbled to shake one of the cigarettes out of it as he lifted the receiver.

"Daddy," Missey said, "Ozzie cut his foot."

"How bad?"

"Poppaw put a Band-Aid on it."

He smiled as he cradled the receiver against his shoulder and lit the Winston. "I'm certain it's going to be okay then." He took a deep drag off the cigarette.

"You sure?"

"Yes, I'm sure."

"Good, Daddy, I love you."

"Love you, too."

In the cellblock, the sheriff waited until Alex finished wringing the mop head in his lavatory, then Langston held out his hand.

Alex walked slowly to the front of his cell. This time when he extended the handle through the bars he didn't extend it quite as far as usual, and used his left hand, while he moved his right side close against the bars.

The sheriff reached for the handle. His hand clasped it. Alex's hand shot forward and grabbed Langston's wrist. Langston froze, then tried to yank his wrist back, and was jerked hard toward the bars. His face slammed into them, stunning him, and Alex twisted him around and grasped him around the neck with his arm and squeezed, his immense strength driving his thick forearm deep into the sheriff's throat. Langston's tongue protruded from his mouth.

"*Alex!*" Jordan screamed.

His other hand came out around the bars and searched rapidly through Langston's coat.

"*Help!*" Jordan screamed.

The door at the end of the cellblock flew open and two deputies ran inside.

Alex found the key to his cell. Jordan saw it. "*No!*" she yelled. The deputies drew their pistols. "*Don't shoot!*" she screamed. They tried to aim around the sheriff who was turning purple and going limp. "*No!*" she yelled again, and ran at the cell. She grabbed the mop leaning against the bars and jabbed its hard, rounded end into Alex's face. He swiped at the handle. She jabbed it hard again at his eyes. He jerked his head back, his hand barely hanging onto the sheriff's neck. She jabbed the handle again. He suddenly lunged forward under it and grabbed her wrist and jerked her against the bars, let go of the sheriff—who slid down the front of the cell—and grabbed her throat with one hand while pulling her arm through the bars with the other, and sunk his teeth deep into her forearm.

A deputy fired, the shot missing Alex's head and slamming into the rear wall, splattering a shower of concrete chips into the air. Alex jerked his face back and forth like a dog tearing at a bone. Jordan screamed and tried to pull her arm free—and he suddenly jumped back away from the bars and raised his hands above his head, grinning toward the deputies.

Jordan, sobbing, stepped back from the cell. She stared down at her bleeding forearm.

"Oh, God, no!"

CHAPTER 25

"You'll try to find a cure now, won't you, Delaney?"
Alex smiled from behind the bars.

The wide corridor between the cells was empty except
for a solitary moth flying lonely circles around a dim,
grid-covered overhead light at its center.

"Won't you, Delaney?"

His words echoed down the empty cellblocks.

Darrell stared at the wound.

"I flushed it with alcohol," Delaney said. "Left it
exposed to air."

Darrell took Jordan's forearm into his hands. Alex's
teeth marks were as clear against the skin as if they had
been made in paraffin, twisted where he had tried to tear.
Delaney looked at the marks. Had he flushed any virus
from the wound, or into it? he thought. On the hurried
drive from the jail to the research center, Jordan had held
the wound down toward the floorboard, hoping to let it
drain. They couldn't think of anything else to do. Their
minds had raced so they almost couldn't think at all.
They had been reduced to not much more than novices,
reduced to stunned victims no different from any others.
What else had there been to do? He visualized the viruses, their tiny size making them the same as children's
marbles rolling into the giant Grand Canyon of the

wound. How did you flush marbles out of the Grand Canyon? And now were the marbles, like tiny flakes of dust in a vast water main, rushing through her system, looking for living cells to cannibalize and take over? He closed his eyes at the thought.

The office telephone rang.

Delaney looked at Darrell examining the wound, then turned and walked toward the office as the telephone rang a second time.

It wasn't the regular laboratory telephone, but Feltenstein's fax machine. The older agent normally manning it was in the restroom near the rear of the lab. Delaney saw the paper start to roll out and turned to go back to Jordan, when he saw Alex's name—and then hers.

Regarding: Dr. Alex Brister. Dr. Jordan Jeffries. Orders confirmed concerning transportation team. In route. Will arrive at 1330 hours tomorrow as previously indicated. Your end will be responsible for secure transfer to national guard air transport.
   Continued—
   Text of national security advisor memo follows:
   CDC concludes no possible cure. Advise immediate incarceration in secure government bacteriological facility to prevent any further incident. Final disposition will be determined later.
   Continued—
   Text of Presidential response.
   Proceed.
   Continued—
   Respond that instructions are understood.
   End.

Delaney's gaze went back up the fax.

Final disposition will be determined later.

He felt a wave of nervousness sweep over him. In a secure government facility. Where all that might happen will go unseen and unknown. *Until final disposition.*

He looked into the laboratory and then reached for the fax. Its return address was printed across the top of the page. He grabbed a memo pad off the desk, jotted Feltenstein's name and "Instructions received" on the top sheet, slipped it into the machine, and punched in the proper numbers.

He waited until the message was sent, stuffed the fax and the memo sheet into his pocket and leaned back against the wall, trying to think.

But what was there to think? To do?

His gaze went to the wide map of the Americas taped to the wall. Red magic marker lines drawn by Jordan before they left on the expedition traced their upcoming route. He remembered the smile on her face. She had remarked how much fun it was going to be. Work and enjoyment at the same time. "You don't get an opportunity like that very often," she had said.

And what had they gotten? The heat and the dampness and the stinging insects and the Indians and . . .

His eyes narrowed. He stared back at the map for a moment, then turned and walked quickly into the laboratory.

"Jordan."

She looked over her shoulder at him as Darrell finished bandaging her forearm.

"Missey and Ryder," he said. "I want to see them."

She looked at him strangely. Did they have a right to be around the children until there was no doubt left that there was any other way to transmit the disease but by body fluids? she had to be thinking. But what kind of a charade would it be for her to tell herself that she would see them later—after this was all over? She nodded.

As he walked with her across the lab toward the door, he looked toward Darrell, going toward the electron microscope. Darrell's search would be fruitless now, but a few hours from now, a day or two at the most—it only took the monkey hours to develop the full-blown disease—there would be hundreds of millions of the viruses by then.

And then Feltenstein—at the jail at the moment, he would be coming soon. It wouldn't be long until he would begin to wonder why he had received no further messages. Delaney quickened his pace, causing Jordan to look toward him.

As they walked out of the lab and turned toward the building's exit, Delaney saw Feltenstein striding up the hallway toward them. Two younger men in dark suits hurried to keep up with him.

"I'm sorry," he said when he stopped in front of Jordan. He looked at her bandaged forearm. "You don't know how sorry I am. But we're going to have to restrict your movement now." He glanced at the bandage again. "At least until we see what happens."

Delaney felt his stomach twist. He had waited too long. He had stood in the office thinking instead of just running. He looked at the two behind Feltenstein, one as tall and broad as an NFL tackle, the other of slim build, but tight with lean muscles.

Maybe he could gain time. "No. Not now. You know there is no need to do anything this quickly. Darrell is checking now. We'll monitor her blood every couple of hours if you want. We will anyway. But until there is a sign, nothing's changed. We're going to see our children. We'll be back in a couple of hours."

Feltenstein had a look of terrible regret on his face. But he didn't move out of the way. The two men stepped to his sides.

Delaney glared. "I said no. Haven't you got any feelings for—"

"She has to be quarantined," Feltenstein said in a low voice. "You know that as well as I do."

"I told you that—"

"No, Delaney. It has to be this way."

"I'll be back," Jordan said. "In less than two hours."

Feltenstein slowly shook his head.

"I'm not going to allow this," Delaney said. "You're being unreasonable. If . . . if later she . . . we'll talk about it later." He grasped Jordan's arm at the elbow to walk her down the hallway.

Feltenstein shook his head again. "Delaney, I know I can't be as sick at my stomach about this as you are. But I swear to God I am sick at my stomach. But I don't have any choice. The possible consequences are too big to let two people stand in the way of being certain the virus doesn't spread. I'll . . . I have to do whatever it takes."

Delaney felt Jordan's hand on his arm. He looked at her. She nodded. "He's right." She tried to force a soft smile, but didn't do a very good job of it. "We'll know pretty soon and . . ." Her lip trembled. ". . . and then we'll go see Missey and Ryder."

Delaney stared at Feltenstein, turned toward her, circled her shoulders with his arm, and started back into the lab.

"No," Feltenstein said.

Delaney stopped and turned back around.

"I'm sorry, Delaney, but she's going to have to go to Rankin County."

An actual fear swept across Delaney, causing his hair to rise on the back of his neck. Once Jordan was in jail there would be nothing he could do. A second message would come down. He shook his head. "No."

"I'm sorry, Delaney."

"You don't touch her."

The men to Feltenstein's sides stepped forward.

Delaney held his hand up. "I'm warning you."

"No," Jordan said, "they're right."

He didn't care. "She'll sit in the lab until Darrell knows one way or another. If she's infected, she'll go then. But with this already on her, you're not going to pile more. There's no need. Nobody, not Paul or Alex, not any of the animals, lost control when the virus first manifested itself. There's time. There's time."

The smaller agent reached for Jordan's arm.

Delaney slapped the man's hand away.

The larger agent whipped back his coat, exposing his holstered automatic.

Jordan quickly stepped to Dr. Feltenstein's side. "Here, I'm ready," she said.

CHAPTER 26

An agent in a wrinkled brown suit had just drawn a sample of Jordan's blood and left the cellblock. She stood behind the bars in a cell directly across from Alex's. Langston had wanted to put her at the opposite end of the floor, as far away from Alex's presence as he could, but she had said no. She wanted to be where she could see him. If she was to become like him, she wanted to see everything she could in the hope it might tell her something. Something she could tell Delaney. Something that might help. Something.

Dr. Feltenstein stepped to the bars. "I am sorry."

He reached out his hand and laid it over hers on the crossbar. She stared at his touch, and then back into his eyes. Instead of an uncaring, driven federal official, she now faced an older man, genuinely sad over what he had to do.

"I wish you would go easy on Delaney," she said. "You know he was only scared over what was happening to me."

"He's going to be all right. I only made him stay at the lab because I didn't want him down here when we put you in a cell. He's on edge. But he's going to be all right."

She forced what she could of a smile, turned her palm up under his, and gently squeezed his hand, then walked toward the bunk at the rear of the cell. Sitting on it and leaning back against the wall she stared across to Alex's cell as the others walked away.

Alex watched them for a moment, then his face came back to hers.

Darrell looked from the electron microscope back over his shoulder. Delaney waited. Darrell shook his head.

The older agent standing next to the office turned and went inside the door to the desk, reaching for the special telephone there.

A moment later Delaney heard him say, "No sign yet."

A few minutes later, Dr. Feltenstein stepped inside the laboratory. The first thing he did was walk to Darrell. Darrell shook his head again. Feltenstein said, "I talked to Washington on the way back from the jail. The virus is in the soil like you suspected. There's obviously going to be a problem in sterilizing the area. But it's less than a square kilometer in area—it's possible to do it."

As Feltenstein paused, he looked toward the window where Delaney stood. "If your group had come down a couple of hundred yards to the east, you wouldn't have been exposed. The contaminated area ends there on that side, at a stream. Not a bit of contamination on its other side. It's bordered on two other sides by small streams, too." Feltenstein's eyes went back to Darrell's. "It's almost as if the virus can't cross water. Does that give you any ideas?"

Darrell shook his head.

Delaney stared at Feltenstein, at the older agent by the office, and then at the door leading out into the hall.

Jordan looked from her cell across into Alex's again. This time his eyes came back to hers. Previously he had avoided most of her glances. She looked at the barred window at the rear of his cell, and the growing darkness outside it.

"Alex."

"Yes." His voice was soft.

"Do you feel anything?"

For a moment he only kept staring. His face seemed to soften. He looked at his hand, as if he was studying it, and then back to her. He shook his head slightly. "Don't feel anything," he said. "But a feeling."

"I don't understand. Can you explain it?"

"You'll grow sick at first," he said.

She nodded.

"You'll grow sick at your stomach," he repeated. "And you'll start having headaches. They'll start deep inside, and you feel them moving. As if they're trying to . . . as if whatever it is, is trying to get out."

"It starts after dark?"

Alex nodded. "And leaves at daylight. It's like you have a hangover. And then even that's gone. The first few days that's what you think it is—the leftover feeling from a bad headache. But somehow you know it isn't. It's that feeling. Then you start having thoughts. At first it's . . ." He closed his eyes, as if he were visualizing in his mind what he was saying.

"You're in control now," she said.

"No, I'm not."

She narrowed her eyes questioningly. "When the agent was here you were normal. Your voice is level, your thinking is—"

"You don't know what I'm thinking."

"Hate?"

He was silent for a moment. "I hate like you can't understand. Were you close enough . . ." At his pause his face seemed to take on a different look. He glanced across his shoulder toward the rear of his cell. He looked back at her, then slowly turned and walked toward his bunk.

"But you can control your actions. Your appearance."

"Yes," he said without looking back at her. He leaned

over the bunk, moving his hands under its mattress to its metal frame.

"Yes," he repeated.

Feltenstein napped on the office couch. The large federal agent and the smaller one talked in the laboratory doorway. Darrell leaned over the electron microscope. His hand froze at the controls. Delaney caught the motion and shut his eyes. Darrell looked back at him. Delaney looked toward the doorway, and then walked in its direction.

The two agents faced in his direction. He stopped before them.

"I'm going to see my children."

They told him no by staying squared toward him.

"Why?" Feltenstein asked.

Delaney looked toward the office, and then toward Darrell. Feltenstein followed his eyes. Darrell nodded. Feltenstein took a deep breath. "You can't tell them," he said.

"Hell, are you crazy? I wouldn't . . ." He felt the agents behind him move closer. He forced his voice lower. "I wouldn't put them through that. I just want to see them."

Feltenstein's tongue touched his upper lip as he thought. "I can understand your feelings, Delaney, but we're not supposed to be leaving the lab. And then if I let you and you should say—"

"I'm not going to say anything, for God's sake. I just want to see the children."

"Okay, Delaney, I have to call it sooner or later. I'm calling it. I'm a hundred and ten percent certain now. It's only body fluids. It has to be with all we've seen. It can't be spread any other way. But there's still the panic that can be caused if word of the disease gets out. Others we have in quarantine don't know why—except maybe they've been exposed to some disease. They have families who will talk to the reporters—the word's already get-

ting around. But it's just a disease as far as they know.
It could be a resistant tuberculosis. Hell, I don't care if
they think it's the black plague. But you, you are an
eyewitness to what it really is. If you were to say anything to anybody—about a disease that drives you mad—
and it got out, that could sound a bell on a panic that
might well could not be handled. But I understand your
feelings about wanting to see your children, too. Especially with Jordan having . . .''

Feltenstein took a deep breath, thought for a moment
longer. ''If you give me your word . . .''

Alex's hands worked on the frame under the cot's mattress.

''Alex.''

''Yes.'' He didn't look back. His voice was low, the
same kind of low it had been ever since he had turned
toward the cot.

''Alex.''

''Yes, Jordan.''

''What are you doing?''

''You know.''

CHAPTER 27

The moth disappeared as the light went off. Jordan looked down the cellblock. A face momentarily darkened the viewing window in the steel door and then the light from the booking area reappeared. Its glow dimly lit the center of the corridor for a few feet, then faded into the shadows between the cells. She could hear Alex still feverishly working his fingers against the steel bunk.

The bigger agent's name was Mueller. "Karl Mueller," he had said. "Karl with a K." He had blond hair and a long face with a prominent, square chin. From his temperament, Delaney could easily imagine him as a member of the SS had he been born in Germany at the time. As Karl parked his car on the short concrete apron in front of the garage, he looked across the seat. "Do any talking we don't like, and you'll all be going back with us."

The agent sitting to Delaney's right opened the passenger door. His name was Bob, and he seemed as easygoing as the name sounded. But he did do his job. Delaney slid out of the car and walked toward the iron gate.

Mrs. Daniels answered the doorbell. "Delaney, the children will be so glad to see . . ." She smiled politely at the men behind him, and looked past them. "Jordan's not with you?"

"She couldn't get away from the lab."

He stepped on into the house. The agents shut the door behind them. Missey and Ryder's door was closed.

"They've been asleep about thirty minutes," Mrs. Daniels said.

"I'll speak to them in a minute." Delaney walked toward the living room.

Mr. Daniels came off the couch as they walked into the living room. "Where's Jordan?"

"She couldn't get away."

"Missey and Ryder will be tickled to death to see you."

"Jordan needs some clothes."

Mrs. Daniels nodded. "Did she say what?"

"Something comfortable—some jeans and blouses, I guess. A couple of changes. A pair of tennis shoes."

Mrs. Daniels walked toward the bedroom.

"Is it going to take you much longer?" Mr. Daniels asked. "To do whatever it is you're doing there?"

Delaney shook his head. He looked at Karl. "You mind getting me a couple pairs of slacks and shirts?" He nodded toward the open bedroom door. "She can show you where they are."

Karl stared at him for a moment, then walked across the carpet in the direction Mrs. Daniels had gone.

"It's something you're working on for the government?" Mr. Daniels questioned. He glanced at the agent still in the room.

Delaney nodded again, looked toward the bedroom, and walked in its direction. Bob came close along behind him.

Mrs. Daniels and Karl were in closets opposite each other in the dressing area between the bedroom and the bathroom. Delaney walked toward a chest of drawers against a side wall and reached to its top drawer.

"Wait a minute," Bob said. "I'll get what you . . ."

Delaney yanked the drawer open and grabbed inside it. Bob whipped his coat back and reached for his holster. Delaney faced him with the revolver.

Karl, a pair of dark slacks draped over one arm and carrying shirts on hangers in his other hand, stepped back into the bedroom from the hallway. He froze at the sight of the revolver. He slowly shook his head. "You crazy bastard."

Mr. Daniels stood in the doorway to the living room. His eyes were wide.

Delaney glanced toward him. "Get me the tape out of the drawer next to the refrigerator."

Mr. Daniels didn't move.

"Damnit, get it."

Mrs. Daniels's hands came to her mouth.

Dr. Feltenstein spoke on the phone to Washington. "No, sir," he said. "I don't think that Delaney'll say anything."

"Think?" the gruff voice came back across the receiver. "You sure as hell don't. What if he slips them a note?"

"He won't. He wouldn't put them through knowing. He just wanted to see his children. I can understand his—"

"Take them into custody."

"Sir, he's not going to—"

"Take them into custody. This isn't going to get out."

Feltenstein took a deep breath to control his anger. "Yes, sir, but I'm running out of men. The ones out there with him have been up sixteen straight hours now."

"How many do you have at the jail?"

"One on duty, two sleeping in the booking area—they're rotating."

"Wake the two up. Send them out. Take the Danielses to the safe house in Madison. And then don't let Delaney back out of the lab under any circumstances."

*   *   *

The agents who had accompanied Delaney to his house, their hands bound behind them, their mouths gagged with washcloths, and white tape wrapped around their bodies until they almost looked like mummies, lay side by side on the bedroom floor. Delaney pulled several folded hundred-dollar bills from the dresser, stepped outside the room, and closed the door behind him.

Mr. Daniels stared at him. "What in God's name is going on, Delaney?"

"Jordan's contracted a serious disease."

Mrs. Daniels gasped.

"The government doesn't want it out. That's why they were with me."

"Want it out?" Mr. Daniels sputtered. "The government? What . . . I want to go see her."

"It's contagious. And if you tried to see her they would take you into custody. If they even find out I'm telling you what I am, they'll take you into custody. You have to stay with Ryder and Missey."

"I want to see my daughter," Mrs. Daniels said.

Delaney looked at Mr. Daniels. "Please. I'm going to tell you. All of it. You're going to have to be strong, and then you're going to have to trust me."

The screech of metal was apparent, and then the pop. Alex rose from his knees beside his bunk. He faced toward the front of his cell, and Jordan's cell beyond it across the wide corridor, and then walked toward the bars.

Jordan's eyes were accustomed to the dark now, and she could make out his shape clearly, but only the solid outline of it as he stopped at his cell door. She heard the sound of metal on metal. She caught a glimpse of his white teeth as he smiled. She looked down the hallway toward the small, lighted window in the door to the booking area.

"Alex," she said, her voice strained by her nervousness.

The only answer that came back was the sound of metal working against metal.

"Alex, if I call them they might hurt you."

The sound of metal upon metal continued. She looked toward the lighted window again. "Alex—please."

Dr. Feltenstein spoke on the telephone to the jail. "If Delaney's still there when you get to his house, he's not going to like you taking the Danielses into custody. Be ready. He's upset. But don't hurt him. . . ." He took a deep breath. "Unless you have to."

In the booking area, the agent placed the receiver back on its hook. "Feltenstein says they go to Madison."

A few feet away, a lanky, middle-aged agent with thinning brown hair brought his hand to his mouth and yawned. "Then maybe we can get some damn sleep," he said, and walked toward the elevator.

The only other agent in the area, a stocky, red-haired man in his late thirties, glanced over his shoulder as the two stepped on the elevator, then faced back to the counter.

"Gin," the jailer said and laid his cards down on the counter, then gathered them back up and started shuffling the deck again.

The agent wrote the score on a pad next to his elbow, frowned down at it, and then yawned.

The noise of metal on metal continued.

Stopped.

Another sound—a click.

The door to Alex's cell swung open. Jordan backed away from the bars. Alex's dark shadow came quickly toward her cell.

She stared toward the lighted window at the end of the block. "Help me!"

A screech of metal on metal as Alex worked against the lock to her cell.

"Help me!"

She glanced frantically around her. The toilet, the sink, the bunk bolted to the back wall—there was nothing that could be used to beat Alex away from the bars.

"Helllp meee!"

The cellblock lights came on. The door at its end burst open. The red-haired federal agent rushed inside. Alex stared at him. The agent drew his pistol and dropped into a crouch.

Delaney came up the exterior concrete stairs to the steel door at the south side of the jail. He held his revolver down at his side and partly behind him, hesitated a moment, and then knocked sharply on the metal.

The door swung open. The jailer's face was flushed. "The maniac's gotten . . ."

He stared at the revolver. His hands slowly came up above his head. He glanced back over his shoulder. "He's loose."

Delaney looked toward the open cellblock door. *Jordan.* "Back up!"

The jailer moved backward. Delaney, circling around him, moved to the open door.

Down the wide corridor, the agent, his hands clasped around the butt of his automatic and in a crouched position, aimed the weapon directly at Alex's chest.

"Alex, please," Jordan said.

"This is your last chance, buddy," the agent said.

Alex looked past him at the jailer being pushed ahead of Delaney as they came down the hall. The agent didn't turn. The jailer coming up behind him, anything coming up behind him, was the least of his concerns.

"Okay, bastard, I warned you," he said. "I'm going to count to three and if you're not back in your cell you're dead where you stand."

The jailer stepped beside the agent. The cold steel of Delaney's weapon pressed against the agent's neck. His hands still clasping the automatic in front of him, the man's face came around. His eyes widened. He looked back at Alex. Delaney jabbed the revolver's barrel hard against the man's neck. Alex took a sudden step toward them. The agent fired, his weapon deafening in the enclosed space of the cellblock.

Alex was knocked backward to the floor. Jordan screamed. Delaney raised his revolver and brought it down hard against the back of the agent's head. The man's knees buckled, and he collapsed forward to the concrete.

Jordan stared in shock. Alex squirmed, made a sound that almost sounded like a growl, and kicked his feet spasmodically. A piece of metal flew out of his convulsing hand and slid across the floor. The jailer's eyes were wide.

Alex moved again. Jordan knelt at the front of her cell close to him.

"Get back!" Delaney said.

She looked up at him.

"Get back!"

She scooted away—just as Alex's hand cupped into a claw. He stared at her. His fingers relaxed. Delaney raised his pistol and pointed it directly at Alex's face.

"No!" Jordan said. "My God, Delaney, have you gone crazy?"

Delaney kept the weapon pointed. "You're going to have to crawl back into your cell, Alex. I'm not coming any closer. If you can't crawl, I'm going to kill you."

Alex lowered his head back to the floor, staring toward the ceiling. His body seemed to relax.

"Alex, I don't have any choice. Somebody could be coming. If they come in here, I don't have a chance. It's you or me."

Alex made no attempt at moving.

Delaney cocked the revolver.

"No!" Jordan shouted. "No, what are you—"

Alex's arm snaked out from his body and reached toward his cell. Slowly, he turned over onto his stomach and began to slide in that direction.

Delaney glanced back across his shoulder toward the booking area. The jailer's eyes looked toward the pistol. Delaney looked back at him. The jailer took a deep breath and looked toward Alex.

Alex dragged himself painfully across the floor. He raised slightly, almost coming to his elbows and knees as he pulled his body through the open doorway into his cell.

Delaney nodded toward it. "Close it."

The jailer, walking slowly, his eyes glued on Alex lying just inside the bars, moved toward the cell. When he caught the door, he swung it shut with a clang and stepped forward, bracing his arm against the bars. In a moment he had inserted his key in the lock, turned it, and the bolt slid into place. He moved back away from the cell.

Delaney nodded toward Jordan's cell. The jailer moved in its direction.

When the door swung open Jordan didn't step outside.

"Come on," Delaney said and glanced up the cellblock.

"Have you gone totally mad?" she asked. "What are you doing?"

"Damnit, Jordan."

"We'll know in a day or two," she said, "maybe hours. I'll be out if . . ." She shook her head. "I'll either be out or we'll know I can't be out."

He had no time to say it any other way. "We already know."

Her eyes widened. The jailer stepped back away from her.

"Jordan, I'm not going to let you rot here or wherever they end up taking. . . ." He didn't finish. He shook his head. "I can't. To hell with the whole world, I just can't. We have a chance, but you have to come with me."

She looked across the cell at Alex, lying on the floor, staring back at them.

"Damnit, Jordan."

Her eyes came back to his. She still made no move to come outside the cell.

"Jordan, I swear to God I'm taking you out of here—one way or the other. I would rather see you dead now than going through what Alex has, what's going to happen to him. If anybody comes in here, I'll do what I have to do, but I'm not letting you stay here."

CHAPTER 28

As he drove through the Natchez Trace underpass Delaney knew his plan had ended before it had a chance. Behind them, blue lights flashed rapidly and a vehicle sped toward them.

He looked down at his lap, stared a moment, and lifted the revolver.

"Oh, God, Delaney," Jordan said. "Don't do it. Please." She grabbed his arm. "Please." She grabbed for the pistol.

He moved it away from her reach. She pulled against his arm. The car swerved into the left lane and then back to the right. He yanked lose from her grasp.

"Please, God, Delaney, don't."

He stared in the rearview mirror at the blue light. If they had only been allowed another ten minutes. The cruiser pulled out into the passing lane to come up beside them. He raised the revolver across his chest.

Then he lowered it. He couldn't do it.

He took his foot off the accelerator.

The patrol car sped on around them, and, its blue lights flashing rapidly, quickly opened distance between them.

He kept his foot off the accelerator, his car going slower and slower, until the blue lights had disappeared, and he turned off into the small darkened airport.

Jordan stared at the Cessna.

"Delaney, running's not any good. How can I run away from—"

"We're not running."

She stared at him.

"We're going back there," he said.

"Back there?"

"Brazil." He drove past the darkened airport office toward two wide, blocky buildings at the end of the field.

"Brazil?" she questioned.

"Why, Jordan—why was an Indian there?"

Before she could respond he said, "Feltenstein said a hunting party. Maybe it was. But maybe it wasn't. Maybe it was Indians who live there. Maybe they know how to stop the virus." He shook his head in frustration. "I know that doesn't sound possible—an unsophisticated tribe, discovering how to stop a virus that modern science can't. But if they are there, we at least have to try and find out."

He stopped in front of the last building.

The stocky, red-haired agent, his face at the barred window of the cell, yelled at the top of his lungs. The jailer stared across the hall at Alex, back at his bunk again and working feverishly with his hands under the mattress. The blacktop street down the short slope at the rear of the jail brightened. A car came along behind the lights. The agent shouted toward the street. But the car, its windows up, drove on by. Alex worked harder. A drop of sweat rolled down the jailer's long nose and dripped to the floor. The moth lay partially on its side in the center of the wide corridor between the cells, its wings fluttering, its soft body turning in short circles against the concrete floor.

The padlock broke under the pressure of the tire iron and the door at the side of the hangar swung open. Delaney hurried inside. He was afraid to turn on the lights and used only the illumination he had, the short flame of a cigarette lighter—he could cover only a few square feet at a time.

A quarter mile from the hangar, Jordan parked the car in the student parking area at the rear of Madison-Ridgeland Academy. If nobody drove around behind the buildings until morning maybe the car would be lost among a couple of hundred other vehicles.

She stepped outside and started jogging in the direction of the airport.

Delaney set an empty two-gallon can next to the three five-gallon cans he had found earlier. But they needed more. The tire tool in his hand, he hurried toward the last building.

Five minutes later he stepped back outside the building with two five-gallon cans in his hands. They were all he could find. Enough containers for twenty-six or twenty-seven gallons at most. Almost not worth the effort of filling them. But it would be better than nothing—a couple of hundred more miles of range. He gathered the cans and hurried toward the fuel pump. In a minute he had broken its lock and was filling the containers. Then he noticed the car coming down the road along the side of the airport.

He crouched behind the pump.

The car slowed.

It was another police cruiser. A spotlight flashed on at its far side. The beam was not directed toward the airport, but on the open field across the road.

Jordan.

Jordan dove to the ground as the beam of light swept toward her. She kept her face down, hoping her dark hair would blend in with the night. The light came past her, then swept back over her again. She shut her eyes, caught herself closing them as tight as she could, as if in her not seeing the police they couldn't see her.

The light went out. The cruiser resumed its way along the road, slowly at first, then picking up speed. She didn't move a muscle until the red taillights were completely out of sight.

And then a sudden frightening chill swept her body.

She closed her eyes. But it was still there—a slight nauseous feeling in the pit of her stomach.

The chill swept over her again.

The storage space in the cockpit was so limited that Delaney had to set the last five-gallon can upright in one of the rear seats. He strapped the safety belt across it.

Jordan looked across her shoulder from the copilot's seat. "Do you think that was them, already looking for us?"

"They wouldn't have just flashed the lights across the field and driven on down the road." He turned and slid into the pilot's seat.

Jordan reached out her hand to his. "I love you," she said.

The engines coughed and came to life in a loud roar, and he taxied the plane out toward the darkened runway. Seconds later, their navigational lights left off, they sped down the hard surface, and lifted off the ground.

He purposely flew northeast until they had climbed high into the bright moonlight, held that course for better than a mile and then swung the Cessna into a sweeping turn toward a southwest heading.

"I hope somebody heard us heading northeast," he said, thinking aloud as much as making a statement. Jordan still held his hand.

Two deputies hurried down the cellblock past the dead moth. Alex, blood soaking the front of his jump suit, quit working a piece of steel against his lock. They kept an eye on him as they stopped in front of the cell containing the jailer and the agent.

"There's another set of keys in the bottom drawer of the filing cabinet," the jailer said. "Watch that bastard, he's trying to pick his lock."

Feltenstein answered the telephone in the office off the laboratory. His face reddened. "What!"

There were only a dozen federal agents of the special type in Jackson, but they were helped in their search for Jordan and Delaney by every car of the city police, highway patrol and sheriff's departments across a three-county area.

One of the cruisers circled around the rear of Madison-Ridgeland Academy. Its lights framed the lone car in the parking lot.

An hour after he left the lab, Feltenstein spoke into a cellular phone outside Alex's cell. "Can he fly a plane?

"A plane, damnit," he added. "A plane."

A moment later he slammed the phone case shut. He shook his head. "They're going to find out."

Darrell stared back at him. He knew. Who at the medical center didn't know about Delaney's passion for flying? He also knew what his not telling—if they got away—might mean. And yet he still found the words difficult to bring forward.

"He owns a Cessna. He keeps it out there."

Feltenstein flipped his phone open. In a matter of seconds he had somebody on the line.

"They're in the air. What in the hell do we do? Radar. Is there radar here that could pick him up?"

The party on the other end of the line said something.

Feltenstein's eyes tightened in anger. "If I knew, damnit, I wouldn't be asking you. Find out. Get hold of the air force. Where is the nearest air force base?"

He nodded at the answer. "Okay, get hold of them. See if they can get some jets up. Those damn things have radar that can see for miles. They can catch them in a few minutes no matter which way they went. Hell, get as many up as you can. Send them in every damn direction.''

He listened for a second. ''Hell, I don't know. Call the friggin' Pentagon if you want. Call anybody. But get the damn jets up. Call the states that border this one too. Jesus, how fast can a Cessna fly?''

He was asking a question. He looked at Darrell.

Darrell shrugged.

Evidently Feltenstein received the same kind of response over the telephone. ''Well, find out, damnit. You know they're flying as fast as the thing will go. We ought to be able to calculate how far they've gotten from here, where they are right now. Do it.'' He closed the phone again.

Darrell stared into the cell. ''You're going to have to crawl over here, Alex, lay with your head close to the bars where we can get the anesthesia to you.''

Alex shook his head feebly.

Feltenstein stared at him. ''Well then, you're just going to have to damn die. Nobody's coming in that cell until you're out cold.''

Alex's eyes came around to Feltenstein's and stared. Then, slowly, he slipped off the bunk to his feet and, amazingly, still possessed the strength to walk toward the front of the cell.

CHAPTER 29

Delaney took the Cessna down as low as he dared. Lower than he wanted to be. Jordan scanned a chart unfolded on her lap by means of the muted glow from a small, handheld pen light.

"No transmission lines," she said. She looked out the window at the dark tops of the trees only feet below them. "We'd be flying under them anyway at this altitude."

If she was making a joke, her grim tone didn't show it. She looked at him. "How do you know the radar can't pick us up this low, anyway?"

"I don't."

She looked out the window as they passed the last of the trees on the west side of the Mississippi River and the topography turned to flat Louisiana farmland, and he dropped the Cessna even lower.

She looked back at the chart.

Columbus, Mississippi, air force base dispatched fighter jets, an entire squadron of them. That was all that would be needed, the Pentagon had decided. They could fly farther in a couple of hours than a Cessna could in an entire night. But, spreading out in every direction, like spokes running out from the hub of a wheel, the jets grew farther apart the farther they flew. Even they didn't have radar that could reach forever. But the Cessna couldn't be that far anyway.

One advantage in the search was that it was only an hour until dawn. If the jets hadn't made contact by then, all types of law enforcement aircraft could join in the search, not to mention that occupants of vehicles on the ground could look upward and out to the sides, too. The order that had been given, should one of the jets positively identify the Cessna, was to shoot it down on contact, the first time such an order had ever been issued to an intercepting aircraft in the sky over the United States of America.

It was shortly after the order was given that Father Eli Dunnigan was pulled from his sleep by the telephone ringing on his bedside table. Uncharacteristically irritated by the sound, he stared at the telephone a moment before jerking the receiver to his ear.

Habit forced his voice to remain polite. "Yes."

It was one of his parishioners, Rowella Lopez. He knew her situation well. Within an hour, just as the sun rose over Miami, he parked in front of her little house off Biscayne Bay. Despite being obviously built cheaply, it was attractive in its way, its wooden siding silvered from the salt breeze; a child's sliding board and swing sat in a neatly trimmed backyard. But inside the house, not all was well. That was why he was there. And it was also where he first experienced a disquieting sensation. It was only a feeling of irritation, and most would say deservedly so after the many months he had worked with the woman. He looked across the worn, wooden kitchen table at her; heavy-set and holding her infant child in her arms. The pock marks dotting the heavy flesh under her forearms were quite evident. There were several new ones.

And she still didn't seem to care. That had been evident in her just-given flippant response about "getting around to stopping."

And that was when he had felt the mild irritation—almost an urge to reach out and slap her. Why had she called him in the first place if she was going to be so flippant? But that was when she was still trying to resist the compulsion to inject the narcotics. Now she didn't care. But he still felt the irritation. Finally, he made a successful effort to push the feeling from his head. He said a quick thanks in his mind, then looked across the table at her again.

"We expected backsliding, Rowella . . ." Despite the seriousness of his work with her, he nearly smiled at his choice of the word backsliding. That sounded more like he was a Baptist preacher. No doubt the lingering effects of his childhood spent in south Georgia.

"Rowella," he began again.

Darrell trimmed the last stitch and straightened from where he had been working on Alex, not only still unconscious from the anesthesia, but spread-eagled on the bunk with his hands and ankles cuffed to its four corners. Darrell pulled off his gloves and dropped them into the trash can they had moved into the cell.

"I don't know," he said. "I'm a long way from a surgeon. He had a lot of damage. I don't know how he kept standing."

Feltenstein looked at the agent hurrying the trash can from the cell. "Wrap it in plastic bags," he said. "Two or three bags. Don't spill anything." He looked at the other agents. Their hands gloved, they half crouched, afraid to kneel on the floor, as they scrubbed the bloodstains Alex had left.

Outside the cell, an agent held the crude keys that Alex had fashioned from pieces of material he had twisted from the steel strap that ran under the mattress. He shook his head in amazement.

"I couldn't have done this with a pair of wire pliers," he said, "and he bent them with his fingers."

*   *   *

They landed in a seemingly endless tract of pasture land in East Texas, and rolled the Cessna under the cover of a half dozen thick oaks grouped close together. The tail section wasn't quite concealed, and they covered it with wide, leaf-laden branches from bushes growing along a narrow creek running to a side of the oaks. It was the best they could do. Good enough, Delaney thought, except maybe for an eagle-eyed spotter in a slow-moving helicopter. He brushed that possibility from his mind and pulled Jordan closer against his shoulder as they sat at the foot of a tree.

"Delaney."

"Uh-huh." He squeezed her shoulder tighter.

"When it happens . . ." She closed her eyes a moment. "When it happens, you have to stop me."

He squeezed her shoulder still tighter, but didn't say anything.

"We have to talk about it, Delaney. I've thought about it. As long as there's a chance, I want to go on living— I guess."

He looked at her.

"But I don't want to go on living bad enough to do this to somebody else. When I start getting sick, when we know what I'm heading for, if there's some place where I could be put . . . safe. Where I can't get out. I want you to promise me you'll do that. If we're not where there's a place like that, I want you to promise me you'll—"

"I don't want to talk about it."

She brought her hand up to the side of his face, gently cupping his cheek in her palm. "Baby, I don't want to talk about it, either, but we have to. Do you want to be like this? If it were you with the virus, I wouldn't want to contract it. I don't want you to. I don't want anybody to be like this—me be the cause of it. I can't be allowed to be."

He stared across the rolling grass, swaying gently in the warm breeze.

"Delaney, I want you to listen to me, because I don't want to have to kill myself."

He caught her shoulders and moved her back from him, staring at her.

"I mean it, Delaney. If I could have your word, so I can trust what you're saying. When it starts, I want you to take me to some place where they can lock me up. I want you to tie me up, do whatever you have to do to keep me away from you—away from everybody—until you can get me someplace. If I don't believe you, then I'm not going to let myself get that far."

He continued to stare at her. Her determination was such that her eyes were almost cold. He nodded. "I promise."

"Delaney, I don't want to just hear you say it. I want to believe you."

"I swear."

She shook her head a little, unsure.

"Jordan, I swear. I don't want you hurt, either. If you reach that stage you could be hurt, I'll take care of you. And I'll take care of you afterwards. And I won't let you hurt anybody. I wouldn't let you hurt me, especially. If you did, how could I take care of you?"

She still stared at him. He was doing all he could to convince her, while not knowing if he meant anything he said. How could he know until that time? When it came. When it happened.

"I swear," he said again.

She stared a moment more, nodded, and slowly moved back against his shoulder. He slipped his arm around her and ran his hand through her hair.

Her voice came softly. "You're the only thing Ryder and Missey have left. You know it wouldn't be the same with Mama and Daddy having to take care of them, no matter how hard they tried."

He closed his eyes in despair. Missey and Ryder. How could he chance leaving them without either a father or a mother? Jordan was right. Three days, four days. However long it took. And then he would have to do something.

God help me, he thought, *let there be an answer where we're going.*

But what? A tribe of half-naked Indians streaked with white paint certainly hadn't developed a cure for a virus. This was not something a puff of gray smoke from a medicine man could cure.

But something had happened. Something that kept them—if they were there—free of the disease. There had to be something. If not, they would have wiped each other out in a rage of killing, first one and then another, finally all of them affected by the bites and scratches of their kinsmen.

He tried to think. To imagine a possibility. To guess. But nothing came. And he kept thinking.

Not an inherited immunity. That was the one thing he knew for certain. You had to have a genetically lucky few overcoming the disease and bearing resistant children. But who would be sick and recover when all those around them were going mad and killing? There would be no one left to recover.

The last victim, perhaps, a hundred years ago. A single man or woman left torn and bleeding standing among the dead bodies? But even if that one victim did recover, a one in a billion, ten billion, chance, who would be left for them to mate with, to start a new tribe?

And who, if recovered, could bear to live at the same place, a place of such terrible carnage, and start a new tribe there?

No, there had been no immunity developed. There had been no medical cure. But there was something. He could feel it. There had to be, for Jordan's sake. And then he noticed that she had fallen asleep, breathing softly, nestled against his chest.

How? he wondered. How could anybody sleep with the knowledge of what was coursing through their veins?

But maybe she hadn't slept since she had been taken

to the cell. He hadn't—and there was a limit of how long anyone could stay awake.

He moved his head into a more comfortable position against the bark of the tree, closed his eyes, and tried to will himself to sleep.

Overhead, a jet fighter swept through the clouds at full throttle.

CHAPTER 30

Feltenstein hammered his fist on the desk. "What do you mean, just disappeared? Planes don't just damn disappear."

They poured the last drop of the gasoline into a wing tank, left the containers lying at a side of the creek, and took off just after dusk.

Delaney flew so low now that perspiration kept popping out on his forehead. To make things worse there was a thick cloud cover over the moon, making the ground harder to see. And then they were past the scrub trees, past the sand, and beyond the coast. Ahead of them the water stretched out endlessly.

"Well, here goes," he said looking at the fuel gauges.

Jordan looked at them, too, and then pulled the chart back into her lap, opened it again, and traced her finger along the line she had calculated—the way they had flown from South Texas to the coast, and, ahead of them, the couple of hundred miles they had to go before she showed a line turning back east at an angle toward Mexico. The coast was already out of sight in the darkness behind them.

"Answer me, coast guard," the captain pleaded into his mike. "They've all gone mad."

The pounding on the outside of the steel door to the small radio room increased in its intensity. The chair wedged against the door vibrated.

"Mayday. Mayday. Mayday."

They started slamming something metal against the door now.

"For God's sake, answer me."

On the coast guard vessel, its commander stared through a pair of rubber-coated binoculars toward the freighter. He lowered them when an ensign stepped up beside him.

"Sir, base still says stand off of them at our current distance. They repeated that we are not to board the freighter under any circumstances."

The commander's expression showed his continued disbelief at the orders they had been receiving. He raised the binoculars back toward the darkened freighter.

At its bow, two men struggled against the rail. The man who had been attacked by three others on the stern deck now lay motionless. Two of the attackers had fled. The third one was down on his hands and knees, his head leaned forward against the body's chest, as if he were listening for a heartbeat.

"My God!" came the voice of the man at the large mounted telescope outside the bridge.

The commander walked out onto the exposed wing. The crewman stepped back from the telescope. His face was ashen. The commander lowered his eyes to the powerful instrument. Through the lens, he saw the crewman had focused on the same scene he had. His mouth gaped at what he saw. The crewman leaning over the body had raised his head. The upper portion of the body lying in front of him had come up with his movement. He had used his teeth. At the man's neck—sunk them into the man's neck.

"Commander."

It was the ensign.

"New message from base. If one of them goes overboard we're not to pick him up. We're not to let him on the cutter under any circumstances.'' The ensign looked toward the freighter. ''Even to the point of using deadly force,'' he added.

The commander brushed past the ensign onto the bridge, and walked quickly to a radio.

The chair splintered. The steel door sprang open. The long metal beam the crewmen had used for a battering ram slammed to the deck with a loud clang. The captain dropped the radio mike and grabbed for his pistol.

The first man snarled. The captain fired. The second man dove across the crumbling body into the captain, slamming his chest, turning him over backward in his chair to the floor.

The others came through the opening. One bit into the back of the neck of the man on top of the captain. The bitten man turned on his back and snapped at a hand going past him toward the captain's face.

In Jackson, Dr. Feltenstein had been getting reports, secondhand, relayed from the coast guard cutter to its base, to the southern command, to Washington, and then to him. But he was now on a conference call with all parties trying to speak at once, interrupting each other. Even with what Feltenstein knew about the disease, he was stunned at the viciousness reported taking place on the freighter. *The same thing that would take place everywhere if it was allowed to spread.*

A voice cut into the argument between an admiral at the Pentagon and a doctor in Atlanta. The men immediately hushed. The president spoke again.

''Order the navy to sink the boat. But wait until daylight. We have to be certain there are no survivors.''

A thought sweeping through Feltenstein's mind chilled him to his very marrow.

''We can't.''

''Who's speaking?''

"Dr. Feltenstein, in Jackson, Mr. President. A monkey, a rat, and a guinea pig all contracted the disease. If we sink the freighter, how can we be certain that we won't be spreading . . ." The thought was almost too terrible to comprehend.

"Out with it, man."

"The sharks."

Delaney jammed the Cessna's controls to the left to avoid hitting the dark shape sitting in the water in front of the plane. The Cessna barely avoided the freighter's stern. Jordan looked back at the ship.

"Damn!" Delaney exclaimed at the sight of the running lights ahead of them. It was a coast guard cutter. He cut the Cessna hard to the right, pulling back on the yoke at the same time.

Behind them, to the right, the freighter floated in darkness. On the coast guard cutter tiny figures lined the rail, looking up at them.

The club was little different from countless others like it in Miami, a simple, one-story, cement-block building once painted white, but now a dingy gray. It made no difference. The steady stream of customers entering the door didn't come for the atmosphere, but for the young women stripping on stage.

Father Eli Dunnigan stopped at the building's entrance and glanced at the larger-than-life-size figure of a naked stripper painted on a wall to the side of the door. The doorkeeper, a thin, dark-skinned man with a long chin, stared at him. Father Dunnigan smiled politely.

"Mr. Estrada is expecting me."

The doorman, a quizzical expression across his face, hesitated a moment, then nodded and disappeared inside the club. A young man in a brightly painted shirt, jeans, and cowboy boots passed Father Dunnigan, stopped at the door, glanced at the priest, then slipped his billfold back into his pocket and walked on inside the club. An older gray-haired man on his way from the car to the club saw Dunnigan's uniformlike dark garb, stopped, and hurried back toward his car.

Johnny Estrada walked from the club. His slight frame was clothed in a shiny black suit. He had a broad smile across his narrow face. He extended his hand in greeting.

"Father."

The two shook hands. The door behind Estrada opened and two heavy-set, dark-skinned men stepped outside and came up behind Estrada. Father Dunnigan caught a glimpse of pale flesh at the bright area in the center of the dimly lit club. Estrada looked down at the sidewalk.

"We can go around this way to my office," he said.

It took a moment to get the door open. Estrada, working the key in the lock, glanced over his shoulder. The men behind him were glancing over their shoulders, too.

"I hardly never use this entrance," he said. The door came open and he stepped back and gestured with a sweep of his hand for Father Dunnigan to enter. Before he could, one of the heavy-set men passed him and stepped inside the room.

Estrada frowned, then looked back at Father Dunnigan, waited for him to step inside, and then stepped inside behind him. The other heavy-set man remained outside, shutting the door.

Father Dunnigan looked around the room. It was small, surprisingly so, he thought, and furnished with the cheapest of furniture: a worn, bare wooden desk, a chair behind it, and two straight-back chairs in front of the desk. The door at the far side of a dingy gray carpet was cracked open and a thin stream of tobacco smoke curled into the room from the club's interior. The heavy-set man who came inside with them walked across the room and outside the far door, closing it behind him. The scratchy country tune from an old jukebox could still be heard, but it was much quieter now. Estrada stepped behind the desk and waited for Father Dunnigan to sit before he did.

"It is an honor to have you in my office, Father."

Almost like making a bargain with the devil, Father Dunnigan thought, but got to the point. "Mrs. Rowella Lopez is a parishioner of mine."

As the Father paused, the little man smiled politely. "I'm afraid the name doesn't ring a bell."

"You have a thu . . ." Father Dunnigan started, then phrased it differently. "There is a gentleman named Maury Soles who works my parish."

The little man's thin eyebrows knitted. "Father, let's not mix religion and business, if you don't mind."

"I'm not. I know that would gain me nothing. But there is this one woman. She is only twenty-three and has four small children. She's into drugs heavily. But she's redeemable. Three times now I've been able to persuade her to stop. She actually did. Cold turkey. Then Mr. Soles came by to visit her, asked her where she'd been, and gave her some free samples. She's only a human being, not beyond temptation. Not when it is brought right into her house."

Estrada steepled his short fingers under his chin. "I see."

"Can you help me? With this one woman?"

The little man smiled sweetly. "Father, you do me an injustice by even having to ask. Of course I will. I was not aware of the situation. We only provide a service to those who would otherwise use somebody else. It is not our intent—never has been—to try and cause addiction." His smile grew sweeter. "You understand?"

"I thank you." Father Dunnigan rose from his chair.

"Don't you wish to visit longer? It is not often that I am able to speak with a priest."

"I can always be found at my church."

Estrada nodded slowly. "I understand that. But I have many enemies. For me to attend your services would mean bringing several of my bodyguards with me. To do that would be disruptive to your other parishioners. In particular, the carrying of guns. Somehow I have always felt that would be profane—inside a church."

Father Dunnigan stared down at the little man. There had been a genuine tone in his voice. "Maybe you should trust in the Lord."

The little man shook his head wistfully. "If the word got out on the street that I was without my bodyguards . . . you just don't understand."

"No, my son. It is you who don't understand."

CHAPTER 31

The fuel gauges neared empty. Delaney didn't know how much was left in the tanks when they registered that. He had never flown his fuel to near as low a level. Jordan's expression spoke her concern. The water stretched out endlessly, dark, in front of them.

Then, there it was. A tiny gray line in the dim moonlight seeping through the clouds.

"There," Jordan said.

Moments later the line had broadened into a thin white strip of sand with a dark jungle rising behind it.

As the beach broadened and the trees grew taller, he glanced at the fuel gauges again. The one on the left tank, the one they were using now, dropped below the red line as he pulled back on the yoke and climbed above the jungle. Jordan looked at the chart. He already knew the compass setting and turned the Cessna in that direction.

The engines sputtered.

He waited a moment before switching back to the other, nearly empty tank, as if the last choking gasp out of the engines could carry them a few feet farther. But they made no sounds now. The props only windmilled. He switched to the other tank. Jordan leaned back in her seat, her expression obviously concerned, *pale . . .*

* * *

Father Dunnigan entered his house and shut the door behind him, his senses immediately assailed by the loud roar of a vacuum. The gray-haired Hispanic woman pushing it smiled toward him and nodded in deference. She went around the couch, then brought the vacuum back in front of it. He walked past her toward his study.

Inside the small room he shut the door. She immediately had to vacuum the area outside of it. He frowned at the door. The noise lessened, then came back up again. His frown tightened. He tried to force his mind to his work, opening a side desk drawer and pulling out a thick sheaf of papers.

The damn thing went by the door again.

He came to his feet and strode to the door, swinging it open.

She stared back at his expression.

She turned the motor off.

"Father?"

He slammed the door shut.

The engines sputtered. Delaney tightened his hand on the yoke. They were at ten thousand feet now. The end of the jungle and the start of the desertlike plains was a mile away. A little over five thousand feet to travel with ten thousand feet under them. That would be no problem with the Cessna's glide rate. But what then?

"Delaney."

Jordan was looking toward the ground. Barely visible in the moonlight, a thin brown ribbon snaked through the thick trees. A road of some kind. Someone would eventually drive down it. Meanwhile, the Cessna would be less likely to be seen there than exposed on the open land beyond the end of the jungle. As he nudged the yoke over to glide back toward the road, he wondered if the tips of the Cessna's wings would fit between the growth on each side of the narrow way. But what choice did he have? The trees below them were constantly growing larger.

*   *   *

"Spread the search wider," the general said.

The tall colonel standing across the desk from him in the Pentagon nodded.

"Double the distance they could have traveled in this time. Send aircraft to the very perimeter of the circle and back," the general continued.

"One vector will cross into Mexico."

"We have permission."

"Including firing on the Cessna over their territory?"

"Including firing on it over their territory," the general repeated.

They would have never seen the building under them in the dark except for the glint of the moonlight off the top of a tin roof. Jordan looked back over her shoulder out the window.

"Try to keep its bearing," Delaney said. "Maybe they'll have fuel." He lined up the nose of the Cessna with the very center of the road.

The moonlight cut off as they dropped into the narrow canyon created between the tall trees rising to their sides. Across her shoulder, Jordan saw the close branches whipping in the wind at the wing tips. The road curved to the right in a gentle turn. Delaney eased the yoke in that direction. The plane ever so imperceptibly slid to the left. He tightened the yoke. The white sand of the road rose to meet them.

"Delaney!"

He saw it, a thick stand of trees growing across the road a couple of hundred feet in front of them. He slammed the yoke forward. The plane dropped sharply to the road. The landing gear dug into the soft sand. The Cessna bounced, hit hard again. The yoke jerked in his hands. Weeds sped past the wings. Delaney jammed on the brakes. The plane, sliding forward, tilted toward its nose, slammed back to the ground—and slid to a stop a few feet from the thick, dark trunks rising in front of them.

Delaney slowly dropped his hands from the yoke. Weeds were bent back across the wings and molded to their metal surfaces. Behind the plane, grass rose waist high as far as he could see. It wasn't a road, but an old airstrip.

Abandoned.

He slammed his fists against the yoke. Neither of them saw the shadowy shapes stepping out of the trees on each side of the plane.

CHAPTER 32

Jordan gasped as the man climbed up onto the wing on her side. Delaney grabbed for his revolver in the door pocket to his left—and stared into a rifle barrel pointed through the Plexiglas next to his face.

His fingers froze on the revolver's handle, and he slipped his hand back out of the pocket. His door jerked open and the end of the rifle yanked sideways, motioning for him to step outside onto the wing.

He looked back at Jordan, her door open now, too, and she was staring into a revolver. They were light-skinned, more Mexican than Indian. They wore no uniforms, only loosely fitting shirts and pants. And to come up so abruptly and so heavily armed . . . drug runners. A clandestine laboratory in the jungle. What else could it be? The rifle moved again. Delaney stepped outside onto the wing to stare into a wide face atop a thick neck and a short, heavily built body. The eyes were cold.

Jordan's door opened. Delaney looked back across his shoulder as she came out of her seat and stepped onto the wing. The man there grasped her shoulder with one hand and pushed her toward the ground. The man facing Delaney looked him up and down, as if searching for a weapon.

"We ran out of fuel," Delaney heard Jordan say from the ground on the other side of the plane.

The man nodded Delaney off the wing.

On the ground, he saw there were a half dozen figures in all, a couple of them darker than the others, and all dressed in the same kind of clothing. And all carrying weapons.

Jordan said something as she came around the tail of the plane. The man holding her arm near her shoulder still hadn't spoken. The man in front of Delaney looked toward her, ran his gaze up and down her figure, and grinned.

The voice came from the dark trees a few feet from the plane. "Who are you?" It was deep sounding, almost hoarse. Delaney looked in its direction. The man in front of him stepped to the side, and a tall man, bigger than all the rest, walked from the dark into the dim moonlight.

"Who are you?" he repeated.

Delaney stared into the dark eyes.

"There's a sickness in Brazil," Jordan said. "We're going there to try to stop it."

Delaney looked at her.

"You're doctors?" the man asked.

Delaney knew the man meant medical doctors. Jordan did, too. She said, "Yes—volunteers." Was she thinking that would be enough for compassion to be shown?

"Come with us," the man said.

They didn't walk in the direction they had glimpsed the tin roof, but directly away from it into the dark trees to the opposite side of the runway.

The men moved as if they knew wherever the vines and undergrowth were, but Delaney constantly scraped against something or felt something pull against him. Jordan fell once.

Ten minutes later, they walked into an encampment fashioned by large tents spread out under the tangled, matted overgrowth at the top of the trees. Delaney and Jordan were made to wait as the man in charge of the group walked toward one of the smaller tents.

Delaney looked at the largest tent in the group, actually several canvases sewn together and held up by thin poles. On a wooden platform under the canvas were boilers, tubs, and long tables: the laboratory where the drugs were refined. He looked back toward the tent where the man had gone. A large, bare-chested man wearing only a pair of baggy shorts and sandals walked out of it toward him. His arm was in a sling. Perspiration dotted his forehead.

"You're doctors?" he said as he stopped before them.

Jordan stepped toward him and reached her hand to the sling without saying anything.

"Snake bite," the man said and lifted it toward her. "That has passed, but there is infection now."

More than just infection. The skin was black at the edges where someone had made a slit to let the venom run out. Dark red lines faded into thinner red ones running up his arm toward his shoulder.

"Do you have any antibiotics?" Jordan asked.

The man nodded.

"What kind?"

"We have penicillin."

"You been taking any?"

"I started last night."

Jordan slid the sling back under his forearm. "I'll have to clean it. Do you have anything that will lessen the pain?"

"Come with me," the man said, and turned toward his tent.

Jordan followed him. Delaney started forward, and felt one of the men grasp his arm. He pulled it loose. Two men grabbed him.

The man walking toward the tent turned back to them, stared a moment, then nodded his okay. They let go, and Delaney followed after Jordan.

Inside the tent, the man moved to a cot at the rear and sat down. He nodded toward a cardboard box with a red cross on its side. Jordan moved toward it as he removed the sling. In a moment she stood in front of him with a syringe.

Delaney glanced around the tent, looking for a weapon, but saw none. There was a metal standing locker to the far side of the cot.

"You are both doctors?"

The man was addressing him. Delaney nodded, and then moved toward the box with the red cross. From it he removed a package of sterilized scalpels, a pair of small tweezers, and gauze and bandages, then walked to the bunk where Jordan was already injecting a line of painkiller around the jagged wound.

The man showed no signs of feeling the needle pricks, but watched her carefully as she injected the anesthetic. Finally, he looked up at her. "You actually are doctors?" he said.

"Yes. We told you we—"

"There are competitors," he said.

Jordan shook her head. "Doctors," she repeated.

"How are you, in a small plane—going to Brazil?"

She stared at him a moment. "We couldn't get permission."

The man's eyes narrowed. "Permission? You could have taken an airliner. There's no medical equipment on your plane?"

The man was not only the group's leader, at least in the camp, but obviously intelligent, one characteristic that didn't always go with the other. Was he compassionate too?

But how could he be? They knew where the base was now. But what other way was there for them to plead? Delaney waited until he caught eye contact. "We need your help in getting out of here—fuel. There's no way we would ever say anything about this place."

The man didn't respond.

"There's a source of a disease there. It's fatal. There's a potential for thousands dying."

He wasn't going to say anything more about the disease. He had said enough to arouse the man's compassion—if there was any to be aroused.

And then he thought of the way the men had stared at Jordan's figure, and decided if what he was going to say wasn't able to gain their release, it would at least make her end easier.

"Jordan's infected with it."

The man stared up at her.

"It's not contagious except by the transfer of body fluids. You can't contract it—catch it—unless she is bleeding."

The man flinched as Jordan debrided a piece of the worst flesh. She moved the tip of the tweezers back into the wound.

A dark face poked in between the tent flaps. It was the tall man who had been at the plane. He stared a moment, then slipped back outside. Delaney looked back at the man on the bunk. He was still staring hard at Jordan. His eyes were narrowed—not in a glare, but more in a questioning manner. He wanted his forearm doctored, he knew what blood poisoning could do, but he was unsure about Jordan being so close, too. Real unsure.

Real unsure, Delaney repeated in his mind. Maybe if . . . his mind went to the fax message in his pocket. He pulled it out. The man looked toward the folded paper.

Delaney held it out. "Can you read English?"

The man took the fax into his hand and unfolded it.

Delaney waited a moment, watching the man's eyes. When they narrowed, Delaney said, "The disease is so contagious that when blood *is* transferred, it's guaranteed to cause some infection. And it's not just fatal, it's . . ."

As he paused he shook his head, as if picturing the aftermath of the disease. "It's horrible. The eyes hemorrhage. The head swells up like it's full of water. . . ."

Jordan's eyes came around to his.

"The pain is indescribable."

Jordan looked back at the man.

Delaney inched closer to the cot. "Yes, the pain is the worst of all. You pray to be dead." He shook his head dramatically, being sure to grimace as he did.

"No, not pray—you curse," he added. "At first, anyway. Then the throat swells so tight you have to . . ."

The man pushed Jordan's hand away from his forearm, glanced down at the fax again, and stood.

". . . have a tube stuck down your throat to breathe," Delaney continued, "and still you feel like you're suffocating. Yeah, you can see how bad it is by the fax—the president's involved, it's so bad. But what you don't see is that it's not just blood-to-blood transfer that spreads it—it's really any body fluids. She could spit on your arm and you would be finished."

The man stepped toward the front of the tent. Delaney lunged forward, grabbing him around his thick neck, and slipping around behind him. Jordan ripped the sling back from the man's forearm. He tried to jerk his arm loose, but she hung on, nearly being lifted off her feet. Delaney pulled his forearm as tight into the thick neck as he could. The man's frenzied breathing became a squeaking sound.

But he didn't attempt to cry out. He had had time before his air had been completely cut off, and he hadn't tried to yell. Not while Jordan was so close to his wound.

Not after seeing the proof in the fax.

Not something so horrible the president was involved.

The man stared at Jordan with wide eyes. Both her arms wrapped around his forearm now, she held it close to her face. His cheeks grew ashen from his lack of breath. His knees weakened. He tried to shake his head no. Delaney eased the pressure of his forearm. He spoke softly into the man's ear.

"Have the plane fueled. Have it turned around and pointed back down the cut leading to the strip."

The man nodded. His eyes never left Jordan's.

"And have them not do anything to it. You're going to fly out of here with us. If it goes down, you go down."

Delaney noticed the perspiration dotting Jordan's forehead. The man did, too, and stared at it. Their weapon— her body fluids. And the man's belief, his certainty, they were telling the truth. But she could get out of position. He could knock her out of position, or break away. Or start having doubts about what they said despite the fax. Delaney tightened his forearm again.

"Now."

The man's first words came too hoarse to understand. Delaney eased the pressure of his forearm.

"Hernandez," the man shouted.

The face immediately poked through the flaps. He couldn't have been but a couple of feet away. His eyes widened.

The one Delaney was holding spoke in English. "Fuel their plane. Don't do anything to it. They are taking me with them."

He could have spoken in Spanish. He wanted to be certain they knew he wasn't misleading them. His eyes still stared at Jordan's. The man at the flaps disappeared.

Delaney glanced toward the locker. "Is there a weapon in there?"

The man nodded. Delaney inched him toward the locker, moving carefully, giving Jordan time to move with them.

It was a revolver. Delaney held it in his hand, close to the man's back, but still kept his other arm around the thick neck.

And then the worst part came, the waiting, standing in the same position, tight as three embracing lovers, Delaney's breath against the back of the man's neck, the man's wide eyes only inches from Jordan's, with her clasping his forearm high against her chest, her mouth close to the wound.

How much time passed? It seemed like hours. Then

the face poked back through the flaps. The man's eyes studied them. Thinking, Delaney knew. He tightened his forearm. The man he held shook his head.

The man at the flaps nodded. "The plane is ready."

CHAPTER 33

Through the dark jungle, moving awkwardly, Delaney visualized scenes of a kidnapping taking place and an FBI agent staring at the perpetrators through the scope of a high-powered rifle. Only glimpses of the swarthy men silently shadowing them could be seen—but they were there. Delaney had first thought to have the man order them to stay in camp. But if he had, and they hadn't remained behind, what would happen then? If they called one bluff it would embolden them to call another. He had decided it was better for him to not say anything, just remain in charge by keeping the man in a tight grip, close to Jordan.

And then—twenty minutes, thirty minutes, an hour, he didn't know—and they were at the Cessna. It had been turned around where it sat and now faced back down the cut toward the runway. Still holding the man in their tight embrace, they moved awkwardly up onto the wing, half climbing, half crawling.

Partially inside the cockpit, Delaney felt the man's body stiffen. For an awful moment of pounding pulse, he thought the man was going to call their hand. Then the man's muscles loosened again, and he allowed them to move him on inside the plane and over into the rear seat.

"Jordan."

She took the revolver he held out to her and moved its barrel under the man's chin, pressing the weapon's end into his skin. The click of the hammer being cocked was clearly audible. But it was her face the man still stared at. His body was so soaked in sweat it looked as if a bucket of water had been thrown on him. Delaney switched on the engines.

They gained speed along the angled cut leading to the straight strip of runway. Going around the slight bend, he pushed the throttles hard forward. The Cessna seemed to squat, then, engines roaring loudly, jumped forward.

A hundred feet. Two hundred. Three hundred. Particles of grass and weeds whipped over the wings. Four hundred feet. Delaney pulled back on the yoke, and the Cessna lunged into the air and climbed sharply toward the sky.

The bullets he feared would fly their way at the last minute did not come. The man *was* important, at least to those on the ground.

He turned the yoke, swinging the Cessna back in the direction of the flat plains beyond the jungle. A thin pink line showed across the far horizon. By the time it had grown into a wide glow, they had left the trees far behind them. A road appeared, running across the desolate land below them. This time a real road, paved. Delaney pressed the yoke forward and slightly to the side, lining up with the surface.

In moments they touched down and rolled to an easy stop.

When the dark-skinned man came out of the aircraft, he sprinted wildly down the road, as if his fear of Jordan had reached such a point he could no longer control himself, even though he was away from her now.

She slid from the back seat into the front.

"I have to be crazy," she said. "All the time I was holding his arm, I was worrying about making sure none of my sweat dripped into his wound." She stared directly into his eyes. "God, what would we have done? Would it have infected him that way? We couldn't have taken the chance, could we? We would have had to kill him."

She stared at him a moment longer, then dropped her face into her hands and started sobbing, crying as much in fear for herself as the horrible thing they would have been forced to do.

As the F-16 streaked across the sky, Captain Fellows hoped there was no screwup. Scrambled out of their bunks before dawn, his squadron had been ordered at top speed in all directions, as if a Russian badger was heading toward America and no one knew from which direction it was coming. And he didn't stop at the Mexican border. In fact, his orders were to fly all the way to the Guatemalan border if necessary. Somebody damned sure needed to have gotten permission first. Surely they did. Surely it was not that big a screwup. He wondered what the Mexican Air Force flew, and if they fired without warning. Surely not. But that thought kept coming back. He looked down through a break in the thick clouds to the jungle below him. But that wasn't how he was searching, not by sight. That was what his radar scope was for, set on its farthest range possible.

He looked back at it, and caught the blip. That was the fourteenth time since he had crossed the border, one target coming right after the other. Three of the targets had been close enough that he had been able to vector slightly off course and visually identify them. The others had called in their identity when challenged. Eight airliners . . . or was it nine?

Nine. The others had been private aircraft. All of them had filed flight plans and were exactly where they were supposed to be. He smiled. Eventually somebody was going to spot something like a crop duster, something without a listed flight plan, and its pilot was going to be shocked to look up and see U.S. fighter jets circling around him like swarming bees. Then Fellows's smile vanished. If he were the one to run upon the Cessna, he had already thought about calling in engine trouble and breaking off the pursuit; let somebody else do the dirty work. Shooting down a toy airplane wasn't exactly what he had been taught at the Air Force Academy. He reached for his radio.

The blip disappeared.

He waited a moment.

He worked the controls, heightening the radar scope's intensity by pulling it back to a shorter range.

Still no blip. Whoever it had been, it had hit the deck, and was staying there, if not crashed, then flying low. *Eluding.* Contacting his base, he reported the sighting and that it was gone, and asked permission to change course to make visual contact.

"Roger, go ahead. Don't spare any fuel."

They landed on the highway and taxied toward the pump in front of the old wooden building. A tall, older Indian with long graying, black hair and wearing a T-shirt, jeans, and boots stared from the doorway. Delaney slipped to the ground and lifted a fuel nozzle. Jordan walked toward the man.

"Lower on fuel than we meant to be," she said. The Indian stared at her, looked past her to Delaney stretching the hose up toward the wing tanks, and shook his head.

"This no plane fuel," he said.

"Gas works just as good in these engines."

A short, heavily built woman looked out past his shoulder. She pulled at the man's sleeve. He said something back over his shoulder, and shrugged.

Jordan, working through her headache, smiled politely. "It's not the best thing for the engines, but you can run them for a long time on straight gasoline. After a while it gums them up." The noise of an engine caused her to look over her shoulder.

It was an old flatbed truck with crooked wooden posts for rails. The half dozen dark-skinned laborers in its rear

stared at the Cessna as they went by. A man leaned out
the passenger window, held his wide-brimmed hat to his
head as he stared at them, and then disappeared back
inside the cab.

They had to turn the plane around to fill its other wing
tank, and the Indian couple helped.

Captain Fellows looked down at the little blacktop airstrip, and the small private jet landing on it. Off to the
strip's side a Rolls Royce and a Mercedes sat waiting. A
couple of hundred meters to the east, a bright orange
home as big as a small fort was surrounded by luxu-
riously landscaped grounds. The ranch's grounds spread
for miles.

"Unconfirmed blip is a private jet," he said, and
swung his F-16 around in a wide, sweeping turn toward
his original course.

The smoke had been billowing out of the stern of the
freighter for hours. Flames flickered out of the aft hole
now, but nobody was fighting the blaze. In fact, only
once in the last hour had they seen anybody, and that
was a squat man with only one hand, naked and covered
with blood, dashing along the starboard rail.

The sickness was troubling, but not nearly as troubling
as the terrible thoughts. Father Dunnigan recoiled in
shame. But he couldn't stop thinking them. On his knees,
he looked up at the ceiling of his room and prayed as
hard as he ever had. "Please, God, stop him." It had to
be the devil; there was no other force that could make
him think the thoughts he was.

CHAPTER 34

The little coastal town was as they remembered it: the buildings mostly wooden, a few concrete block, some of them not much more than shacks; the narrow main street paved with cobblestones, the dirt streets running off it. They entered the town, passed the medical clinic, shuttered and darkened, with only a dim light showing through the window of living quarters at its rear, and moved toward the saloon at the center of town, the only place that would be open after dark.

Not more than a half dozen people walked the streets, and Delaney could see all the way to the other end of the town. The saloon did have lights showing. Two young Brazilian women wearing bright shirts and blouses and too much makeup stood on the wooden sidewalk outside talking to a young man in jeans and a T-shirt. Delaney approached them.

"Do you speak English?"

The women looked at Jordan.

"Yes," the young man said.

"The old helicopter at the end of town." He guessed it was still there. "Who owns it?"

"Mr. Callahan."

"He's an American?"

"He's English."

* * *

Callahan was tall, thin, had thick red hair, a drooping handlebar mustache—and had already gone to bed. He rubbed his eyes as he stood in his open doorway.

"Yes?"

"We need to rent your helicopter."

Callahan looked past them to the bright moon hanging low over the jungle behind the town. "Tonight? What are you, bloody smugglers?"

"In the morning would be fine," Jordan said.

"You would have to rent me too, mates. I don't let anybody fly her but me."

Delaney nodded. "Say at dawn?"

"Dawn then. But if I'm getting up at such an awful hour, don't make me wait."

"We won't."

"Rates sixty dollars an hour—American. And hours will include my flying time back here if I'm leaving you somewhere."

Delaney had only the money he had taken out of his dresser drawer. Originally a dozen crisp hundred-dollar bills, but nearly all of that had been spent at the Indians' station and the little airports where they had taken a chance on stopping to refuel since then.

Callahan noticed the hesitation. "You have that much money?"

"Of course," Jordan said.

"Dawn then," Callahan said, and turned back into his house.

When the door closed, Jordan glanced up the street. "So what are we going to do—rob a bank?"

"When we get him to the helicopter, we'll just have to persuade him. We've gone too far now to stop."

"I knew that's what you were thinking." She looked at the bulge where he had slipped the revolver inside his shirt.

Then she looked at her engagement ring and wedding band. "I'd rather use these."

He didn't say anything. There was no choice, for there

would be more needed than for just the helicopter ride: ropes to let them down to the ground, helmets, gloves.

And they would need weapons other than just the revolver too. The Indians had fired darts. They had to protect themselves from that. Even if they found out nothing, there was still hope—as long as they remained alive.

He shook his head in disgust. How in hell did you talk to somebody who might be trying to kill you? And how in the hell, if you could, could you make them understand you when you didn't speak a word of their language? The whole thing was crazy. The whole idea of coming to Brazil was crazy. But what else was there?

As they stepped away from Callahan's door and started up the street, Jordan moved her hand to her forehead. Delaney stared at her. "Headache?"

She nodded. Neither one of them said anything. She glanced at her watch. "We have over five hours to wait. If I had a little sleep it might help. I wish we'd just stayed in the Cessna."

"Maybe we can find someplace." He looked toward the saloon. One of the brightly colored women and the young man had disappeared. The other woman was now talking to an older gray-haired Brazilian in a loose shirt, baggy trousers and sandals. She said something to the man and spread her hands apart. The man drew a billfold from his pocket. The two disappeared inside the saloon.

"It has beds," Jordan said. "But I don't know if I want to sleep in one of them."

Then she shrugged. "Hell, if it's a bed, who cares?"

Three older men playing cards looked toward them when they entered the saloon. Jordan's nose wrinkled at the stench. "On second thought, I'm not so sure I'm all that tired."

The man wearing an apron behind the bar looked up at them from drying glasses with the tail of his shirt.

"You have rooms?" Delaney asked.

"Sim," the man answered in Portuguese, and nodded.

"Delaney," Jordan said.

Coming through a doorway in the far wall was Police Captain Manuel Dominguiz. A young, dark-skinned woman in a red dress gave him a peck on the cheek, then walked toward the tables where the men played cards. Dominguiz looked toward the bar.

"You think he knows?" Jordan said.

Delaney doubted it. But he hooked his thumb in his waistband, close to the revolver. Dominguiz walked toward them.

"Doctors."

They returned his nod. He looked at Jordan's jeans and blouse. Delaney knew his own clothes were wrinkled and soiled. Dominguiz's tongue ran under his upper lip. Then he smiled politely.

"No freighter has returned," he said. "No helicopter entered town today." He spread his hands in front of him, asking for an explanation.

"We hitched a ride in on a truck," Delaney said.

"I see. And you are by yourselves?"

"There are others—up the road."

"At the next town?"

Delaney nodded. They would be gone at dawn, before Dominguiz could check. "We're here to talk with the people, see if any of them have ever heard of medicinal qualities we might not be aware of in local herbs."

"Yes," Jordan said. "You wouldn't have heard of any, would you? Anything the local women use. Old legends even?"

"No. I have not."

Jordan shrugged. "Probably won't be any," she said. "But it's part of our follow-up."

"You are staying here tonight?" Dominguiz asked. He glanced toward the dark outside the door. "What there is left of it?"

Delaney nodded. "We were busy talking to people

until after dark. Then we walked down to the beach and just sat there.''

Dominguiz smiled. "Lovers in the moonlight."

Delaney forced a smile. "Sort of."

The bartender said something in Portuguese. Dominguiz looked at him, and then back to them. His expression was slightly changed. But he said nothing.

Delaney looked at the bartender. The man averted his gaze. Delaney moved his thumb nervously in his waistband.

"I see your neck healed properly," Dominguiz said.

Jordan touched the side of her neck. "Yes. You didn't hear any more about Indians in the area, did you?"

Dominguiz smiled.

Delaney waited a moment, then spoke when Dominguiz didn't. "Did you?"

"Indians?" Dominguiz questioned, then smiled again. "You asked if I heard—not if there were any."

"Excuse me?" Jordan said.

"We have a famous explorer gracing our little town," Dominguiz said. "Famous, anyway, to hear him speak of himself. But then I am being too harsh in my judgment. His name is Edgar Langdon Lorden. He was a legend—before my time. He is a drunk now."

"He knows something about the Indians?" Delaney asked.

"As I said, he is a drunk now. The only thing he has left is the little children who come listen to his stories and learn English from him. Some of the words he teaches them are a little colorful for the women in town. I have had complaints. He told me there was a tribe there. Not a tribe; but the remnants of one, according to him. It was over thirty years ago. He had diverted his boat off a river there and came up a side stream. He said Indians streaked with white paint"—Delaney noticed Jordan's glance—"came out of the bushes with their blowguns poised. He said they turned out to be friendly. But they wouldn't have been, according to him, if he had been on the other side of the stream. Evidently it was their holy land, forbidden to be trespassed upon, including by themselves.''

''You said remnants of a tribe?'' Jordan asked.

''He said they told him there were only a few of them left.''

Developed immunity, Delaney thought, as hard as that was to believe. There would be antibodies in their blood. A sample might lead to a vaccine, even a cure. ''You said they were on the side of a stream?''

''Yes,'' Dominguiz said. ''A hidden stream, according to Lorden's romantic interpretation. A tall wall of thorns on each side, and overhanging limbs of trees above, hiding the stream from sight.'' He smiled again. ''Not far from where the pilot said you came down.''

''In which direction?'' Jordan asked.

Dominguiz looked at her. He stared for a moment. ''They are still on your mind?'' He nodded at his own question. ''Yes, there were Indians there who shot at you. A hunting party from another village up or down the river, I expect. But maybe . . .'' He shrugged.

''In which direction?'' Jordan repeated.

Dominguiz turned to the bar and slid a napkin close to him. He pulled an ink pen from his tunic pocket. He drew an X on the napkin, two parallel lines, and another X.

''You came down here,'' he said, touching the end of the pen to the first X. ''A couple of hundred meters to the east is the river.'' The two parallel lines. He jabbed the pen at the final X. ''It is here where Lorden met the Indians—he said. Despite the unlikeliness of the story, I drew a map for a man here representing your government. It is my job to be as helpful as I can.''

''A man?'' Delaney questioned.

''Yes. He was from your embassy, here yesterday making a report on your incident.''

Jordan looked at the napkin. Dominguiz looked at her,

and then glanced at his watch. "Well, friends, I will see you in the morning."

As his bulky, wide shape passed out the door of the saloon and into the night, Jordan said, "He doesn't know about us, but he knows there's something."

"What could he think?"

"I don't know, but he thinks something."

"He'll check in the morning. But we'll be gone by then. Trinkets," he added. "That's something else we'll need." He looked toward the men playing cards. "And an interpreter."

Jordan looked toward the table. "For ten dollars American, they'd carry our equipment all day. But there's not enough money made for them to talk to a bunch of Indians who might try to kill them. And what about us?"

"At least we have a chance now to really find out something."

She laid her hand on his forearm. "It's crazy. It was crazy when you first came for me in jail. You knew it and I knew it. But knowing what I faced, I panicked; I would have jumped at anything. We ran to the plane. Flew here refusing to think about how crazy it was. But we know. I know and you know. How is it any better for me to get myself killed by a bunch of Indians? At least I'm alive right now. Feltenstein, and every other government scientist you can think of have to be working on this—something could come up. We can tell them about the possibility of there being Indians immune to this. And what about you? What about Missey and Ryder without either one of us? We need to find Dominguiz and tell him everything. Let him call them to come after us."

He shook his head.

She squeezed his forearm gently. "Delaney, think about it. There's nothing else we can do."

He looked at her.

"It's really all over, isn't it?" she said.

It wasn't what she said, but her coloring that bothered him. She was pale, as she had been ever since dark had fallen. But at the same time there was a faint redness high around her neck.

CHAPTER 35

Father Dunnigan kicked his sheet off. He kicked his bedside table over. Saliva seeped from the corners of his mouth. He stared at his door.

Then he stared back at the handcuff around his wrist. The chain ran over his headboard. He yanked his hand with all his strength. The headboard shattered. The chain tightened around the concrete column.

He stared at it. There were three such thick columns on each side of his study. He had moved his bed into the room and placed it against the middle column on that side. The chain was a heavy one he bought at the hardware store. The handcuffs he borrowed from a detective member of his parish. He had carefully assembled the rig, cautiously snapping the handcuffs closed a good two hours before dark. The maid had the key.

"Estella!" he roared. He shook his head in anger.

"Estella!" His eyes bulged.

"Estella, damn you, you whore; bring me the key!"

Jordan lay next to Delaney in the small bed. His back was to her face. Her forehead was dotted with perspiration. She closed her eyes and turned onto her back. *Please,* she thought. But it did no good. She couldn't keep from thinking as she was—blaming him for what had happened. *If he had not talked her into going on the expedition in the first place* . . .

Her jaw tightened with her growing anger. If he hadn't . . .

She shook her head in desperation. *It wasn't him who had talked her into it. She had wanted to go.* But she couldn't stop her anger. She turned suddenly toward him and shook his shoulder.

He looked back at her.

"Delaney, it's getting worse."

"The headaches?"

"The headaches and the nausea and the . . . the thoughts have started." She shook her head again. "You promised," she said, "when it started . . ."

"It's not that bad yet."

"Delaney, you don't know. My thoughts are . . ." Her hand came to her mouth. Her cheeks paled. She slid out of the bed and hurried toward the little bathroom. In a moment she was retching violently into the toilet.

He knelt beside her and slipped his arm over her shoulders.

She looked back at him. "Delaney."

"We're so close," he said. "Just a few more hours."

"Delaney, I—"

They both heard the doorknob turn. He looked back over his shoulder.

Silence.

A knock sounded.

He came to his feet and stepped back into the bedroom. "It's occupied," he said.

The knock came again. Jordan stepped into the bedroom. The knock came once more, louder. He walked to the door and opened it.

Dominguiz stood there.

"You're under arrest, my friends."

Walking beside Jordan across the dirt street toward the old, two-story jail, Delaney looked up at the transmitting tower rising high above the building.

"I spoke to you once about the technology your government shared with ours," Dominguiz said from behind them. "Smuggling is our two governments' highest priority. You should have known."

Smuggling? Feltenstein had guessed where they might be going. At least he knew it was a possibility, and smuggling was a charge he could level against them without taking a chance of creating a panic. He would know if they were taken into custody that they wouldn't say anything about the disease. The man from the embassy—was he there looking for them, too?

He looked at Jordan. She was still pale, her eyes half closed as if she were trying to fight back her nausea.

Inside the jail, Dominguiz nodded them across a dark, dusty, concrete floor toward three empty cells along the rear wall.

His automatic in his hand, he moved around them, opened one of the barred doors, gestured them inside with a motion of the pistol, and locked the door behind them.

He leaned against the bars. "To smuggle drugs is very serious, friends." He shook his head, as if deeply concerned about their fate. Then his eyes dropped to Jordan's rings. "What would it be worth for you to escape?" he added, and his eyes came back to Delaney's.

Delaney glanced at the rings, then back into the dark face on the other side of the bars. Dominguiz had made an offer, that was obvious. But why? Why didn't he simply take the rings and then deny there had ever been any? Who would take drug smugglers' words against that of a police captain?

And then Delaney suddenly realized *why*.

Drug smugglers weren't two people but an organization, a cartel, a group with a lot of other people involved. Dangerous people. And they weren't safely behind bars.

He tried to keep his face relaxed as he thought, not wanting Dominguiz to see any stress in his expression, but instead see a confidence born of power—the power of the cartel.

A poor police captain in a lonely, out-of-the-way coastal town on the fringe of the rain forest—who really cared about him? But who might care about him if he were responsible for the arrest of two members of the cartel, especially if they were important members?

Two or three men coming into the town one night, bullets fired into a police captain asleep in his own bed, and the men gone again. How much of an investigation would there be? And even if there was a determined one, what would there be for the investigators to learn?

In the end, a posthumous medal for Dominguiz. His name on a dusty plaque hanging in a police station somewhere. That wouldn't be nearly as nice as two diamond rings while he was still alive. And members of the cartel, instead of upset, grateful for the escape of two of their members.

"What are they worth?" Dominguiz asked.

"A lot," Delaney said.

Dominguiz smiled. "They look like they are."

Actually they were. Especially the big solitaire in the engagement ring. It was worth much more than Delaney could afford when he became engaged to Jordan. But he hadn't had to pay for it. It had come down from his mother, who had received it from her mother in turn.

And now it was as if the solitaire was a guardian angel that had passed down through the family for three generations. That is, if he could pull off what he was about to do. He stared back into Dominguiz's dark eyes, and spoke slowly. "American officers will be here soon, won't they?"

"Very soon."

Delaney purposely, theatrically, tightened his jaw and shook his head as if he were greatly disturbed.

"But you don't have to be here when they arrive," Dominguiz said.

Delaney stared at him, wrinkled his forehead and bit

his lip as if he were in deep thought. "The rings are nothing," he suddenly said. "There can be more. If you're willing to help us."

It was Dominguiz's forehead that wrinkled now. He had already made his offer in exchange for the rings only. Why the offer of more?

Delaney looked directly into the dark eyes. "Did they tell you the details?"

"Details?"

"About us. What we were doing here—earlier."

"No."

A carrot and a stick, Delaney thought. What might happen to a police captain foolish enough to hand over two members of a cartel to American officers was the stick. Five hundred thousand dollars would be the carrot. Five hundred thousand for a police captain who wouldn't see that much money in his lifetime. Most importantly, five hundred thousand dollars for a captain who had already made it plain what he would do for money.

"We didn't know the DEA had placed agents among the specimen teams."

Dominguiz waited a moment. "Pardon me?"

Jordan looked off across the room, her expression blank, but listening intently.

"They knew we were going to pick up the money. Or at least that someone from the teams would. We got the word. We left the money in the forest—where it had been left for us. Five million dollars."

Dominguiz's eyes widened. "Five million—"

"They have a man who knows the money is here—a traitor. He'll be coming with them. We have to remove it before they arrive. For your help we'll pay ten percent—five hundred thousand."

Dominguiz's Adam's apple bobbed. "Help?" he asked.

"We were to pick it up in the trees the last day we were here. We need to go back there, but we'll need ropes to get down from the helicopter—and clothes and helmets that will protect us going through the branches.''

And now the final persuasion—a little more of the stick.

"We have men coming—in a couple of days. But we can't wait now.'' He held his next words for a moment, then spoke them while looking directly into Dominguiz's eyes. "Because of you. You are the reason the money might be lost.''

He pictured Dominguiz visualizing men slipping into his bedroom at night.

"But you can make amends for that—and make five hundred thousand dollars as a token of our appreciation.''

Father Dunnigan, his eyes open wide and staring at the morning light coming in through a window, lay stiff on his bed. He heard the sound. His head turned slowly toward the door.

It cracked open.

A thin brown hand extended into the room. A key lay in a pale palm, turned up and trembling. His maid was doing as he had asked her. As he had asked her in God's name. Her trembling hand extended farther into the room, and she pitched the key to the floor at his feet and slammed the door shut.

She should have known better.

He quickly undid the cuff and hurried after her.

But just before opening the door, he fell to his knees, forced himself to stay there.

"*Oh, Almighty God, please help me,*" he prayed.

CHAPTER 36

It was near dawn, a faint glow showing on the horizon beyond the ocean. Tentacles of steam rose to form a fine mist which lay over the jungle behind the town. Delaney and Jordan walked along a narrow dirt street.

"So we look for the tree where the money is hidden," Jordan said, "and keep looking—hoping for signs of the Indians. What happens when the first sign is a dart?"

"Dominguiz said Lorden spoke of them being friendly," Delaney said.

"That was thirty years ago," Jordan said. "He wasn't there when they shot at us."

"We were on their forbidden land. The land infected with the virus—somehow they know its boundaries."

"If—by a miracle—they're there," Jordan said, "and they don't kill us, how do we suddenly tell Dominguiz to forget about the money and start interpreting—that it's actually the virus we're interested in?"

"We still have the rings."

She looked at her hand. Despite her nervousness, an amused expression crossed her face.

"What?" he asked.

"When the first explorers wanted to talk to Indians, it only cost them a few glass beads. There's been a little inflation since then, I'd say."

He smiled. "How are you feeling?"

"Better. A little. It's getting better."

He glanced toward the glow of the rising sun, then back in front of them. The helicopter sat a hundred feet ahead on a concrete pad next to a metal shed. Callahan worked atop the craft on a connection to the rotor blades. Delaney hoped the rotor was in better shape than the rest of the helicopter, its paint faded, and even rust showing at some of its rounded corners. Dominguiz turned to face them. He held up a submachine gun.

"In case there actually are any Indians," he said. He slid the weapon inside the helicopter door and looked back at them.

"Ropes, helmets, machetes—everything you ordered," he said. "And there will be no charge—not for five hundred thousand dollars as my part."

He had spoken loudly. Delaney looked up at Callahan, looking back at them. Callahan smiled. "Partners, blokes," he said. "Fifty-fifty, share and share alike. Me and the captain been partners on many a deal—but none so handsome as this." He climbed down from the helicopter's roof.

The helicopter engine roaring loudly, the blades spinning overhead, Delaney leaned back against the bulkhead and watched the trees flash by below. Jordan leaned close.

"So now we not only have Dominguiz to worry about," she said, "but Callahan, too."

Delaney shook his head. "Callahan will be waiting back in town for our radio call. It will only be Dominguiz—until we know one way or the other."

"We can set down here," Callahan shouted back over his shoulder from his seat.

Delaney came to his feet and walked to the front of the craft. Ahead of them, several trees had been felled outward in a fan-shaped fashion, leaving a wide space for them to set down.

"American Army rangers," Dominguiz said. "There's been a whole regiment of them in here for days. I assumed they were conducting maneuvers.'' Dominguiz looked over his shoulder. ''You don't think your government knows more about the hidden money than you think, do you?''

''Just a coincidence.''

Callahan worked the controls. The helicopter began to descend.

Delaney shook his head quickly. ''No, we're not going to land there.''

Callahan looked across his shoulder. ''Why? It's almost the exact position you came down before.''

''The money isn't there.'' *In which direction was the stream?* If there were Indians, the helicopter had to land outside the forbidden area. The Indians had been friendly once, according to Lorden. That was the way to keep them friendly again—he hoped. He pictured the map Dominguiz had drawn on the napkin. Where was the damn stream?

''Which way?'' Dominguiz asked.

Delaney purposely wrinkled his brow—as if confused. ''Somehow it looks different,'' he said. ''It was close to a little river—more like a stream.''

Dominguiz smiled. ''Lorden's hidden stream.'' He looked down at the trees. Callahan glanced back over his shoulder again.

Delaney kept searching the ground.

A glimpse of brown water.

''There!'' Dominguiz said, looking back across his shoulder. ''We just passed it.''

Callahan whirled the helicopter around.

''Slower,'' Delaney said.

There it was again, a thin thread of brown water with walls of thick thorns on its banks.

''Now,'' Callahan said, ''to find a place to land.''

Delaney looked at him. ''You can let us down through the trees.''

Callahan shook his head. ''With that much money at stake, I want to be going along with you. What if it's ten million instead of five million?—that'd be a million dollar commission.''

Dominguiz looked strangely at his partner. ''You going to argue with the cartel? A half a million is enough for me.''

Callahan didn't respond.

''There,'' Dominguiz said. It was a smaller clearing than the last one, but made in the same manner, trees dropped out in a fan-shaped fashion from its center. It was three hundred yards past the stream, and downstream a couple of hundred yards.

CHAPTER 37

Delaney looked down the narrow passageway leading through the wall of thorns to the stream. On the opposite bank, past fifty feet of yellow-brown water, a similar growth of thorns rose ten to twelve feet. A passageway could be seen there, too. The passageways had to have been purposely cut—otherwise the walls of thorns ran unbroken out of sight down both banks. Back in the center of the water, two rounded, scaly eyes gently broke the surface and stared at him.

That amused Dominguiz. "It is good we did not land on the other side and come across," he said.

Delaney looked to his left. In another few hundred yards they would be in the spot Lorden had indicated that the Indians met him. And what to do then—keep banging around trying to attract attention? "It's this way," he said.

Jordan glanced at him, then at the submachine guns the other two carried.

They heard a voice.

Callahan's head jerked in its direction.

It had been metallic sounding. It came again. A radio? It came again. A different voice. Still metallic.

People speaking to each other over radios.

"Rangers," Callahan said. He moved toward the concealment of a thicket of vine-twisted cane.

*   *   *

They heard the metallic talking for several more seconds.

Then two men appeared.

Dominguiz's eyes widened.

It was as if they were witnessing a scene from a lunar landing, with the two men covered in bulky white suits with air canisters on their backs, and wearing helmets with wide glass faceplates. Except men on a lunar mission don't carry weapons. Each of them carried an automatic rifle across his chest.

Behind them came another man, dressed the same, also carrying an M-16.

Following him was a line of men in the suits. A couple of them carried instruments that resembled short, stainless steel posthole diggers. The rest carried or had strapped to them several small metallic cylinders.

They walked slowly but purposely, being careful where they stepped, their faceplates constantly moving back and forth as they scanned the ground in front of them. In a few minutes they were out of sight behind the wall of thick thorns on their side of the stream. The metallic sound of a query over one of their radios floated back through the undergrowth.

Delaney looked at Callahan and Dominguiz, staring at him.

"What is happening?" Dominguiz asked.

"Those are bacterial contamination suits," Callahan said. "The air canisters—they don't even want to take a chance of breathing whatever. . . . What have you led us into?"

Delaney didn't answer.

"There isn't any money, is there?" Callahan said. "What are you here for? Tell me." His submachine gun came up to point at them.

"A disease," Jordan said.

Dominguiz's eyes widened again.

"When we were here on the expedition, one of our members contracted a disease. We're back to find its cure. You're in no danger. As long as you don't cross the stream. That's where its source is.''

Callahan stared. His finger moved around the submachine gun's trigger guard. Then he looked in the direction the rangers had gone.

''You're in no danger,'' Jordan repeated.

His eyes came back to them. ''Whatever's here, you're going to get to stay with it. But first . . .'' He held out his hand.

Jordan glanced at her finger, then pulled her rings off and stepped forward, handing them over.

Callahan and Dominguiz hurried in the direction of the helicopter.

Jordan closed her eyes. ''I thought we were going to be shot.''

''We would have been if the rangers weren't still in hearing distance.''

''They're looking for the Indians, too.''

''Whatever they're doing, with that many men and guns they're going to scare them off—if there are any.''

A hundred feet away, in a matted thicket growing out from a side of a tall tree, several pairs of eyes stared at them, two lone figures, standing by themselves.

Delaney looked at Callahan and Dominguiz disappearing into the undergrowth. He suddenly felt like an impulsive child, madly going about whatever struck him, sure in his own mind it was the thing to do, that it made sense, and then, when it was too late, suddenly realizing it made no sense at all. What had he brought them into?

''I'm frightened, Delaney,'' Jordan said.

But her coloring was good.

The sun was bright.

CHAPTER 38

The room had a long conference table with a dozen chairs on each side. But nobody was sitting. Instead, Ph.D.s in civilian clothes, and a mixture of M.D.s and Ph.D.s in Army uniforms, stood at the end of the room where a wall-sized map hung on the plaster. A two-star general used a long pointer to touch the places he was describing.

"Here, here, here, and here," he said, using the pointer to indicate the four sides of a relatively small section of the Amazon jungle. "The topography is slightly depressed compared to the area. It's almost a slight sinkhole, approximately one kilometer by one kilometer."

"Go in either direction these ways"—he used the pointer to indicate two sides of the area—"and you're out of the infected area. Go south, where the start of this rise is, and you're out of it again."

He moved the pointer to the far north end of the section. "Across this stream—and you're out of it again."

He turned to face the others and rested the pointer across his thighs. "First of all, we can thank God the contaminated area is not any bigger than it is. If it had been hundreds of square miles . . ." He shook his head to emphasize the impossibility of ridding an area of that magnitude of the virus.

"You can also thank God that exposure to oxygen kills the virus. That means it is unlikely to spread on the wind. But it's not anaerobic, either. Three inches down in the soil, there's not a trace of live virus. So we have a situation where a thin sliver of soil up to an inch thick is the only place the live virus exists—nothing below that, nothing above it."

He looked back at the map. "Now if you can tell me how we can remove three inches of dirt from the entire area—and do it cleanly?"

Delaney hadn't realized why his eyes kept going back to the long-limbed monkey moving through the high tree-tops until now. "That's the first one I've seen."

"What?"

"The monkey. That's what was missing." He glanced over his shoulder in the direction of the stream, now out of sight a quarter of a mile behind them. "When we were here the first time—did you see any wildlife? Anything living, other than plants? I don't even remember any birds."

Jordan looked at the monkey as it disappeared into the thick foliage of an adjoining tree. "The monkey at the research center developed the virus almost immediately," she said. "Monkeys come to the ground. They occasionally have cuts or scratches—skin parasites if nothing else, leaving open wounds. It would just take one animal being infected, and then attacking the others."

He nodded. "If they came onto the contaminated land. But why wouldn't they? They couldn't know. There's no way they could know."

"Maybe instinct," Jordan said.

When he looked at her, she nodded. "Why not?" she asked. "What is instinct? It's a learned behavior built up over time. Maybe long ago, thousands of years ago, they did come onto the land—they went mad, maybe—there were orgies of killing. Over the centuries they learned not to go there. I don't know, Delaney, but I don't remember anything alive there either.'' Her brow narrowed. ''There was the crocodile.''

''Uh-huh, but he was in the water. Maybe he didn't go up on that side. Maybe the contaminated soil doesn't reach all the way to the stream. Hell. I don't know. Maybe there's a difference between warm-blooded animals and cold-blooded. But I don't remember seeing anything.''

He looked around him, back in the direction of the stream, and in front of him—to the matted thicket fifty feet away that blocked their view.

The coast guard cutter commander stared through his binoculars. The first smoke had come out of a cargo hole near the freighter's stern. Within minutes, flames had jumped out of the hole, brightly illuminating the half-dressed shapes of men lying sprawled about the decks. That had been hours before. Now the entire rear half of the freighter was ablaze.

Feltenstein's thoughts were filled with horror as he spoke rapidly on the phone. ''They have to stop it from sinking. They have to. Everybody on board must be infected. There's blood everywhere. When it goes down . . .''

He looked at Darrell, staring back at him from the office doorway, and shook his head.

Out in his cage, the injected monkey screamed and screamed and screamed—and then was suddenly silent.

Delaney held back a limb and Jordan stepped under it. When he let it go, it scraped against his hand and he immediately looked at his palm. It wasn't scratched. He saw Jordan look at him.

He tried to force a smile.

''Delaney, I'd give anything if we hadn't come here.''

''That's nonsense.''

''What have I got to lose? But you, you have everything.''

"Jordan, you're going to have to quit—"

Her eyes turned to where he stared. Twenty feet ahead of them, a tall Indian, girded with a loincloth, wearing a headdress of bird feathers and painted with wide white stripes down his body, held a three-foot-long, thin, jagged rock over his head.

Two other Indians came from each side. Blowguns poised. Pointed.

"Easy," Delaney said.

The Indian with the rock said something in a coarse dialect. He began to pump the rock out in front of him. Behind the blowguns, brown cheeks swelled, puffing to an exaggerated proportion, and breath was exhaled suddenly—but over the tops of the blowguns instead of through them.

Delaney held his hands out, palms up in a supplicating motion. The thrusting of the rock suddenly stopped.

The Indian lowered it to his waist. He stared at them for a long moment. And then his eyes dropped to Delaney's waist. Delaney's hands moved slowly, pulling open his shirt first to expose the revolver, then reaching slowly for its handle.

The blowguns fit against poised mouths.

Delaney pulled the weapon out and let it drop to his feet.

The blowguns lowered slightly. The Indian in the headdress grasped the handle of a long, sheathed knife at his side, and gestured with a sideways motion of his head for them to walk past him in the direction he indicated.

CHAPTER 39

In less than a hundred feet, the ground began sloping upward. But the rise could only be felt underfoot, the wide tree trunks and thick underbrush every few feet making it impossible to see any change of elevation in the land.

Then the trees began to space farther apart, the underbrush grew less prevalent, and the slope became noticeable to the eye as it grew ever steeper.

Moments later, the side of a hill rose in front of them, and they were going up it, approaching an area of barren rock that sloped sharply upward.

And then the rock began to open, swinging back on long timbers, revealing the mouth of a wide cave flickering with the illumination of a light source coming from within it.

Delaney felt Jordan brush against him. He glanced at her. She stared openmouthed at the entrance. In front of them the Indian stopped and held the stone high above his head, remained in that position for several seconds, then started forward again.

Delaney felt a cool wave of air come down the side of the hill, washing over him from the interior of the cave, and then the end of a blowgun nudged his back, urging him forward again.

*　　*　　*

Rows of long torches projecting out from the rock walls to each side of the wide cavern illuminated its interior in a bright glow as they stepped inside it.

And then Delaney saw the white man.

He was in a cage of thick poles bound together by twisted vines close against the rock wall on the left of the cave.

"Delaney," Jordan whispered.

The white man stared at them. Off to the cage's side, two young Indians, blowguns in hand, sat facing him.

The Indian in the headdress stopped in front of the cage, lifted the long stone over his head, and brandished it toward the wooden poles, then stepped to the side, motioning with a gesture of his head for them to come closer.

The Indians who had been sitting on the ground rose to their feet and lifted their blowguns to their mouths.

Delaney stared at the man. He was middle-aged, with hard, wide shoulders covered with a yellowed T-shirt, and was heavily bearded. A pair of tattered, knee-length shorts and rough sandals completed his dress. He stared back at them, then raised his hands to the poles at each side of his face and clasped them.

"I'm Richard Little," he said in a hoarse voice.

It took Delaney a moment to find his voice. "Delaney Jeffries." He couldn't help but stare. The man's arms and legs were absolutely pale, as if he hadn't been out in the sun in years, but his face was as red as if it were sunburned, especially his cheeks and forehead. A fetid odor, carried on the cool wind coming from deeper in the cave, swept past Delaney, and he saw the melon rinds sitting at a side of the cage, big green flies buzzing around them, and the bucket, crusted with the man's dried excrement.

"I'm . . ." Jordan started, then had to clear her throat of her nervousness. "I'm Jordan Jeffries."

The man nodded slowly, then looked over his shoulder toward the far side of his cage. Past the poles, Delaney saw another Indian sitting cross-legged on the ground a few feet from the cage. Unlike the others, he wore no paint, and had long black hair hanging to his shoulders.

"He understands some English," the man said. "Portuguese. Several Indian dialects. They want you to talk— so he can listen."

The sitting Indian's face remained expressionless, except for his intense stare. Beyond him were three more cages in a row, but empty.

"If you don't talk, they're going to start jabbing you with those blowguns," Richard Little said.

Jordan had been looking at the other cages. She turned her face back to the man. "Why do they have you in there?" she asked.

"Because they're damn savages," Little answered sharply, his sudden change in tone startling. Then his voice was back to low again. "They caught you in the forbidden land?"

Delaney looked at the Indian with the headdress. "We weren't on the other side of the stream."

The Indian sitting cross-legged said something in his dialect to the one with the headdress.

"I think he just said that you know what the forbidden land is," Little said.

Jordan nodded. "We heard about a man. Edgar Lorden. He was here thirty years ago. They told him about the land."

Little's forehead wrinkled questioningly. "Here, and they let him go?" He shook his head as if confused.

Jordan nodded.

The man waited a moment, as if he were still thinking about the man who had been turned loose. "There's not anybody else with you?"

"No."

He looked toward the entrance to the cave, now closed again. "What's going on down there? There's been something going on down there. These savages have been agitated for days about spirits."

"The army. Army scientists—in biological gear."

"They won't come after you?"

"They don't know we're here."

The Indian, staring intently, narrowed his eyes.

"Don't know?" Richard said. "What are you . . ." He shook his head.

"They just don't know," Jordan said.

"In biological gear?"

She nodded. "Protective suits."

"I wondered why the Indians didn't go after them. It's their religious duty, they think. Run intruders off. They fire darts at them. They're not poisoned. Not unless they can't run 'em off. They were scared. They hadn't ever seen anything like that—the suits. Damn stupid savages."

Delaney glanced toward the Indians.

"Don't worry about them," Little said. "They won't hurt you no matter what you say. I curse their chief every time I see him, the gray-haired bastard. Even curse their head scientist there—the medicine man. Name's Bombussa." He nodded toward the tall Indian in the headdress.

"That's him. He's the top dog. Curse him like the heathen he is, I have. Curse their gods, too—when I'm really upset. It doesn't make any difference. They won't hurt you. It's against their religion to harm anyone. You'll go in a cage, just like me. And you're going to stay here till you rot. But they won't hurt you."

He took a deep breath. "Unless you run. If you run they will kill you. I wish I had run when they first caught me. Anything but this."

As he paused again he took another deep breath. "But I was too sick then."

"Sick?" Jordan asked.

"Real sick—delirious."

Delaney saw Jordan's eyes come around to his. He looked back toward the cage. "Hallucinating?" he asked.

"Yeah. Fever high, I guess. Nightmares was more like

it. Why are they wearing biological gear?''

"You're not sick now?" Jordan asked.

"Do I look sick? You sound like these savages. That's the only reason they don't let me go—they say. I'm sick—possessed, is the way they put it. I could do a dozen push-ups, stand on my head, turn flips in the air, if one of the bastards had a thermometer I'd let him stick it up my ass and see. But it wouldn't do any good. It's their legend. Crazy, heathen bastards live by it—their whole lives are structured around it. Now, you were saying—biological gear."

"Mr. Little," Jordan said, "what were your hallucinations?"

"What are you, a doctor?"

"Yes, we are," she said.

"*Monbombo*," the sitting Indian said to the one in the headdress.

Little smiled.

"Mr. Little," Jordan said, "were the hallucinations a growing anger—a hate?"

He narrowed his eyes as he stared back at her.

"Mr. Little, were they? Were you dreaming about anger, growing worse at night? Did it seem to go away in the daytime and then reappear at dark again?"

Little's brow wrinkled now. "What are you here for? Tell me what the damn biological gear is for?"

"There's a virus here."

"A virus?"

Jordan nodded.

"Not here," Delaney said. "It's across the stream—the forbidden land. That's why we're here, trying to find a cure for a disease it causes. We thought if there were Indians—maybe they knew something. There has to be some reason they didn't contract the disease."

"Mr. Little," Jordan said, "were you across the stream—before you got sick?"

"That's where I was when they got me. Put me in this damn cage. I'm not sure but with the draft and all, this damn cold dampness, that that's what kept me sick for weeks before I got over it.''

"But you got over it—you're well now."

"What do you want me to do, dance you a jig to prove it?''

"It's just that we . . .'' Jordan shook her head. "If we had just waited?'' she said.

"Waited for what?'' Little asked.

Delaney felt his stomach turn with regret.

"*Moran dau bonfa*,'' the medicine man in the head-dress said.

"Bombussa's wanting you to go with him,'' Little said.

The Indian pointed deeper into the cave.

The sitting Indian said something.

"*Monbombo*,'' Bombussa repeated. He held his hand out again toward the rear of the cave.

Little smiled. "*Monbombo*—that's their word for a medicine man. You might be their captive, but looks like you're a big shot in their books now that they know you're doctors. That's holy to them.''

"*Monbombo ral caa radada*.''

Little stared at Bombussa. "I think he's saying he wants to show you something.''

Delaney felt the end of a blowgun jab him in his back, urging him forward.

"Tell him to wait a minute,'' Jordan said.

"Hell, lady, you tell him. I can understand a bit of their prattle. But when it comes to me speaking it, I'm lucky if I can pronounce their words for different kinds of food. And that's after three years.''

The Indian sitting on the ground said something. Bombussa nodded.

"Three years,'' Jordan murmured. She shook her head, then took a deep breath. "Why are they immune?''

Delaney looked at her.

"I want to know, Delaney,'' she said. "Why? And if they're not immune, how do they keep from getting the disease? Remember, Lorden said they didn't go into the forbidden land themselves. But the one who shot me did. And the ones who brought Mr. Little out did—he just said they did.'' She looked at the medicine man. ''Why are you here?'' she asked, staring at him.

''I know a bit about that,'' Little said. ''They were defeated by another tribe, buddy over there tells me.'' He gestured with his head back over his shoulder toward the sitting Indian. ''It was long ago. They can't even tell you how long ago—they only count back eight generations. After that it's just 'the others.' Well, the others got their butts kicked, evidently. They were run off from their village and ended up here. They were religious people even then. I guess all heathens are, in their own way. I told you they wouldn't hurt you. That's part of their religion. You know, the Thou Shalt Not Kill bit. They had always been like that, then got their butts whipped; didn't know how they had displeased the gods. They didn't live in this cave when they first came here. They built their village on the near side of the stream where there was water and fish for the taking. A few of them became possessed, started attacking the others. They had to kill them. Some of those who had been injured by the ones who were possessed, became possessed, too. They say it was because the possessed ones got close enough to exchange an evil spirit for the other ones' souls. They even have a word for souls. It translates directly.''

A one-sided smile came to his face, and he shook his head slightly.

''Anyway—their legend—one night an old woman saw a bat fly into a tent. She went inside. The bat had changed into a man, attacking her children asleep there. The fools are as certain of that as they are certain I'm standing here talking to you. It's gospel to 'em. So they became bat killers. That's a hell of an occupation, isn't it? They found the biggest colony right here in this cave. They decided this is where the god of the underworld emanates from—out of a hole in the ground at the rear of this cave. Somewhere back there is where they're supposed to have their early warning system, is the way I understand it. But they're not afraid. Some big honcho medicine man years ago—back before eight generations ago—told them the evil god wouldn't send any more bad spirits out as long as they were brave enough to live here where anything would have to pass them before it got loose out into the world. Their whole existence—like I said, their religion is based on it. Loosely translated they call themselves the guardians, though that's a title more commonly specifically applied to the few young ones who go into the forbidden land when somebody trespasses there—the ones painted with white streaks. There's not all that many young ones left—any of the tribe left, for that matter. Maybe a few dozen in all— counting women and children. They say they used to number hundreds. It's living in this damn damp cave is what it is. They're dying of real sicknesses. Not some imagined possession. And it's good enough for them.

"But even if every last damn one of them dies, the final one alive will still be a guardian as long as he can stand. Still keeping the evil god from bringing forth more bats from the underworld to fly out and look for blood."

"*Golomkar*," Bombussa said, gesturing with his hand for them to follow him, and turned and started deeper into the cave.

"*Golomkar*," Little said. "I know that one. That's the ones I was telling you about, the ones you see with white paint. The guardians, the ones who watch over their crazy damn forbidden land—the only ones their religion allows to set foot in it."

A blowgun pushed against Delaney's back, urging him after the medicine man. Jordan was nudged too. "Where are they taking us?" she asked.

"I don't know," Little said. "I never went any farther than right here."

CHAPTER 40

The coast guard commander stared at the freighter engulfed in flames, its steel sides glowing red hot like the walls of a blast furnace. The stern slowly dipped under the water, a loud hissing sound and heavy cloud of steam rising into the clear sky. A flame amidships pointed toward the elevated bow. A naked man standing there, blistered and charred, his hair burned off, swiped at the horrible heat with his hands, screamed, and ran forward, disappearing into the conflagration.

The bow rose higher. It hung there, and then, almost imperceptibly, began to slip backwards. The flames burned a bright, raging orange.

More steam rose from the steel plates sinking beneath the water; the deck glowed blue-white, buckled, and the freighter sped backward, disappearing beneath the clear water, leaving a large cloud of gray steam billowing upward in its wake.

The commander looked down at the cutter's starboard rail, at his men, dressed in life jackets, ready to go.

Stop it from sinking at all costs, had been his orders.

But the orders had come only minutes before; there was nothing he could have done.

Delaney followed slowly behind Bombussa. Despite the bright, flickering light from the torches spaced along the walls, he had to walk carefully over the rough, uneven rock surface to keep from tripping and falling. Jordan leaned close to him.

"Vampire bats. Any animals that were infected in the forest—the bats would have carried the virus after feeding on them. Vampire bats can pass on almost any blood disease. The bats fed on some children one night— maybe others later. For a panicked mother, who saw a bat fly out of a tent where her children had been sleeping, and then her children went mad—it would be an easy story to get mixed up in the retelling. Especially with adults going mad later. It became a bat flying into the tent and changing into a man. So they're not immune. But then how are they alive?"

Delaney wondered how she could still be rationally thinking about the disease, rationally thinking about anything, with a cage awaiting them. Three years, Little had said. Until you rot, he had said. That's all that kept going through Delaney's mind—and that it had been he who had brought her here.

He wouldn't let her be caged. Whether that was an irrational thought or not, he meant it. Somehow. Bombussa stopped in front of them. The two Indians who had been following them with blowguns stopped a few feet away.

Delaney looked toward a narrower passage leading off the one they were in.

A squat, older, gray-haired Indian, unpainted and backed by two younger ones, also unpainted and carrying blowguns, stepped from the passageway.

Bombussa bowed his head toward the squat Indian, then held his chin to his chest for a moment before raising his face once more. *Their chief?* He spoke to Bombussa, then stepped around him to face them at a distance of three or four feet. He gestured with a motion of his head for them to follow, and turned and walked still deeper into the main cavern.

"Jordan, I said there couldn't have been an immunity

developed by anyone living in the infected area. The ones who went mad would attack the others, kill them all out. But maybe that's not right. In a jungle village, it's not like in a city where those with the virus could be anonymous. Here, they would be isolated and easy to track through the jungle or caught if they came back to the village. We could go coast to coast before they could travel a couple of hundred miles. Any outbreak would have stayed isolated here. It's happened in Africa. Viruses there have killed whole tribes without spreading out of the area where the virus originated. There are no highways here, no transportation for an infected person to catch a ride on and spread the disease.''

The squat, gray-haired Indian veered out of the main tunnel toward another narrow opening. In a few steps it began to widen, and then jumped into an immense room with only a single, low-burning torch jammed into the wall at the far side.

The Indian walked farther into the shadows. Delaney and Jordan followed.

They saw the stones then.

They were like the one Bombussa had held over his head—three to four inches wide, long, and jammed into the floor—dozens of them. The floor felt soft under their feet. Dirt, not stone. The gray-haired Indian said something and swept his open hand across the room. Bombussa spoke.

"*Golomkar.*"

Delaney looked back at the stones.

Bombussa nodded. "*Golomkar,*" he repeated.

The gray-haired Indian hooked his thumbs in the waistband of his loincloth and smiled broadly. "*Golomkar,*" he said again, an obvious note of pride in his voice. He again swept his hand across the room.

The medicine man cocked his head to the side. There was an expression across his face like he was confused, or thought they were. He straightened his head and looked toward the stones, and then walked to the nearest one.

Delaney smelled the odor of death now, a dry, decayed scent. It was so strong he wondered why he hadn't noticed it before. He looked back at the stones. *Headstones.* They were in a graveyard? *Golomkar.* A guardians' graveyard.

Bombussa was scraping his foot back and forth, kicking dirt from around one of the stones. Delaney looked at Jordan.

Her nose moved. She was just then noticing the smell, too. "Headstones," she said in a low voice.

The gray-haired Indian moved to help Bombussa. They kept kicking their feet back and forth. A murmur came from the unpainted Indians behind Delaney, and he glanced over his shoulder as they slowly dropped to one knee. He looked back at the two working at the grave. Bombussa crooked his finger and motioned with it for them to come. Delaney stepped forward.

He looked down at the stone—transfixed squarely through the dried bones of a human chest.

"*Golomkar,*" Bombussa said proudly.

CHAPTER 41

They moved deeper into the vast cavern, following the older Indian and Bombussa.

"My God, it's like we're in Romania instead of Brazil," Jordan said. "It's the same legend. Men changing into bats in the middle of the night, stakes through the heart—those long stones. It's exactly the same—not vampire bats, but vampires that they fear. They're wasting their whole lives guarding against a legend of vampires."

"And dying," Delaney said. "They go into the contaminated area and scratch themselves—they don't have any idea that's how they're infected. Over the years, one after another of them goes in there and gets infected. They're filling the graveyard." He thought for a moment. "Little says they don't believe in killing unless they have to. Those other cages—the empty ones. They're for their own people who get sick—become possessed. Do they leave them there until they grow old and die? They didn't kill Little, and they think he's possessed. But all the ones with stripes on them are young. Unless an infection hasn't occurred in an awfully long time, wouldn't one of them be in a cage, still alive?

"Or maybe they treat outsiders and their own people differently. Maybe it's something to do with their religion. They don't kill outsiders, but they do their own people when they're infected. Maybe the punishment has something to do with being a guardian in the first place.''

But whatever the case, Little was in a cage—had been for three years. And until he rots. Until they rot.

And all because the Indians worried he and Jordan might turn into vampires. He could see how the legend got started. A bat flying into a tent, and maybe a maddened man there already, attacking the children. The attacks themselves could lead to the Indians believing the maddened people were after blood. The biting and scratching as they killed a victim; it left blood all over the place. Splattered blood would create a vivid memory for someone who had lost somebody close. Over the years the story could easily change into the blood being why the attack was made in the first place.

But it wasn't. It was a virus causing the attacks, a disease, not possession. If only there were some way to make them understand. It wasn't bats or men, but a little organism too small to see.

Monbombo. A doctor. The Indian name for medicine man. And now he and Jordan, also *monbombos.* Something the Indians respected—revered.

Could he use that?

Bombussa said something to attract their attention, and then pointed ahead of them to a passageway veering off the main cavern. It was barely wider than where a man could walk.

It led into another room, this one only eight or ten feet in width, but widening as it ran back twenty-five feet to a stone wall.

Immediately in front of the wall stood three large blocks of stone, laboriously chiseled into uniform squares. Upon each of them sat a life-sized replica of an Indian's chest, shoulders, and head. Two of the busts were brown with age and, though wiped clean, stained where mold had grown in the cave's dampness. The third one was new, some of the chipped and polished corners still showing the faint sheen of freshly exposed rock.

The gray-haired Indian went to one knee. Bombussa dropped to both his knees. The Indians behind Delaney murmured. He glanced over his shoulder to see them motioning for him and Jordan to kneel.

As he went down on one knee, Jordan came down beside him, and then the Indians at their rear were kneeling and leaning their bodies forward, reaching out and placing their hands on the stone floor in a gesture of supplication.

Bombussa spoke without rising. "Gods."

The English took Delaney aback. He looked at the statues. For the first time he noticed that against the wall behind the statues sat baskets of melons and herbs.

Bombussa came to his feet as did the gray-haired one. They slowly backed toward the entrance. Delaney came up, then he and Jordan backed in the same fashion. They were well into the narrow tunnel before the two in front of them turned to face them. There wasn't enough room to pass and so Delaney turned and followed the younger Indians who had been trailing them out into the wider main tunnel.

As they stopped and waited to see which way they would be led this time, an enlightened expression crossed Jordan's face.

"We're getting the grand tour because we're doctors—medicine men. *Monbombos* representing gods. They're hoping we'll see something that will better help them fight the . . . the whatever it is they're guarding against. Something we might know because we're medicine men ourselves in their eyes. Something maybe our gods might tell us."

Gods, Delaney thought. Spoken in English. The Indians had learned that word from Little. And their gods—the busts in the small room—looked human. Were human?

The cavern began to narrow. Soon not only the walls closed in, but the ceiling dropped to barely above their heads. They walked single file again. Delaney looked past Bombussa's shoulder, waiting for the cave to suddenly widen or to see guards at the spot Richard talked about, the place where the cave dropped off into a hole to the underworld.

He saw neither. Instead he saw the gray-haired Indian look back at him and bring his finger to his mouth in the universal symbol for silence. The young Indians behind them stopped where they were. The two in front now walked slower, more carefully. Jordan's face was beside Delaney's shoulder and he looked at her. When her eyes tightened suddenly, he looked back in front of him.

Bombussa and the gray-haired Indian had stepped to the side of the passageway and pressed their backs against the wall to allow a view past them. Twenty feet down the corridor, two torches illuminated a man laying on his side on a thick bed of animal skins spread wall to wall.

But not a man either. Rather the scarred and ridged grayish white figure of a man hideously burned—more a hard body resembling a mummy, wrapped in the dead layers of his own hard skin. Ridged streaks ran up and down his length. His hair and eyebrows were gone and his eyes were white and hard as stone. The one leg sticking out of a deer skin loosely draped across his middle showed his toes had fused together.

And then his arm moved.

"He's alive!" Jordan blurted.

Bombussa stared hard at her, but the burned one didn't move at the sound. His ear was seared into no more than a bump rising from the ghastly white skin at the side of his head. Bombussa hadn't been worried about him hearing, but wanted quiet out of respect.

And then the mummylike form shifted again, and turned laboriously over onto his stomach. The back part of his body now exposed was as brown and soft as any of the other Indians. It was like he had been baked on hot coals on one side and never turned. Jordan's hand cupped her mouth.

Delaney looked past the torch in the wall beyond the man, and saw the cavern narrow to a funnel no bigger than a basketball goal, and then turn sharply downward—the passage to the underworld. The figure in front of them was the early warning system Little had spoken of.

But Little had also said the Indians' religion prevented them from harming anyone. What kind of savages would do that to a man, and why?

Then Delaney caught the faint sweet scent of incense. He noticed the tiny flickering flame coming from a small, round clay bowl past the figure's head. There was a bowl at his feet too. The animal skin lying across his middle was obviously soft, draping his body like a fine satin sheet. The women, or the guardians, had worked hard to chew it that soft.

A reverence they were paying him? To harm him as they had and now pay such reverence? Why? And then Bombussa held up his hand and motioned for them to move back the way they had come.

When Delaney and Jordan stepped back into the main passageway, Bombussa spoke. *"Boran doo ramm."* He pointed with an index finger to his stomach.

"Boran doo ramm," he repeated. He poked his stomach.

Delaney shrugged his not understanding.

Bombussa held up three fingers, and glanced to his left up the narrow passageway they had just exited. Then he dropped two fingers, continuing to hold one up.

He pointed again into the narrow tunnel, wiggled one finger, then looked back over his shoulder, pointed up the wide cavern, and raised three fingers again.

"The three busts we saw in the other room?" Jordan said. She looked down the narrow tunnel. "The man in there is one of them?"

The reverence, Delaney thought.

Bombussa stared at him, then turned and started back up the cavern.

Reverence, Delaney thought again, and glanced back over his shoulder. The three busts in the other room.

"Tepes," Jordan said.

Delaney looked at her as if she had said a word of the Indians' language.

"Tepes," she repeated. "Count Vlad Tepes. I knew his name would come to me. He was the one in Romania on whom the original vampire novel was based. He lived in the fifteenth century. He's said to have killed a hundred thousand people. His favorite method was to impale them on long wooden poles. I was thinking about the poles of Little's cage and it came to me. Tepes often drank his victims' blood, too. The original Dracula. It's amazing how much legends are alike all over the world. You know there are caves in Europe where ancient people drew pictures on the wall that look like flying saucers, and show men wearing what resemble space helmets, sitting in them. The drawings even show fiery exhausts. At least that's what it appears to be at the rear of the saucers.

"The identical drawings have been found in caves here, in South America. They were all drawn by people who lived thousands and thousands of years ago. They weren't visiting each other. How did they come up with identical concepts? Religions too. It's amazing how many sprang up in different isolated places with the same tenets and practices."

Had she totally removed her mind from their situation? It was like she was a tourist, strolling casually through a cave display.

But then Delaney realized she wasn't just idly speculating. The look on her face was both reflective and thoughtful at the same time. She was trying to make something spark an idea, like thinking of the poles of the cage reminded her of the poles on which the original Dracula had impaled people.

And his mind suddenly clicked.

"What happened to him?"

The Indians stopped at his sharp tone.

They looked at him.

"What happened to him?" He pointed back down the cave in the direction of the passageway they had just come from. "What happened to him?"

Bombussa stared questioningly.

Delaney pointed down the cave again. He drew his arms up close to his shoulders and bent his hands into twisted shapes, similar to how the form's had been.

"What happened to him?"

CHAPTER 42

At the cages, Bombussa spoke to the Indian sitting cross-legged on the ground. Delaney saw the man's eyes come up to his, and then the Indian came to his feet and walked to him.

"What happened to him?" Delaney said.

"*Roglain bar coo.*"

"What?"

"Burn," the Indian said.

"Yes, him. What happened to him? He had the virus. . . . He was possessed, wasn't he? What happened to him to . . . to cast the possession out of him?" He shook his head in frustration at Bombussa's questioning stare. "Damn. He doesn't have the faintest idea what I'm saying." He looked at the cage, and Richard Little staring back at him with his eyes slitted and dark against the background of his red face.

"Can you help? I want to know what happened to the man at the rear of the cave. If he was infected and got well. If he's there because he did get well, he was powerful enough to cast off the possession. He's their main guardian now. . . .

"I want to know if I'm right."

Little looked at the Indian. "*Par fono . . .* crap. I don't know the . . ." Little pointed toward the rear of the cavern. "*Par fono . . . don rel ron . . .* hell, you little brown bastard, you know English some. Help me out.''

The Indian looked at Bombussa, said something in their dialect, and waited.

Bombussa nodded.

The Indian looked back at them. ''Possessed. Run.''

Delaney nodded. ''Yes, he was possessed. Your people were chasing him. He was a guardian himself, wasn't he? That's how he became possessed. He had been in the forbidden land.''

The Indian nodded.

''And you were chasing him,'' Delaney prompted. ''Where did he run?''

The Indian stared, unsure.

''Run,'' Delaney repeated. ''Where run?'' He spread his hands. ''Run?''

''*Romboa.*''

''*Romboa?*'' Delaney said. ''*Romboa?*''

The Indian pointed in the direction of the entrance to the cave. ''*Romboa.*''

''The forbidden place?''

''No.''

''What's *romboa?*''

The Indian looked back at Bombussa and said something in their dialect. Bombussa walked toward the wall between the cages. Delaney saw the wet stain. It was a place where water dripped down the stone surface. Bombussa held the side of his hand close against the rock until he had a tiny pool of water in his hands. He turned and pointed toward the torch twenty feet away. He used his other hand to touch his fingers to the water, then suddenly flared his fingers up dramatically above it and pointed back to the torch.

''Fire coming out of water?'' Delaney said.

''A geyser,'' Jordan said. ''A hot spring.''

Delaney nodded. ''He ran into an area of hot springs. They couldn't follow him. He was overcome by the heat, or an injury—something. He fell, landed on the side that's scalded. But, no, those burns were too deep. He crawled through a geyser, a few inches deep, on the side he's burned. Or passed out and ended up laying there unconscious, maybe on some ledge heated by the springs. In any case they couldn't go in after him. Or didn't see him until he had been there long enough to be horribly burned.''

"Delaney, what are you getting at?"

He held up two fingers and looked directly at the Indian in front of him. "He is one of the three busts in the little room where we went, isn't he?"

The Indian wrinkled his brow in confusion at the words.

"Three," Delaney said. "The three in the little cave off this one. The three who . . . damn." He held up his fingers again. "Three down there." He pointed down the cavern. He placed his palms together and put them to a side of his head, like he was sleeping on them. "Three. He is one of the three. All of them were possessed. All of them got over it some way. They were . . . they're almost living gods. They were. There's one left now."

"Gods," the Indian said.

Delaney nodded. "Three of them. Living gods."

"Living," the Indian said and nodded.

"What happened to the other two? What happened to them before they were cured?"

"Delaney, what is it?"

"Heat, I think."

"Heat?"

"I think they were all subjected to heat in some way. The one we saw burned. What happens in the lab when you're working with viruses and you leave them out too long?"

"I don't follow you."

"When you leave viruses out too long—at room temperature."

Her eyes narrowed as she glanced back into the cavern. "They die."

"Every medical student knows that. The vast majority

of viruses have to be stored in a refrigerated environment—or they would all die. They're much more sensitive to heat than bacteria. In your body, they take over other cells. Even though they're at body temperature, sometimes even up to a hundred four or five when you have a fever, they're protected by the cells they've infiltrated. But if they weren't protected . . .''

Jordan looked at Richard Little, looking back at them.

"You had a fever," she said. "A raging fever, you said. Maybe one that overcame . . ." She shook her head slightly. "It can't be that simple."

CHAPTER 43

Delaney looked past the Indian who had been trying to interpret, and spoke directly to Bombussa. "You have shown us your living god. Now I'm going to show you what our gods can do."

Bombussa looked back at him.

"Our gods," Delancy repeated. "We are doctors. *Monbombos.*" He touched his chest with his fingers. "Our gods spoke with your gods. They sent us here to cure the disease—the possession—for all time. To honor you by doing so." He looked at Richard Little.

Little stared back at him for a moment and then looked toward the Indians. "*Monbombos. Monbombos foran da* . . . what's the damn word for cure? You've told me I'm sick often enough. Sick, damnit. Sick." He spread his hands wide.

"*Simmon,*" the interpreter said.

"Yeah, sick, damnit. What's the opposite? *Doomano. Doomano,* that's it." He pointed to Delaney and Jordan. "*Doomano,*" he repeated. "*Com doomano caarm.*"

Bombussa's eyes narrowed. "*Pom?*"

"How?" Little said. "He wants to know how you cast out possession."

"My gods sent the means."

"Gods?" the interpreter said.

Delaney nodded. "Gods." He took a deep breath and

pointed toward the closed entrance to the cave. "A potion. But we hid it when our gods told us you were coming."

Little stared back at him.

It took nearly a half hour, with Little and the interpreter getting only a fraction of the words correct, and Delaney attempting sign language almost as much as the spoken word. But, finally, he got the point across. His gods had sent him with a potion as a gift for their gods. A potion that could help to rid the world of the spirits from the underworld. Whether the Indians thought he meant permanently or only a potion to be used in an individual case, Delaney never could be sure, but they finally did understand it was a powerful medicine.

They wanted to go after it where it had been hidden, and it took Delaney almost another half hour to get the point across that only he and Jordan, emissaries from their gods, could retrieve the medicine without it being ruined. It had to be delivered directly to the living god at the rear of the cave.

The Indians agreed, and indicated they would take him and Jordan to the spot where it was hidden when the sun rose again. But, though growing late in the afternoon, it was not yet dark. And if they didn't go then, if Jordan and he were forced to remain there overnight, they would never be allowed to go—not after Jordan grew sick. The Indians would be sure then that going after the potion was only a trick of ones possessed.

"We must go now," Delaney said.

"*Roon*," Jordan said, the Indian word for *now* that Little had spoken in trying to help them.

"*Roon*," Little repeated.

"Now," the interpreter said.

Bombussa nodded reluctantly.

"I'm going, too," Little said.

Delaney looked toward the cage.

"Or nobody is," Little added.

The Indians stared now.

"You figured it out this far," Little said. "You figure it out the rest of the way now."

Delaney knew that would never happen. The Indians thought Little possessed. They had not allowed him outside the cage in three years. They wouldn't now.

Jordan spoke softly toward the cage. "We'll be back." She had spaced her words carefully. She repeated them, making a point. "We'll—be—back."

Little's hands caught the posts at each side of his face "I haven't seen the sun in three years. I exercise, eat— if you call that eating"—he glanced at the melon rinds at the side of the cage—"and I slowly die. They bring their own people and put them in the other cages after they've been in the forbidden land. They're here two weeks, and then they're turned out. But if they had showed a sign of being sick they would never be turned out again. They saw me sick. It's now or never for me."

"Please," Jordan said.

Little shook his head.

Then a strange thing happened. His cheek ticked.

"No," he suddenly said.

Delaney stared back at Little as his red face seemed to grow into a dark color and twisted into a grimace— or anger he couldn't hold back.

"No. Damnit. I'm telling you now. No."

Little's hands tightened around the posts.

"Don't stare at me like that. I'm ..." His eyes went to the raised blowguns. *"And you bastards can rot in hell!"*

Two darts thudded into the posts next to his face.

His eyes widened. Sweat broke out on his forehead. His hands trembled at the posts. New darts were quickly loaded into the blowguns.

He stepped back.

He stared directly at Delaney and Jordan.

His mouth opened—and a guttural sound came from deep within his body.

*   *   *

The tall doors at the entrance to the cavern slowly swung
open. Bombussa led the way outside, and then stepped
aside to let Delaney and Jordan take the lead. Four Indians followed them.

Jordan looked back across her shoulder toward the
cave. "The raging fever—it didn't cure him. It's not heat
that's the answer then."

Delaney stared straight ahead. Jordan spoke again, her
voice in a whisper.

"They're not going to let you pick up your revolver.
We can't just run. We wouldn't get twenty feet." She
looked at him. "So what are we going to do?" she asked.

She didn't say anymore. She didn't have to, her expression said it for her. She wasn't going back into that
cave.

He wasn't either.

CHAPTER 44

"*Hom!*"

Delaney stopped his movement toward the hidden stream.

"*Hom*," Bombussa repeated, and shook his head firmly. The four Indians behind him had their blowguns raised halfway up their chests. None of them wore the white paint of the guardians. Bombussa shook his head again.

"We're not going across," Delaney said.

They stared at him without understanding.

He held his hands a couple of feet apart, to indicate the width of the stream, and then pointed under his left hand. "The medicine is hidden on this side of the bank—under it."

They still stared. The tall thorn wall on the near side of the stream was still more than a hundred feet away. He dropped to one knee and quickly drew the shape of the stream on the ground. He pointed to the near side of the drawing, and dug his finger into the ground. "It's there."

Bombussa raised his gaze toward the stream, stared a moment, then nodded.

Delaney walked forward. "Remember the thorns," he said in a low voice.

Jordan looked at him and then toward the prickly wall

of stiff, long spikes. At the entrance to the passageway leading down to the water, he stopped. He moved his head slowly back and forth, and then nodded, and stepped forward. Jordan wasn't close enough to him and he looked back at her and stared. She came closer to him. Out of the corner of his eye, he saw the blowguns being raised. He stopped at the edge of the water and looked down at his feet.

Jordan stopped beside him. He used his hand in the small of her back to push her a few inches closer to the water. He looked down the stream to where it turned sharply to the right.

"It's more than a hundred feet until it goes around the bend," he said in a low voice. "Can you make it underwater?"

Bombussa's eyes tightened. He spoke sharply in his dialect. The Indians behind him quickly stepped forward. Delaney shoved hard against Jordan's back and dove for the water at the same time. They hit it together and went under.

Delaney's arm bumped against Jordan's elbow once, and he felt her hand brush his side. Then he lost her.

Jordan thrust her hands out in front of her face and pulled them back repeatedly. She had sucked in as much air as possible till the very second her face hit the water. She could already feel herself growing lightheaded. She stroked harder.

The lightheadedness became a concentrated dizziness. Her chest burned. A light gray film passed briefly before her closed eyes. She turned to her back, opened her eyes, and, still stroking, gradually began to rise. She saw the faint yellow glow of light near the surface.

Her face broke into the air. She gasped in a breath and arched her back, pulling as hard as she could with her arms. Four darts hit the water where her face had been.

She was under again.

Turning her face she reached as far as she could out ahead of her and stroked her arms back hard.

Delaney, growing dizzy, felt the mud of the bank on his left brush against his elbow, pushed off of it hard to his right, made the last three strokes possible to him, and burst high out of the water, screaming air into his lungs.

He yanked his head around. He was behind the bend. Jordan wasn't anywhere to be seen. He heard the Indians through the thick thorns and bushes on the bank. Jordan's head burst the brown surface in a violent spray of water. Her gasp for air sounded like she was almost crying. He pulled on her arm and they stroked toward the bank bordering the contaminated land.

There was a two-to-three-foot span of mud between the edge of the water and the thorns on that side. They came up onto the mud, first sinking past their ankles, then jerking their feet loose and trying to take long steps, being sucked back and falling forward, burying their hands to their wrists.

Delaney pulled his hands free and lunged forward once more.

"Delaney!"

He thought an Indian had gotten a clear shot at her. But she was staring at the base of the thorns.

He took a step back toward her. A narrow channel maybe two feet wide and partially filled with water ran under the thick limbs with their dagger spikes. Jordan dove head first into the channel and pulled herself, half underwater and half out, underneath the thorns. He dove after her.

Twenty feet, thirty feet. Scrambling on hands and knees. They were breathing hard. He felt his shirt hang and rip—and a thorn dug into the small of his back. The pain was such his hand came around involuntarily toward his back—and then stopped. *The mud covering his fingers.*

The dirty water he was in. He tried to keep his body

where the water only soaked his front, and it slowed his progress, Jordan coming out of the thorns and to her feet several feet ahead of him. She was sprinting as hard as she could.

He came out from under the wall, yanked off his shirt, throwing it out to the side as he ran after her. He glanced back across his shoulder. The trees and undergrowth were so thick he couldn't see more than a few feet behind them. The stream could be crossed at will. But he was counting on the Indians' religion to stop them. Only Bombussa wore white paint, and maybe his was only symbolic, because he was the medicine man. Maybe.

Still running madly, hopping over small bushes and dodging around taller ones and thick tree trunks, Delaney could feel his lungs screeching for air. Jordan's face was growing blue. She tripped and sprawled forward on her face.

He caught her shoulder, trying to pull her to her feet, but she stayed where she had risen to all fours, gasping, her breath wheezing into her lungs.

He looked behind them.

Only the brown tree trunks. The dark undergrowth. The stillness.

"Delaney!"

He jerked his head toward her. She stared at his back. Her eyes came to his. He shook his head. "I hadn't touched it. I don't think any—''

She closed her eyes. He grabbed her arm. "Come on," he said.

She came slowly to her feet, staring into his eyes as she did. "The stream," she said. "You were in the water. Your shirt was soaked with—''

"Come on," he said, turning her around and pushing her toward the trees in front of them.

She looked back over her shoulder.

"Damnit, Jordan, go on."

*   *   *

Only a couple of minutes passed before she had to stop again. She was breathing so hard she could only look at him and shake her head.

He glanced back across his shoulder. He looked to each side. He listened for the sound of someone coming through the bushes.

"Delaney . . . where?" Jordan gasped.

He looked ahead of them. "Feltenstein said the contamination only covered a square kilometer. We'll keep going until we're certain we're out of it. Then we'll think about what to do."

A hundred feet farther and Jordan stopped. In front of her, her helmet sat on the bundle of specimen boxes. Paul's rifle lay a few feet away. The radio directional beacon sat just where she had left it.

He stepped forward and lifted it into his hands.

"The rangers didn't touch anything," she said. Her eyes moved down his bare upper chest. He had already looked. He had no scratches other than where the thorn had dug into his back. The feeling of stickiness there made him want to reach back and feel the place. "Go on," he said.

He had already flicked the switch on the beacon's side.

As soon as they were past the specimen boxes and into the trees beyond them, he saw the open area of sunlight, one of the places the rangers had cleared to land their copters.

He looked at the radio beacon.

Was it working after lying in the sweltering dampness so long?

"*Delaney!*" Jordan shouted.

Bombussa charged out of the trees from the right.

Delaney saw the knife, held low and ready to be swung upward. He waited until Bombussa was nearly on him, then jumped to the side.

The Indian whirled to face him, crouched, and started

edging forward, his knife held out in front of him now. Jordan frantically looked around for some kind of weapon.

Delaney backed slowly away.

Jordan saw a long limb on the ground, and ran to it. Bombussa glanced in her direction. Delaney jumped forward and grabbed him around the neck with one hand, reaching for the hand with the knife with his other.

The blade came around. Delaney caught the wrist, stopping the thrust. Jordan ran toward them. Bombussa was strong. The knife pressed through Delaney's grip toward his stomach. Jordan swung the limb, hitting the Indian hard in the back of the head.

Bombussa's knees buckled. Delaney twisted his wrist. Jordan was grabbing for the knife handle.

With a superhuman effort, Bombussa jerked loose from their grasp and jumped backward.

He stared past them, then suddenly turned and ran.

Delaney looked across his shoulder at the rangers hurrying through the trees toward them. Bulky and awkward in their white protective suits they looked like some kind of bloated, swaying creatures from another world. He looked back at Bombussa disappearing into the brush. Then he turned back toward the rangers.

Rifles were pointed his way.

One of the men stepped a couple of feet ahead of the others. His face was only a shadow behind the wide glass visor, reflecting the dim rays of the sun filtering through the tree limbs overhead.

"I'm Dr. Jeffries and this is my wife."

The bulky figure made no move to come closer, nor said anything.

"I'm Dr. Delaney Jeffries. She's the one who has the virus. Jordan Jeffries."

The face moved slightly behind the faceplate.

"She's Jordan Jeffries. Don't you understand? No, you don't, do you? Probably everybody in the world is looking for us now and you've never heard of us. And the damn Indians you're looking for, that was one of them. They're in a cave across a stream back behind us. There's an infected man with them—a white man.''

Ten minutes later, the helicopter lifted off the ground into the dying rays of the sun. The rangers assigned to guard them, still in their protective suits, sat at one end of the cargo bay. They had made him and Jordan lie down on their stomachs at the other end.

Her face was paler than it had been. He laid his hand across her back. Her eyes came around to his. There was a look of irritation in her expression. He patted her shoulder softly. Her eyes closed.

"I'm sorry," she said in a low voice. "But I can't help it. No, that's not right. I don't think one way or the other about what I'm doing or saying. It's as if my reactions are becoming more and more visceral. That's the transformation—that's what's happening. It's like whatever shield we've supposedly developed through two thousand years of civilization is being eaten away in my case."

"You want to talk about spaceships?" he asked.

She looked at him.

He smiled softly. "A different subject anyway."

Despite her haggard look, despite the pain and nausea she was experiencing, she smiled a little. "Unless it's some damn depressing thing like they're getting ready to invade the earth."

And then her skin suddenly grew paler still, and she pressed her face into the steel floor.

CHAPTER 45

Their trip from Brazil to Jackson was made in cages strapped in the center of the cargo bay of an air national guard transport plane. Jordan spent much of it, all at night, on her knees, vomiting onto the floor of her cage. The big plane had barely taxied to a stop when one of the side doors flew open and Dr. Feltenstein hurried inside.

He strode toward them, cautiously stopping a few feet away from the cages. Jordan looked up at him from her hands and knees and stared.

Delaney moved to the front of his cage. "Did the rangers get to the cave?"

Feltenstein nodded. "The Indians were gone. There must have been another way out of the cave. But the old man at the rear of the cave was still there. If you want to take the chance, I've received permission to try it."

"It is heat then?"

"There's a chance. The busts were of Indians who contracted the disease and recovered. Two of them had definitely been subjected to extreme heat—the one the interpreter talked to, and one represented by another of the busts.

"The third bust—the burned Indian didn't know what happened to that one. He died generations ago. The interpreter said the Indians didn't even have a word for that far back in time; he simply spoke of him as one of the others. But the one he did know about, he lived some fifty years ago. He contracted the disease, ran from the other Indians, hid, and was burned out of the hiding place. Actually not burned out of it, but burned in the fire. He was thought dead. They found his body the next day, charred where he had hidden under a pile of grass he had dampened and placed over him.

"They put him in a cage and waited for him to die. I don't know how he didn't. I don't know how the one the interpreter talked to didn't. As badly as they said he was scarred his body fluids should have seeped out of his burn areas until he did. But he didn't. When he recovered he was free of the disease—the possession, they called it."

Feltenstein glanced at Jordan, still staring at him. "From the way the one at the cave described the earlier one's actions after he recovered, he was virtually brain dead. He only lived a few more months. But the one in the cave wasn't brain dead. It's up to you if you want to go forward."

"*No!*" Jordan screamed. "Don't touch me."

Her eyes widened, she gagged, and without lowering her head, vomited a spray of green bile against her bars.

Delaney closed his eyes.

Father Dunnigan had not owned a gun since he was a little boy, when he had shot a sparrow and then cried for hours. But now he had to have one. It was against God's law to commit suicide. But the Lord was forgiving when asked. Yet how could he knowingly commit a sin at the very second he was asking for forgiveness? But how did he not go forward with his death—to save others he knew he would kill if he remained alive? Tears flowed down his cheeks.

*   *   *

The cages were transported from the Jackson airport to the medical center with tarpaulins pulled down over them to give them the appearance of being packing cases. As they were winched from the big flatbed truck to the dollies that would take them into the research building, Delaney heard one of the agents telling a curious student that the cases contained radioactive isotopes—therefore needing the heavy security deployed in the form of a dozen agents standing around the crates.

Darrell had already drawn a sample of Delaney's blood. Now he stood outside Jordan's cage. He tried again to reason with her.

"We have to, Jordan. We have to take a sample to see if we can kill the virus with low enough heat to be safe to you."

Her eyes cold, she stared back at him.

"Stay away from me," she said. "I mean it."

Feltenstein looked back across his shoulder to the agent with a tranquilizer gun and nodded. As the weapon was raised, Delaney turned his face away from Jordan's.

He heard the dull thump as the gun fired, and her gasp. He couldn't keep from looking back at her.

She had jerked the dart from her thigh and held it in her fist, brandishing it toward the bars. Then she threw it as hard as she could at Feltenstein.

He ducked and the dart flew over his head toward the far wall.

Jordan's brow wrinkled now. She looked down at her legs. Her knees moved, then buckled, and she went clumsily down on them. Her head raised and her eyes stared directly into Feltenstein's. She spat and crumpled forward over onto her face.

The agents stepped forward. The door to her cage was opened. The larger agent seemed to hesitate a moment, then stepped inside the bars.

In moments they were carrying her limp body toward a gurney fitted with a multitude of leather straps.

And the wait began. Finally, Darrell rose from the electron microscope.

"His blood is clear."

Feltenstein stepped forward to unlock the cage and Delaney stepped outside.

"Maybe you were lucky with that scratch," Feltenstein said. "The contaminated area stops well short of the stream. I would have thought runoff would be in the stream. But none of the samples showed it. It's full of fish, and none of them were infected—CDC's checking now to see if they can harbor the virus. The rangers killed a crocodile there, too. And it was free of the virus. All I can say is . . . all I can say is if it stays that way for you, I'm glad."

Delaney nodded, then looked toward the two agents gingerly carrying the howling monkey's cage forward.

He was quickly sedated.

The heart/lung machine, modified for the purpose, was connected to the animal's body.

The warming of his blood began.

Across the lab, Darrell continued to heat different samples of Jordan's blood, carefully monitoring each degree rise in temperature.

It was all Father Dunnigan could do to keep from jumping across the counter and banging the clerk's head against the wall. He didn't even look at the pistol as the man handed it and a box of ammunition to him. How many lives would he save by killing himself? But how many would he ruin, too? What damage would he do to those who believed in him? The young, especially.

A sin, under any circumstances, was a sin.

The viruses infecting the sample of Jordan's blood had become less active at a hundred and two degrees. They had started dying at a hundred and four degrees, and all had been dead at a hundred and six degrees. But that was viruses dying in blood spread thinly across a laboratory slide and openly exposed to heat. Inside Jordan's body, the viruses would be shielded from the heated blood by the body tissues where they hid, by the brain matter, by her very system itself fighting to hold her temperature at a normal level.

And what was that normal level?

Under the tongue it would be the well-known ninety-eight point six degrees Fahrenheit. Yet at the same time as an oral thermometer registered that mark in the mouth, the normal temperature in the liver would be a hundred and five. Was there virus in her liver, living unaffected at that hundred and five degrees? If that was indeed the case, then what was the purpose in trying to raise her temperature enough to kill the virus?—her body couldn't tolerate temperature much higher than that, not sweeping her whole body, not for any length of time at all. Delaney looked at the monkey, strapped sedated to the metal gurney.

His temperature had been rapidly raised to forty degrees Celsius, a hundred and four on a clinical thermometer, and samples of his blood showed the virus infecting the blood, unchanged.

The gauge registering the animal's body temperature now sat at a hundred and five degrees. The blood going back into his veins had been heated to a hundred and twelve degrees to get the body to that level. He had convulsed then. They had decided to hold at that level for fifteen minutes before they raised it any more. He had occasionally continued to convulse. Darrell walked back toward his stool with a fresh sample of the monkey's blood. They were taking one for every half degree rise.

Father Dunnigan sat numb in the front seat of his car as he slipped the cartridges into the revolver. He stopped at three, wondering why he had bothered with more than one, and looked down at the weapon again.

So cold and heavy—a dead-weight heavy.

He continued to stare at it.

Good and evil all in one instrument, he thought—according to who wielded it, and for what purpose. He slowly raised it to his head.

Airtanker after airtanker, their giant bellies fully loaded with diesel fuel, had lifted from U.S. bases throughout the southern hemisphere. The president had sat in the situation room and watched their courses plotted electronically on a wall-sized viewing screen.

When the transports arrived in South America, they had fed the diesel fuel they carried into forty-gallon drums and tanks to be flown into the rain forest by droves of helicopters, a few of them taking the drums inside their cargo bays, many of them carrying the tanks hanging from steel cables beneath their bodies.

It was ironic that with all the fuel they transported several of the helicopters had become dangerously low on fuel for their own engines, as they had waited for the protective-suit-clad men on the ground to fell enough of the big trees for them to land.

The biggest problem faced by the mission had been logistics, with not enough airports in South America with long enough runways to adequately handle the huge tankers; many of the tankers had to circle until others had been emptied.

There had been danger, too, with such a large area being soaked. Had a premature fire ignited, many deaths could have resulted.

But any risk had been deemed necessary by the man who ordered the vast undertaking, and who now sweated it out.

"What are the chances of this working?" he asked.

It was a question that had of course been asked by dozens of technical experts hundreds of times over the last few hours.

And the answer was the same. "There's simply no

way to know if the heat will burn hot enough three inches under the ground, sir.''

"And if it doesn't?''

"We have plan B." Exploding a nuclear bomb, and its radiating of thousands of degrees of heat over the area.

At least there won't be any trees left to shield the ground if we have to go to that, the president thought—not after the first fire. He wondered how many nations would refuse to give their permission to such a request.

It would be done anyway.

Of course there would be a terrible outcry. The launching crew responsible for the ''accidental'' firing of the missile would have to be disciplined. Their careers would be over. But there were other rewards.

As to the endings of their army pay checks—the CIA had a fund that would adequately ease the pain of that.

Darrell looked down at the sedated monkey. ''The virus population has been cut to less than ten percent, but it's still present." And that was at a body temperature of a hundred and five and a half degrees.

A neurologist, who had been hurriedly roused from bed, and shocked by the explanation why, shook his head. ''We can't elevate the temperature any higher in a human without causing brain damage. In fact the level is already too high for me in good conscience to subject a human to it."

"Higher," Dr. Feltenstein said.

The neurologist looked at the cardiologist and anesthetist, brought there for the same purpose, and shook his head again. Behind them across the room, Jordan moaned. Delaney looked at her. Her hands and feet twisted at the straps binding her to the gurney. She tried to rise against the strap pulled tightly across her chest. Her eyes turned as dark as the night outside as they caught Delaney's. Her moan changed to something that resembled a growl.

CHAPTER 46

The monkey's temperature was raised another half a degree and then another half degree. Darrell had dispensed with the use of the electron microscope because they couldn't afford the time it took to look for the virus with that instrument. Not while the monkey lay with an elevated temperature. For the possibility of brain damage or even death didn't lie singularly in how high the temperature was raised, but also in how long a period it was held at any particular elevated level.

So he had constructed a DNA probe. That way a cell population could be removed from the monkey, quickly washed with a permeabilizing agent, and then the cells could be analyzed by flow cytometry. If the virus was still alive, it produced RNA. That viral RNA would be attracted to and bind with the DNA in the probe. By use of a fluorescent tag contained within the probe, the RNA would glow red, the color Darrell was using—and hoping he wouldn't see.

As he drew a second sample of blood cells, the monkey's sightless eyes opened wide and flashed spasmodically from side to side.

The neurologist shook his head.

Darrell hurried back toward the flow cytometer.

Delaney looked at Jordan, lying quietly on the gurney, glaring at the bright ceiling fixtures with a cold stare.

*   *   *

Father Dunnigan, cloaked in sweat, his clothes wringing wet, raised the pistol to his temple for the dozenth time. But again his hand trembled, his arm shook, and he lowered the weapon back to his side.

Delaney walked to a window at the side of the lab. His hands were nervous, nearly trembling, and he steadied them by grasping the sides of the window frame. It was completely dark outside now. The disease always peaked at night. Did the heat of the sun tend to hold back the expression of the disease? Didn't that lend to the theory of heat working to kill the virus? It was cooler at night than in the daytime.

But that wasn't true every place in the world. At least not in actual temperatures expressed. There were continents that were hotter during their nights than other continents' days. So maybe it was due not to an actual change in temperature, but only a comparative difference between periods of heat and cool. Besides, the virus wasn't on every continent, but in the Amazon—and in Mississippi. Hot days and cool nights. At least there had been no exception to that since the original trip to the rain forest. On the freighter, too, in the western Gulf of Mexico—hot days and cooler nights. But then the body's normal temperature would remain the same with such a small change as there was between day and dark. All warm-blooded animals kept their temperature basically the same during periods of moderate outside change. The body did have to burn a few more calories to stay as warm when it was cooler. Did the virus sense the body working to do that as the nighttime temperature dropped? Was it a signal for the virus to become active?

Or was it not the difference in heat and cold that triggered the virus, but the difference in sunlight and dark itself? From prehistoric times to now, some forms of life were brought to activity when dark fell and then rested during the day, while other life forms rose with the sun and slept at night.

Most humans, deprived of the artificial stimuli of clocks and exposed only to dark and daylight, were triggered by an impulse in their brains to come awake with the light, grow drowsy with the dark. Was the virus nocturnal?

Heat and cold? Day and night?

Or was it neither?

Why was most evil, in real life as well as tales, committed at night? Muggers and stalkers and rapists and killers in the dark far outnumbered those in the daytime. In legends, was evil nearly universally said to happen at night because it was dark and scary then, sparking the teller's imagination, or was there an element of truth in the tales that modern man would never know?

That's how it all started, wasn't it?—Jordan in the light, looking for herbs that would make medicines, and now it all ended in a deep darkness somewhere in the brain, from a disease. Now would the heat, the element that originally came from the sun, guide the way?

Or would the coming of the night continue forever—for Jordan? He shook his head, and looked over at her. Then he felt Darrell stepping up behind him.

He turned to face him.

"The monkey is dead," Darrell said in a low voice.

Delaney looked at the hairy animal lying limp on the gurney.

"Almost all of the virus is dead," Darrell added. "But not all of it. Maybe if we hadn't raised the temperature quite so high, but left it elevated for a little longer at a degree or so lower—maybe it would have all died then. But who knows? And with the monkey's system so different from a human's, who knows if the virus reacts the same? All we do know is that heat does harm it. It's your call with Jordan."

Delaney looked toward her, moving silently against her straps.

"But before you make the decision you need to know this," Darrell said. "Alex is dead."

Delaney's eyes flashed back to Darrell's.

"It was his heart. I noticed during the operation after he was shot that his blood pressure was extremely high. I put him on medication, but it kept climbing. It must be a side effect of the disease. That's what killed him. The monkey too—the one we originally injected with Alex's blood. It died, too."

Darrell waited a moment before finishing. "Jordan's blood pressure is . . ." He shook his head slightly. "It's too high to safely subject her heart to the stress of warming her blood. I want you to know that. But it's too high to let it continue like it is, too—and I don't think there's anything we can do to bring it down."

Richard Little's face flashed through Delaney's mind, the glowing red cheeks. Too red. Blood pressure red.

But he had lived. For three years. He looked toward Feltenstein. "The man in the cage in the Indian's cave— was he okay?"

Feltenstein's expression was one of puzzlement.

"The white man in the cage," Delaney repeated. "Was he okay?"

"There was no white man," Feltenstein said. "Not anybody in a cage. Not any cages even—at least that were reported to me."

The Indians had taken Little with them when they had fled? Why? Doing their duty to the last? Remaining guardians as much as they could in the face of swaying, bloated creatures rushing their cave? Delaney looked toward Jordan. "And if we go forward we're going to have to do it in here? We can't use one of the hospital's operating rooms?"

"I'm sorry," Feltenstein said. "Here or nowhere. But we have everything we'll need."

Delaney looked at the cardiologist, neurologist, and anesthetist, standing in a group talking. They were certain the process, while obviously doing the virus harm, would never completely rid the body of it—not completely, there was too much body tissue in which for it to hide.

Alex dead. The monkey dead. Delaney remembered seeing the red color mixed with the pale in Jordan's face. He had thought it an expression of anger.

Alex. The monkey. Both dead. But Richard Little was alive after three years. Was that the odds if they didn't go forward? Two out of three to die, only one to live through the rise in blood pressure. He looked at Jordan again. How could he speak for her? And how could he not? He tightened his jaw and turned toward the window again.

To go forward was obviously to risk her life—at the very least her reasoning powers, what made life meaningful. To not go forward was to not only risk death from high blood pressure, but also to risk the final disposition the fax had spoken of.

"Delaney."

It was Jordan's low voice.

He hurried to the gurney.

Perspiration dotted her forehead and ran down her cheeks to drip onto the sheet covering the gurney.

She glared up at him. Her mouth gaped slightly. Her eyelids quivered. She forced her mouth closed. She seemed to be fighting something.

"Delaney," she said in a low voice. "Please, try it. Please."

CHAPTER 47

Jordan's leg moved though she was sedated. The movement wasn't from the heat starting to work on her brain, but from how light her sleep was. They had decided to put her under just barely, trying to create as little stress on the body as they could. An oxygen mask covered her face—the anesthetist had her on nearly pure oxygen now, trying to make certain they were keeping the blood cells as full of the life-giving gas as they could. An IV tube pumped a solution into her body—to offset the liquid she was sweating away. They were doing everything they could.

Delaney watched as her blood, heated and now coursing through clear tubes, ran back into her body. They had gone to a body temperature of a hundred and five rapidly. The next half degree they had raised much more slowly. There had never really been a definitive study establishing at which point temperature rise became lethal. It could be at a little over a hundred and five degrees—if it raged for a long enough period. The rule of thumb for nearly instant death was one hundred and seven and six-tenths degrees. But that was a rule of thumb formulated only through the conclusions of one experiment. And that experiment was conducted only by going back and studying the records of deaths due to elevated body temperature—a child left in a car during a hot summer, a fever raging out of control. How really accurate had the records studied been, depending as they did on observations remembered after the fact or on temperatures bodies registered when they were discovered dead? Had the temperatures been higher in some cases and the body cooled partially before its postmortem temperature taken?

And what about differences in humans?

As a ten-pound monkey's body was different from Jordan's in both his system and bulk, so was the old Indian's body who had lain at the rear of the cave, and Richard Little's, and the Indians' represented by the other two busts. Some were able to take more of a rise in temperature and survive, some less. And how in God's name could a woman barely over a hundred pounds take what the men had taken?

And for how long? For, again, that was part of the equation, too. Had the Indians suffered a rapid rise in temperature, to whatever it was, or had the rise been not so high, but prolonged?

And yet he had made the decision to go forward.

Then he felt Darrell's soft touch on his shoulder. He looked at him. It was Darrell who had suggested they take her to the "rule-of-thumb limit" just short of brain damage, and hold the heat there.

The rule of thumb again.

And even if that were accurate—for how long?

What was the limit with her system?

A guess.

All guesses.

Delaney looked back at her, and closed his eyes, silently saying the same prayer over and over—to have her back; for him and Missey and Ryder to have her back, and have her back as they knew her.

Darrell patted his shoulder again. Feltenstein handed over a fresh sample of Jordan's blood, and Darrell hurried toward the side of the room.

* * *

Father Dunnigan squealed the tires of his car as he drove it rapidly away from the curb.

Son of a bitch, he thought. *It's not fair. I work with these worthless bastards all the time, and then look what happens to me. Me! It's not right. It's damn not right. I won't have it.*

Ahead of him, an older woman crossing the pavement walked slowly, too slowly, and he knew it, knew his car was coming too fast for her to get out of the way, and he almost ran her over before jerking the steering wheel to the side at the last second and squealing around her.

He stuck his fist out his window and shook it back in her direction.

In front of him, cars paused at a stoplight. His jaw tightened with anger as he stopped behind them—and then he waited and waited and waited.

The light wasn't changing from red. He could hear the sirens of fire engines in the distance.

Making him wait.

His lips twisted into a sneer and he jammed his foot down on the accelerator, his car leaping forward and grazing the rear of a Lincoln in front of him as he went around it.

A fire engine was coming fast. Father Dunnigan stared at it, then at the last moment jerked his steering wheel to the right and ran up on the curb as the engine sped past, its crew cussing back toward him.

He floored his car and gave them chase.

Wide-eyed, they stared at him as he drove the bumper of his car nearly against the rear of the truck.

He smiled. Then he had to jerk his car to the side as the engine slowed rapidly. He jammed on his brakes for a police car parked sideways across the street.

He threw open his door and stepped outside.

A frail, gray-haired woman wearing a shawl hurried up to him. She was sobbing desperately. "My grand-child," she squalled and looked toward the old tenement building, ablaze, with fire shooting out the windows.

"My grandchild," she cried again.

Irritated at her high-pitched voice, Father Dunnigan stared at her.

"Please pray for him to find his way out," she said in a suddenly low voice. "Little Michael. I was downstairs in the laundry room. He's on the second floor. I couldn't get back up to him."

Father Dunnigan looked toward the building and the firemen who had kicked in its front door but gone no farther and were now backing away, their arms held up in front of their faces at the intense heat.

He continued to stare at the building. The woman's frail hands came to his and lifted them, holding them by the outsides and forcing them inward, as if she were trying to press them together in prayer.

"Oh, my Lord in heaven," she said, and closed her eyes. "You are my Father, my Redeemer, my Faith."

Father Dunnigan heard her words deep inside him, in his heart as much as his mind. His eyes narrowed, a strange look passed over his face—and he suddenly sprinted toward the building.

The firemen were aghast when he dashed by them into the fiery hallway.

He didn't even know which way to go, except up to the second floor, and he dashed into the brunt of the heat, taking the staircase in strides he hadn't used in forty years.

"Michael," he shouted into the dark smoke at the top of the landing. "Michael!"

No sound came back to him. The heat fried his skin. He raised his hands to protect his face and stumbled blindly forward.

The first door on his left was open. "Michael," he yelled inside the room. The next one was closed. The doorknob burned his hand. "Michael!" he shouted.

He heard coughing.

It came through an open doorway back to his left. He darted inside the room.

The smoke was terrible. A faint cough came from his right. "Michael!" His hands out in front of him, he moved in that direction.

His knees made first contact with the soft shape. He grabbed down for the boy. He was not more than three. He held a little white fox terrier puppy in his arms. Tears dampened his smoke-stained face.

Father Dunnigan lifted him into his arms and turned toward the door. A wide sheet of flame shot inside the opening. He slammed the door and turned back to the far side of the room. Through the dark smoke he saw a glimmer of light.

It was a window.

He raised his foot and kicked out the glass. Fresh air boiled inside, then heat came at him from his back, and now smoke billowed out the window. He stuck the boy carefully through the glass, leaned out, and looked down. Two firemen rushed to the sidewalk below him.

The boy turned quickly in his arms, reaching back for the puppy struggling loose from his grasp—and the dog was on the floor running toward the doorway.

The boy grabbed Father Dunnigan's neck and fought to come back inside the room.

"No, son!"

The boy's strength was enormous. He pulled himself back over Father Dunnigan's shoulder, squirmed to break loose from his grasp.

"I'll get the damn puppy!" Dunnigan suddenly growled.

The boy ceased struggling, but still kept his hands tightly around the back of Father Dunnigan's neck.

"You promise you'll get him?"

"I give you my word."

The boy released his hold.

Father Dunnigan thrust him forward through the glass, looked down at the firemen, standing with their hands lifted toward the window—and let the boy go.

Straightening slowly, Father Dunnigan turned back into the heat.

He stood there, his cheeks blistering, beginning to peel, his eyebrows starting to curl. For a moment, when the boy had fought him, he had had an urge to throw him against the wall.

He looked at the flames reaching toward him from the hallway.

It was better this way.

"Our Father which art in Heaven . . ." he started, and walked toward the hallway.

An enormous sheet of flame shot in the doorway, burning his face in an agonizing pain. He threw his hands up and stumbled backward. The puppy ran to his legs, yelping, looking up at him. Reaching to his feet, he grabbed the soft body.

The dog's hair smoked as Father Dunnigan lifted it to his chest.

Then he saw the wall of flame, coming at him like the front of a wide, red locomotive, and he dove to the side.

The flames shot past him through the window, roaring in intensity, charring the window frame black. He crawled toward a wall, awkward in his progress because of the puppy under his arm.

His head bumped into the wall and it moved. It was a door. He moved quickly through it and kicked it shut against the following flames.

He was in a bathroom.

The door steamed. Flames licked under it. He felt something soft under his hand and thought the puppy had somehow moved from his grasp. But it still snuggled in his arm. He was on a deep throw rug. He looked at the bathtub next to him.

Grabbing the rug, he stood. He stepped into the tub and reached for the faucets. The water rushed out. He hit the shower button and the spray hit him hard in the face.

Pulling the rug over his head, he lowered himself into the tub. He hunched into a tight ball, the puppy under him, the water spraying down on the rug, and the flames breaking through the door.

Outside, the firemen directed the full force of three hoses through the window into the room—waiting for Father Dunnigan to reappear.

At the front of the building, two teams of firemen, their hoses blasting hundreds of gallons before them, moved in the doors.

Jordan convulsed. Her body stiffened. And it wasn't only because she was barely out.

"Stop it," Delaney said. "That's enough. Stop it. She can't take anymore."

Darrell nodded and the cardiologist quickly reduced the heat. Darrell glanced at Delaney, then leaned to take a blood sample from Jordan's limp arm. Her fingers twitched. Delaney's hands trembled so badly he couldn't force them to stop.

Jordan convulsed again.

Father Dunnigan convulsed. The puppy moved under him, whining as the weight of Father Dunnigan's body, his clothes smoking under the charring rug, grew heavier and heavier—and went limp.

Jordan's body temperature continued to drop back toward normal. Disregarding the possibility of shock caused by the sudden change they were forcing on her body, the cardiologist was bringing the temperature down as rapidly as possible, not wanting to let the temperature linger at the elevated level and risk the attendant chance of what prolonged elevation could do to the brain. He had even employed a fan, blowing directly on her body, now clad only in a bra and panties. The other doctors worked feverishly, sponging her trunk and limbs with alcohol.

Darrell worked at the flow cytometer. "I think . . ."

he suddenly said, his voice excited. "I think it's . . ."

At his sudden stop they all looked toward him.

He slowly turned his head in their direction. He took a moment. Then spoke so low it was hard to hear him. "It's not all dead."

CHAPTER 48

The firemen, in breathing apparatus, kicked in the door to the room. A steady stream of water from four hoses was beating the flames back down the hallway. Another stream poured through the window from hoses on the sidewalk.

"Father!" one of the firemen shouted.

"Over there!" another one said.

It was the charred door into the bathroom. They kicked it open.

In the bathtub, the round hump under the smoking rug, partially under water, was obvious.

Delaney, his eyes moist, held Jordan's limp hand. He stared at her closed eyes. The cardiologist was on the other side of the gurney. The neurologist walked toward the windows at the side of the laboratory. Dr. Feltenstein was already there. He turned and looked back across the room toward the gurney.

"Do you want to try again?"

Delaney couldn't answer.

Feltenstein took a deep breath. "I want to be straight with you, Delaney. They don't give a damn about her. They agreed to this thinking it would either cure her or kill her. She's a liability."

Delaney stared.

Feltenstein shook his head. "I don't mean they will do anything to her. We still haven't come to that in this country. At least I haven't. And I'm going to be apprised and nobody's gonna pull any bullshit with me. But they will take her to a secure facility. They were getting ready to when you broke her out of jail. She'll get good medical care, but she'll stay there until she either . . . she'll stay there until she dies. And neither you nor anybody else will be able to see her. Not there."

As Feltenstein paused he looked at Jordan. "She already told you, Delaney. She would rather be cured or . . ." He shook his head. "She's a gutsy lady. She's fighting it hard. It wasn't just her words, I saw the feeling in her eyes. I'm not going to let her down. However it comes out, I'm going to give her her chance. But I can't unless you okay it."

Delaney looked down at Jordan. Then he raised his face and nodded. "But let's let her come back awake first. The virus is only a few percent of what it was. Maybe she . . . maybe she can talk to us now."

Feltenstein's voice was compassionate. "I'd like to talk to her myself, if she doesn't mind. Tell her . . ." He took a deep breath and walked toward the office.

Delaney heard him slam himself into the chair.

In the office, Feltenstein shook his head grimly as he punched the numbers into the telephone. In a moment he had his connection.

"We tried the experiment. There's still a fraction of the virus left. It'll multiply again. I think the husband wants us to try again. I know she does."

"No," the voice came back. "You had your shot. The president said that if it didn't work to take her on to the facility."

"That doesn't make sense. What's the difference in trying once or twice?"

"That's the president's orders."

"That's supposed to mean it makes sense? Because a chicken farmer said it?"

"What did you say?"

"I said I don't give a damn who said it, him included."

"He's the president of the United States."

"He's a damn chicken farmer, too. Might have founded the largest poultry producing company in the world before he got into politics, but that's still his expertise. He doesn't know crap about virus. He don't know crap about anything but chicken shit."

"Have you lost your mind?"

"No, you have, trying to tell me what to do medically; you and that presumptuous bastard. We're going to try it again. If it doesn't work, it'll at least give us some more information about the disease. And if he doesn't like that, tell him . . . tell him I said stick it up his chicken ass."

"Delaney."

His eyes snapped down to hers.

"Delaney." Her voice was faint. "Delaney, it worked, didn't it?"

He felt her hand tighten around his.

"It worked," she repeated. "I can tell."

He couldn't bring himself to say it.

Darrell looked down at her. "What we are going to do is try again if you want to."

Her eyes moved to his. "It's gone. The headaches and the nausea are gone."

Darrell spoke in a soft voice. "You didn't have any headaches when you were first infected. That's where you are back to now. The virus will multiply again."

"I can tell," she said. "I know."

Feltenstein had walked up to the foot of the gurney.

"Take another blood sample," he said.

*   *   *

The cold water blasted Father Dunnigan's limp body as the other firemen sprayed the man carrying him over his shoulder down the stairs.

He was quickly placed on a stretcher and hurried toward an ambulance. A fireman walked to Michael and his grandmother standing off to the side, and handed the boy the whining puppy. Michael took him into his arms and the animal immediately was silent.

The rear door of the ambulance swung shut and, siren screaming, the vehicle sped up the street. The woman lowered her head in prayer.

"It's dead," Darrell shouted. "It's all damn gone."

Delaney felt his pulse surge.

Darrell quickly prepared another sample.

Delaney held Jordan's hand tighter.

The ambulance swayed as it took a curve fast. In its rear, the young attendant pumped feverishly against Father Dunnigan's chest. The other young attendant stared at the gaunt, smoke-stained face, largely hidden behind the oxygen mask covering Father Dunnigan's mouth and nose. His eyebrows were gone. His hair was charred; short, powdery pieces of it lay on the pillow. A wide blister, swollen with quivering fluid, covered most of one side of his cheek.

All at once the attendant pumping on his chest smiled—broadly.

"He's coming back!"

"How?" Dr. Feltenstein said. "When you took a sample at the highest elevation of her temperature the virus was still there."

Darrell didn't answer immediately. He was still studying the latest sample of Jordan's blood.

A few seconds later he raised his head and turned toward Delaney. Delaney didn't have to ask, Darrell's broad smile told him all he needed to know.

"How?" Dr. Feltenstein asked again.

"The rapid change in temperature," Darrell said. "It has to be that. The virus was almost all dead at the top elevation of her temperature—the remainder of them obviously weakened. The sudden change to a cooler temperature had to be the reason. It was too much of a shock for the virus."

Delaney looked at him. Darrell was right. Delaney pictured the Indians' cave, how cold it was inside the rock walls. The first Indian had been brought back from being under damp, smoldering leaves. The second, after lying in the area of a hot geyser. Both of them carried half naked, wearing only a loincloth into the sudden cold environment of the cave. Richard Little had been carried inside, too. And he only wore shorts and a T-shirt. But he had only suffered a raging fever beforehand. It took more. Much more. A constant, ongoing baking temperature, and then the sudden change to cold. He looked down at Jordan. She smiled up at him.

Father Dunnigan's eyes popped open. The attendants smiled down at him.

His mind was fuzzy at first, and then he recognized one of the faces looking down at him. "You're the same one that had me last time," he said slowly.

The attendant nodded.

Father Dunnigan then remembered the puppy.

"Did the little dog get out okay?"

The medic nodded. "I hate to say I'm lacking in faith. But I believe you have a hell of . . . a lot more faith than I do to walk back in that room to find a puppy."

"I gave my word," Father Dunnigan said.

He remembered that, too. Everything had come back to him. Except the angry thoughts he was having before he went inside the building.

He slowly moved his blistered, blackened hand from the gurney to the medic's hand, and patted it gently.

"Keep trying to believe, my son," he said in a low voice. "The Lord will be ready when you are."

CHAPTER 49

The fire in the rain forest, and its subsequent spread over several thousand acres, burned so intensely it not only disrupted the lenses on nearly all the spy satellites in the world, but created heavy black clouds that dumped soot as far north as Mexico.

Environmentalists everywhere were outraged. The original fire leading to the out-of-control blaze had obviously been set by a greedy Brazilian land owner wanting another section of land to farm. Greenpeace even had evidence of the fire being intentional—in the sticky, black residue of diesel fuel found in the soot that fell from the sky.

The most shocking revelation to come out of the incident was the alleged participation of the U.S. Army and Air Force in connection with the destruction.

More than one witness swore to seeing helicopters laden with diesel fuel taking off from numerous airports in flying distance of the area. And, if that was true, there obviously had been bribes paid, political or otherwise. And such an international conspiracy could not have been carried out unless more than a few square kilometers were to be cleared for exploitation. Much, much more land. The fire was just the beginning. It had to be. And more than one of the member delegations to the

UN, convinced of that, presented official complaints to that august body.

But, of course, the United States, completely backed up by the sworn testimony of the Brazilian delegation, dismissed the allegations as ridiculous.

"Not just ridiculous," the American representative to the UN said, "but . . . ludicrous."

Behind him one of his aides smiled, leaned to another and whispered, "What do they think—that the United States is running so short on fuel that our air force engaged in a conspiracy to acquire new sources from crop residue—run the stealth bomber on ethanol?"

The next thing to draw the environmentalists' attention was the dozens of craft that started shark fishing at a particular point in the western Gulf. Shark after shark was pulled in, hundreds of them, threatening to totally deplete the area of the magnificent creature.

Then, just as the fishing was started to attract the attention of the national media, it suddenly stopped as fast as it had begun.

The report on Feltenstein's desk concluded that between the intense fire on the freighter and then its sudden immersion in the cool salt water, none of the virus in the bodies on board had survived.

Or maybe it was that fish couldn't contract the virus anyway. There was none of the virus left to test with and see. Despite the best efforts of the doctors at the CDC, all the culture samples had died.

For the same reason—the lack of samples with which to conduct experiments—there was never any definitive reason established for why the disease seemed to flare into activity during the night. The guess was that it was the time of day when the body was most relaxed—the virus *was* highly sensitive. But that was only a guess really, based on highly speculative assumptions of what had occurred—what legends are made of in the first place.

* * *

Dr. Feltenstein, Darrell, Delaney, and Jordan were all awarded medals by President Richardson for their dedicated work with the virus. As the president pinned the medal on Feltenstein's new suit, he looked back over his shoulder at his nearest Secret Service agent, then back to Feltenstein.

"Well, Doctor, I hear you told off my chief advisor, my nephew Fred." As the president paused, he smiled. "I wanted you to know that I didn't exactly say what he said I did. He's always putting words in my mouth, but then that's how my brother was, too. Like father like son—that's a little bit genetics, isn't it, Dr. Feltenstein?"

"Yes, sir. You could say it is."

"We did a little scientific stuff with chickens," the president said, winked, and moved down the line toward the others.

Jordan and Delaney were back working in the laboratory in two weeks, though he had to have blood drawn for a full two months before they left him alone. In the long run, it turned out that none of the plants they had brought back from the rain forest had any medicinal value.

But there was always the next trip.

Though Richard Little lived for two more years, staring out from a constantly guarded cage hidden deep in the interior of the rain forest, he was never heard from again.

Nor were the guardians—their lives' work finally complete.

WATCH FOR CHARLES WILSON'S
NEXT NOVEL

EXTINCT

WHERE *JAWS* MEETS *JURASSIC PARK*

Despite the protests of the world community, France detonates its sixth and last underground nuclear test on an atoll in the South Pacific.

The ground turns to bubbling mud, the shock waves course through the water, down the sides of the tall underwater mountains to the deep trenches found in that area of the ocean.

Down ever deeper, past the limit light can penetrate, to the cold, black water where no one has ever gone.

And something huge moves . . .

**COMING FROM ST. MARTIN'S PAPERBACKS
IN LATE SPRING '97**